WAR TORN
(SANDSTORM 4)

A Dystopian Science Fiction Story
Book 4

By
T.W. Piperbrook
Find him at
www.twpiperbrook.com
www.facebook.com/twpiperbrook

To my brother Jeff,
for all your help
with this series. Thanks!

Cover Design

Jeff Brown Graphics

Typography

Alex Saskalidis, a.k.a. 187designz

Editing & Proofreading

Cathy Moeschet

Technical Consultants

John Cummings

Studio A.

Preface

Thanks for sticking it through to the end!

WAR TORN is not only the last book in the SANDSTORM series, but also the culmination of several years of writing.

From a tiny idea I had while driving up the mountain road leading to my house in the Northeast, to a four-book series, SANDSTORM has consumed a large chunk of my life (in a good way), and I hope it has occupied some of yours, too.

While I sit at my "writing place" at the kitchen table, I often envision Neena, Kai, Raj, and Samel in the chairs around me, divvying up their Green Crops and sharing their dried rat. I will certainly miss them (or those that survive!)

But for now...the end!

Darius is dead, Raj is heading down to Red Rock, and somewhere, the monster awaits its next meal.

Are the rest of the Red Rock survivors doomed to die? Keep reading to find out!

Enjoy WAR TORN!

Tyler Piperbrook
January 2020

Recap of Sandstorm (Book 1)

FOR THREE GENERATIONS, THE PEOPLE of Red Rock colony have been stranded on the harsh desert planet of Ravar, where only the scrappiest animals and the heartiest plants survive. Most live without the foolish hope that Earth's supply ships will ever grace the skies again. Most believe they are alone.

Caught in the midst of a severe sandstorm, Neena Xylance encounters a mysterious, injured stranger in the desert and helps him. The stranger, Kai, a man with strange, dark markings on his forehead, explains that he is from a colony called New Canaan. Before they can talk further, an enormous, terrifying creature hunts them from underground. Neena and the stranger, Kai, make their way back to her colony to warn her people of the creature, which he calls the Abomination.

In Red Rock, Neena's brothers, Raj and Samel — the remainder of her orphaned family — complete chores for a grandmotherly figure named Helgid. Raj and Samel are gathering water at the river when a group of bullies, led by a boy named Bailey, ambushes them. The sandstorm strikes, getting Raj and Samel out of their predicament, but forcing them to return to their house and hunker down.

Gideon, the leader of Red Rock, along with his four Heads of Colony Wyatt, Brody, Saurabh, and Horatio, survive the storm in the Comm Building alongside The Watchers, the colony's protectors. Meanwhile, Darius, a crippled old man who used to explore the forbidden caves on either side of

Red Rock, is unable to quell the memories of a boy named Akron, who died in a similar storm.

In the storm's aftermath, Raj and Samel encounter a screaming young woman whose grandmother has been buried by a collapsed house. Raj helps uncover the woman's grandmother, who is dead. They return to Helgid and tell her.

Gideon and the other leaders assess the storm's damage.

Darius resumes an exploration of the forbidden caves, where he thinks Akron might've died. He discovers a passage containing a triangular mark from Akron, and returns to tell his friend, Elmer. Meanwhile, Raj and Samel evade the bullies again, and Raj strikes up a friendship with the young woman whose grandmother he tried to help, a girl named Adriana. Adriana gives him an ancient keepsake in appreciation for his kindness.

Neena and Kai travel through the desert, avoiding a trail of carnage left by the Abomination, while surviving hunger, thirst, and predatory wolves. Neena learns about Kai's colony, and the markings on his head, which he says are spiritual marks of the heavens.

Returning to the forbidden caves, Darius makes an emotional discovery: the remains of Akron. He uncovers something else: the enormous skeleton of a long-dead creature, along with the old corpses of what look like dozens of miners that the creature killed.

While waiting for Adriana, Raj takes a trip to his parents' graves, where the bullies attack him, steal his knife and his keepsake, and toss them in the river. He collapses in pain.

After three days of travel, Neena and Kai make it back to Red Rock. They request to speak with Gideon and the other leaders. In a startling turn, it appears the leaders already knew of New Canaan, and are familiar with Kai's markings. Gideon calls Kai a criminal, and commands The Watchers to take he and Neena to jail.

Recap of Windswept (Book 2)

WORRIED ABOUT RAJ, SAMEL CONVINCES Helgid to let him search for his brother, eventually finding Raj collapsed near the graveyard. With the help of some onlookers and a healer, Samel gets Raj back to Helgid's hovel, where the healer treats him for sunstroke and injury. In the midst of Raj's return, Helgid's neighbor Amos tells her that Neena has been jailed.

Trapped in a dirty cell next to Kai, Neena questions Kai about the leader's accusations. Before she can determine the truth, The Watchers drag him away. Meanwhile, Helgid heads to the Comm Building, where a crowd has gathered to help Neena. Some neighbors tell her about what is happening, before The Watchers break up the crowd.

The Watchers return Kai to his cell and take Neena away. During an interrogation, Neena tells Gideon and his men about the monster, Kai, and his colony. To her surprise, the leaders accuse her of deception and collusion. They tell her that Kai's markings mean he is a criminal, and condemn her for consorting with him. They return her to her cell until they can decide what to do with her.

Darius studies the enormous, strange carcass. Looking at the caved-in wall in the tunnel he found, he makes the astute guess that the creature burst from the sand and into the tunnel, killing the miners before somehow dying. But Akron died more recently. Remembering the covered-up passage through which he arrived, Darius makes another guess: The Watchers sealed up the passage.

In an unavoidable meeting with the young Watchers, Gideon reveals a secret: generations ago, half the population left and formed New Canaan, while the rest stayed in Red Rock. The two colonies considered each other dead for generations, while the leaders kept each other's existence quiet—until the representatives arrived a decade ago. He tells the young Watchers that Kai's markings make him a criminal, but he denies the existence of the monster. He tells the young men that he will arrange a meeting with the colony to downplay the size of Kai's colony, to keep control.

In secret, Gideon, Thorne, some elder Watchers, and The Heads of Colony admit the existence of the monster. They say that if it arrives, they are in grave danger.

Meanwhile, Helgid vows to get Neena out of jail.

In the cells, Kai explains to Neena that he was a thief in New Canaan, and that he escaped to the desert, where she found him. He tells her that his parents are still in New Canaan. Feeling guilty for Neena's imprisonment, Kai devises a plan to free her. Simultaneously, Amos goes to the guards on Helgid's behalf, telling them that Neena's brother Raj is injured and needs her.

After returning to Red Rock, Darius discusses what he found in the tunnels with his friend, Elmer. He decides to attend Gideon's meeting later.

Acting on a plan, Neena meets with Gideon, insisting that she was delusional. Gideon ultimately agrees to release her, threatening to exile her and her brothers if she spreads more rumors. Neena returns to find Raj injured and ill. She's upset, but unable to avenge him, knowing that she would end up back in jail. She keeps the truth of her journey from Helgid.

Darius attends the meeting, where Gideon placates the colony, telling them that Kai's people are a small group and that the monster doesn't exist. Afterward, Darius discovers one of The Watchers in possession of Akron's knife, proving his earlier theory. Speaking with Elmer, he figures out that The Watchers killed Akron to cover up what he found in the cave, and that the monster of which Neena screamed is real. He visits with Neena, comparing stories and confirming the truth. A realization hits them: the leaders will kill Kai. Overhearing a plan, they vow to stop his death.

Neena returns home, reuniting with a recovering Raj.

At night, Neena sneaks out with Darius, stopping several Watchers from killing Kai. Together, she, Darius, and Kai abscond to the caves, where The Watchers hunt for them unsuccessfully. While in the cave, Neena and Kai realize that they have feelings for one another. Meanwhile, determining that one of the fugitives might be Neena, Gideon sets up another, colony-wide meeting to enlist the peoples' help.

Angry about the attack by the bullies, and embarrassed about losing Adriana's keepsake, Raj sneaks away from Helgid's hovel to take revenge on his attackers. Samel follows him. Working as a team, they defeat the bullies, but not without a price: The Watchers arrive in the aftermath, taking him, Samel, and the bullies in the direction of the jail cells.

In the middle of Gideon's meeting, the Abomination emerges, destroying half of Red Rock and killing many people, landing on the podium where Gideon and The Heads of Colony speak, assumedly killing them. The bullies who attacked Raj die during the attack, and Raj and Samel get free of The Watchers. Amidst the chaos, Neena and Kai emerge from the caves, leaving Darius behind while they search for Helgid, Raj, and Samel. Finding them, they head back for Darius and the cave. On the way back, Neena, Kai, and Darius assist several hundred other people to safety, but not before the Abomination devours Helgid.

From the mouth of the cave, the survivors watch as

Thorne and his elder guards unsuccessfully fight the Abomination. They wound it, but ultimately die.

With the attack over, the survivors, led by Neena and Kai, emerge to a ruined Red Rock, finding more people in the Comm Building — including their friend Amos — and some younger Watchers and their families, who survived on the cliffs.

Neena makes a vow to Kai: she will kill the creature before it hurts anyone again.

In a surprising turn, Gideon crawls from one of the Abomination's holes, horribly wounded, but alive.

Recap of Dustborn (Book 3)

WEEKS AFTER THE ABOMINATION'S DEVASTATING attack, the survivors eke out an existence in three caves on the cliffs. Neena and her closest followers stay in the Right Cave, The Watchers and their families live in the Left, and a third group resides in the Center Cave.

Food is scarce, and tensions are high.

Hoping to devise a long-term plan for survival, Neena, Kai, and Darius meet with all three groups, suggesting a scavenging trip to the colony. Arguments break out as people question Kai's past, and whom they should follow. Others interrogate the young Watchers, whom a young man named Bryan unofficially leads. After a while, a healer interrupts them, informing them that Gideon is awake.

Neena, Kai, Darius, Bryan, and some Watchers visit Gideon. Gideon's crippled appearance—and his confused mental state—shocks them. Realizing Gideon is in no position to lead, Neena convinces The Watchers that they all need to work together to scavenge the colony for food. Together, they communicate their plan to the crowd.

Meanwhile, Raj and Samel sneak away from the Right Cave to explore, and Raj discovers a strange, shiny object.

When Neena returns to the Right Cave, she informs Raj and Samel of the scavenging trip. Raj volunteers, but Neena turns down his offer, worried about his safety. Raj storms away. Later, he speaks with Adriana—who has also survived — about her grandmother's lost keepsake. He makes an internal promise to bring the strange object from the caves to her.

Waking up in pain, Gideon decides that Neena, Kai, and Darius are to blame. He vows to punish them for his injuries, and for their part in the Abomination's devastation.

Neena, Kai, Bryan, and seventy-five others head out on the scavenging trip. Things go sour when Bryan's best friend, a Watcher named Gary, dies in a hovel collapse. Another Watcher, Louie, breaks his arm. Bryan and his Watchers decide that Neena and Kai are at fault for the tragedies of Red Rock. They tell Neena and Kai to stay away.

The Watchers isolate themselves in the Left Cave. Unable to make amends with them, Neena, Kai, and Darius visit Gideon again, in the hopes of getting some ideas to defeat the monster. Their meeting yields nothing. After they leave, Gideon — who has been feigning his confusion — tells his healer to fetch Bryan and The Watchers.

Raj sneaks through the tunnels at night, uncovering the strange device. Fearing that someone might take his shiny treasure, he leaves it hidden and decides to tell Adriana about it instead.

In a secret meeting, Gideon regains The Watchers' trust. Together, they formulate a plan to kill the monster, restore the colony, and punish Neena, Kai, and Darius.

Raj sneaks Adriana to the tunnels, where he shows her the device, and they share a kiss.

Later, Bryan and his Watchers hold a private funeral for the dead Watcher Gary, inviting only the Center Cavers, whose unofficial leader is Ed. Bonded by their communal grief — and moved by a rousing speech from Sherry, Gary's widow — the Left and Center Caves unite under Bryan's leadership, with the goal of killing the monster.

Neena, Darius, and Kai approach Bryan to make amends.

Raj and Adriana sneak into the tunnels again, this time

encountering Bryan and his Watchers. Bryan compliments their stealth and lets them go. The meeting bolster's Raj's confidence, inspiring an idea: he tells Adriana they should unveil the device's existence to Neena, Kai, and Darius, so they can gain respect and be heroes. She agrees.

Later, he attempts to tell his sister, Kai, and Darius, but they dismiss him. Dejected and ashamed, Raj loses faith in his sibling and his cave.

Neena, Kai, and Darius make an unsuccessful attempt to reconcile with The Watchers, during which Bryan and Sherry threaten them. The Right Cave grows nervous.

After a chance encounter with Bryan on the cliffs, Raj decides to bring the device to The Watcher leader instead. He consorts with Bryan, Louie, and Gideon to figure out its purpose. After several unsuccessful tests, Raj proposes that they reveal it to Darius to get some answers, while reporting back to Bryan and Gideon.

During a trip for water at a cave spring, Neena, Kai, and some other Right Cavers get into a violent skirmish with Sherry and her crew. A bold woman named Samara is particularly angered.

Bryan develops a relationship with Sherry, who is pregnant with his best friend Gary's baby. Meanwhile, he drills the Left and Center Cavers to battle the Abomination. Together with Gideon, he formulates a plan to use the horns to draw the creature out, bash it against the rock spires, and kill it with their spears.

A Watcher finds evidence that the Abomination is close.

At the same time, Darius determines that the strange device is actually a weapon that shoots small spears. He devises a metal tool that serves as a crank, carves some small, extra spears, and tests the device in the tunnels. Amazingly, the weapon penetrates stone. Unbeknownst to him, Raj watches from the shadows and secretly informs Bryan, who plans to steal the weapon and bring it to battle.

Neena wakes up to find the Left and Center Cavers marching down the winding trail to Red Rock, with Raj in their midst.

In a shocking twist, Kai runs from the tunnels, telling her that Darius has been murdered.

Chapter 1: Neena

"**D**ARIUS IS DEAD?"

Repeating the words stabbed Neena like a thousand, tiny knives. She looked around the empty, middle part of the cave, standing alongside Kai, Amos, and Samel. In the short time they'd spoken, nearly all of the hundred Right Cavers had abandoned their sleeping places and gathered at the cave's entrance. The pungent odor of sweat and fear hung in the air, emanating from their scattered bedrolls, blankets, and bags. Only a few, terrified mothers remained nearby, clutching their children and alternating their gaze between Neena and the commotion outside.

Neena hardly saw them, or heard the noise.

Her attention stayed on Kai.

"What do you mean, he's dead?" she repeated.

"I found him in the chamber where he was working. Someone slit his throat," Kai said, eyes wide. "He was on the floor, near where he was fixing the weapon. His tools were sticking out of him. Blood was everywhere." Kai looked around, as if an attacker might be waiting in the shadows to kill them next.

"By the heavens," Amos whispered, wrapping a protective arm around Samel.

"Whoever did it impaled his belly and his legs with his chisels and knives," Kai added, gripping his spear. "I've never seen something so gruesome, or so malicious. But that wasn't all. They stole the weapon."

"They stole the weapon?"

"It's gone," Kai said. "Someone must've taken it. I assume it was whomever killed him."

"Why were you there?" Neena asked, confused.

Kai blew a frantic breath. "I woke up and found his empty bedroll. Normally, he's back by daybreak, so I went to check on him. When I arrived, I found him dead, and raced back here."

Once again, Neena felt as if she lived a nightmare. She looked from Kai to Amos, processing too many horrific truths.

Nothing made sense.

And yet it did.

Bryan's violent threats, Sherry's sneering face, and Ed's smile flashed before her. Maybe this was the end result of her choices.

The end result of everything.

She took a step, ready to run down the tunnel to Darius, even though it was too late to help him. Kai stopped her.

"Darius is dead," he said, grabbing her arm. "There's nothing we can do for him. But I heard you saying something about Raj. What's going on?"

Her earlier panic returned.

Raj.

"Raj is marching off with The Watchers," she said frantically. "He's headed down to Red Rock."

"What? Why?" Kai looked over to find Amos pointing at Raj's bedroll, where a pile of rocks lay.

"I'm not sure why, but he snuck out with the Left and Center Cavers, who are headed down the trail. We need to get him back!"

Neena stepped toward the cave entrance, ready to

scream warnings—ready to get the attention of *everyone*—until Samel crashed into her.

"Neena!" Samel called, spilling frightened tears. "Don't leave!"

She met his eyes.

"I don't want you to go," Samel said, wrapping his arms tightly around her.

Neena swallowed. Her brother's presence reminded her that he was safe, but Raj was not. "It's going to be okay, Samel. Stay with Amos and don't move until I come back!"

And then she was off with Kai.

Neena's spear shook in her grasp. Her heart pounded. She couldn't stop thinking of Darius, lying on the sandy, rock floor, covered in blood.

Impaled with his own tools.

That fear reinforced another.

What if Raj was next?

Together, she and Kai raced to the edge of the crowd, scanning the shadows. Reaching the back of the crowd, Neena grabbed peoples' shoulders, spinning them around and working her way through them.

"They killed Darius! They have Raj!"

Loud, frightened chatter drowned out her warnings. Those who heard her looked at her as if she were mad. Others scanned behind her, uncertain where the threat was coming from. They were never going to rally in time. She had to do something.

Breaking through the crowd, she and Kai found an open place on the ledge, scanning the cliffs. Far below, about halfway down, a head of curly hair bobbed out of view.

Raj!

He'd just disappeared behind a high wall of rocks bordering the trail.

They had to get to him.

"Come on, Kai!"

Neena and Kai raced along the ledge, heading away from the crowd and toward the precipice that lay beyond the other entrances of the caves. Her brother was more than three hundred feet below — even farther, by way of the ledge.

"Raj!" She cupped her hand over her mouth, screaming.

Her heart thudded wildly.

Too many things were starting to become clear.

She knew Raj had been going through things. But she had no idea of the extent. If not for the pile of rocks he'd left in his bedroll, she might've believed someone had snatched him. But he had clearly left on his own. Whatever the reason, Neena had to stop him.

She and Kai ran along the ledge, contending with loose rocks and sand, sticking close to the cliff wall. A few dozen women and children stood among the craggy rocks at the Center Cave, trading their attention between the marchers and Neena and Kai. Neena looked at them as they ran by. On more than a few faces, she saw sneers.

Did they know what was happening?

She didn't stop to ask.

They continued past, focused on the distant Left Cave a hundred feet away.

A few shadowed women and children poked their heads out, but most stayed inside. Neena kept her spear ready. Down the cliffs, Raj was still out of sight. The high wall of rock had engulfed him and the others. She didn't know what she'd do when she reached the marching line, but she had to do *something*.

Neena increased her speed, shouting for her brother.

She stumbled as something hard struck her in the temple.

Pain stopped her.

Stars blurred her vision.

Too late, Neena turned toward the entrance of the Left Cave, where a shadowy figure stepped from the darkness, moving fast and throwing another rock. More pain struck her cheek. She held up her hands and her spear, too late to ward off an unexpected barrage of stones, which pummeled her stomach and her legs.

"Don't let them reach our men!" Sherry snarled from the entrance, her voice loud and unmistakable. "Get them!"

Through the pain, Neena saw more women step out around Sherry.

Sherry's vicious screaming incited another attack.

Neena held up her hands and her spear, trying to block her face, but she couldn't avoid the deluge of projectiles. She cried out as a few well-placed stones caught her in the stomach, and her head. Beside her, Kai suffered a similar onslaught.

"Neena!" he screamed, ineffectively blocking his body, trying to turn and retreat.

She tried to do the same, but a well-aimed stone struck her in the ankle, pitching her off balance. And then Neena was on her stomach, fighting for wind.

Angry women ran toward her, screaming and shouting.

Neena groped frantically for her lost spear, but the women stomped her hands into the dirt, whisking away her weapon. Pain seared her fingers.

"Get off me!" she yelled, through a mouthful of blood.

She managed to roll onto her side, catching a glimpse of Kai falling over, surrounded by a flurry of women.

And then she was surrounded, too.

The world became a mob of vicious, uncaring faces, spitting, screaming, and kicking. Sherry's voice was the loudest.

"This is for Gary!" she yelled, through gritted teeth, raising a boot over her head and stomping.

Neena's chin hit the ground; she bit her gums. Blood spurted inside her mouth.

It felt as if she was in a dark tunnel, shielded from the light.

She fought to rise, but failed.

She had only a moment to wonder whether Kai was dead, and then the black took over.

CHAPTER 2: Bryan

C OMMOTION DREW THE ATTENTION OF the marching line.

Bryan glanced over his shoulder, joining the staring eyes of two hundred men and women, all of whom looked up the windy trail, trying to see past the craggy, bordering rock walls. He shifted from side to side, but he couldn't see beyond the obstruction of jagged stone. He and his important men strode quickly down the trail, looking for a better view.

"Over there!" Louie called, motioning toward a gap a little further down, where the rock had crumbled away.

Bryan and the others jogged toward the break in the wall, taking turns looking upward. A few hundred feet above them, near the mouth of the Left Cave, a few dozen women surrounded someone. Shouts and screams drifted down from where they gathered. It appeared the women on the ledge were attacking someone, but it was hard to tell exactly what was happening, from here.

Panic rippled through the marchers. A few of them stepped to the side of the trail, looking back up it, but their views were blocked.

"Hold your positions!" Bryan shouted, keeping his people in place.

Rodney, Isaiah, Clark, Nicholas, and Boyle watched him.

"We expected this might happen," Bryan told them quietly, "but I was hoping we'd have more time."

"Do you think someone found Darius?" Louie asked.

"Either that, or they found Raj gone," Bryan determined. "In any case, we instructed our women what to do. They are following their part of the plan."

Bryan looked farther up the stretching line. The people craned their necks, murmuring.

"The good news is that no one else is joining the scuffle," Louie said, peering up at the cliffs. "The Right Cavers are afraid."

"The commotion is contained," Bryan agreed.

Bryan recalled his conversation with Sherry, whom he'd left in charge. At all costs, he'd told her, the line must march unimpeded.

At the same time, he'd told her to keep the baby safe.

Still, he worried.

He'd seen the spark in her eyes. It was the same spark he'd noticed when she returned from the spring. He looked for her amidst the skirmish, but he couldn't pick her out. Still, he was almost positive she was there, fighting for him alongside the other women.

Bryan looked back at the long line of people he'd recruited. Fear knitted their brows. They shifted, clearly losing some of the courage they'd gained on the way down. They were justifiably anxious, but if they turned back now, they'd never find their courage again.

He glanced down at the weapon in his hand, which he'd taken from Darius.

The monster was close.

He knew it, by his men's reports.

The last words he'd spoken with Gideon came back to him.

"No matter how difficult things become, you must account for

those who do not have your faith. You must march them forward, and not let them stop, until they succeed."

The Right Cavers posed no threat.

The time to fight the beast was now.

"Listen, people!" Bryan shouted, drawing the attention of everyone within earshot. The closest men and women swiveled to face him. "Our women are heading off those who might interfere with us, just like they promised! Let us show them that their efforts are worthwhile! Let us slay the monster, and reclaim our colony!"

Slowly, people regained their courage, passing the word to others.

Raising his voice to inspire, he yelled, "Let us show them we are worth fighting for!"

The same brave fire he'd possessed in the cave chamber coursed through him. People arched their backs and lifted their chins. His important men shored up next to him. Those who'd broken from their lines returned to their two-by-two formations, clutching their spears or horns.

"Now is the time of our victory!" Bryan shouted, gaining volume. "Let us make our ancestors proud! Let us make our *women* proud!"

A cheer spread out through the line, as people heeded his words, thrusting their spears in the air.

Together, they marched.

CHAPTER 3: Raj

ORRY PLAGUED RAJ'S HEART. HE struggled to see over the rock wall, but try as he might, he couldn't get a clear view of the cliffs. He wished he were a giant, like the stories in which he believed when he was younger. But those were just stories, and he was a man now: a big, strong man, marching with a fearless army.

Despite his attempts to be brave, guilt pricked his stomach.

Was Neena involved in the skirmish? Was Kai, or Darius, or Samel?

A reflexive anger washed over him.

If it weren't for Neena's lack of faith in him, perhaps things could have gone some other way. Maybe they'd even be fighting the monster together. But he'd gone too far to turn back now.

She'd made her decision, and he'd made his.

He swallowed as he recalled Bryan's last inspiring words. Bryan had stood in front of the crowd in the chamber, while holding up the weapon for all to see. In the early hours of the morning — after Raj had provided him with the weapon's location — Bryan had retrieved the object, bringing it back to the chamber so Raj could demonstrate it. He'd even let Raj pierce stone with it. That was before he'd explained Raj's role in the attack, and reiterated his job with the horn. Raj had been upset at first, until Bryan had convinced him of how crucial his part would be. Without Raj and the other horn blowers, Bryan had said, they wouldn't be able to slay the monster. Now, Raj was excited for his job.

All the pieces were in place to defeat the monster.

All that was left was to execute them.

"You heard what Bryan said," said a round-cheeked man next to him, pulling him from his thoughts. "Stay focused."

Raj nodded, struggling to keep pace.

"The monster is here now," the man reiterated. "We need to do our part in killing it."

Raj looked around him at the ten others carrying horns—five in front and five behind, marching in the line's middle. Even the gravity of their role didn't stop his worry.

"The women are protecting us," said the man, with the same restored confidence as the others around them. "Our ancestors have blessed us."

Raj nodded nervously.

"You're Raj, right?" asked the man.

Raj looked over at his companion, whose underarms were soaked with sweat. "Yes."

"Have you ever hunted anything, Raj?"

"Mostly just rats," Raj said, adding, "But I hunted a wolf and a dust beetle once."

"And now we're going to battle a monster." The man whistled softly. "Probably the biggest creature anyone has fought in our lifetimes."

Fear stabbed Raj's stomach.

"You're a brave boy to join us." The man's smile revealed his yellowed, stained teeth. "I'm a little rusty with a spear, but I'll battle the ugly thing, if it turns out they need reinforcements."

Raj smiled back through his worry. He refocused on the tall, bordering rocks next to them, but he still couldn't see anything above them. Recognizing the man from the colony, he asked, "You're a Crop Tender, right?"

"Yep, I'm Eddie," he said.

Raj let two fingers off his horn and awkwardly greeted his companion.

"I used to live in one of the houses near the water." The man pointed to an area they couldn't see through the rock wall.

Raj envisioned the faraway river, and the distant rows of Green Crops at its southern edge. As brave as he wanted to be, he'd do anything to be there now, celebrating the end of the battle, rather than heading into it.

"Maybe when we're heroes, they'll let us relax while the others do the hard work." A small, nervous laugh escaped from Eddie's mouth.

"That'd be nice," Raj agreed.

"Of course, we'll have to rebuild our homes first."

Raj stared over the heads of the other marchers, glimpsing a sliver of the colony. Nostalgia washed over him, as he remembered saying goodbye to his old home with his siblings, right before they'd come up to the cliffs. Raj only had a few moments to collect his belongings before they'd headed off, leaving the place where he'd spent most of his years behind. The prospect of returning gave him a warm feeling in his stomach, and another pinprick of fear.

He wondered if his old house had weakened in recent weeks and tumbled, like too many others.

His thoughts returned to Neena, Darius, Kai, and Samel. He was still worried they were involved.

Neena had treated him poorly. He couldn't deny that.

But he felt bad for Darius, who had fixed up the weapon, only to have it stolen. And he certainly felt bad for Samel, who would be upset he was gone. He swallowed his guilt and put on a hard face.

Darius and the others wouldn't complain when they had their homes and their colony back. And Raj's bravery would be a huge part of that.

The noise above grew quieter, as they got farther away. Raj breathed nervously.

Soon, everything would work out.

And then Raj would be a person to admire and thank, rather than a person to ignore.

Wiping away his sweat, he struggled to keep up with Eddie.

CHAPTER 4: Samara

"N EENA!" SAMARA YELLED FRANTICALLY FROM the Right Cave. "Neena!"

The ledge outside the Left Cave had become a vicious circle, filled with dust and screams. The crazed, kicking women swallowed up Samara's view of Neena and Kai. All she heard were her friends' agonizing groans, echoing along the ledge and back to the Right Cave. The other Right Cavers covered their mouths, stepped back, or shielded their children. Some screamed for Neena and Kai. Of course, no one rushed toward the ugly mob. They were terrified.

Finding Salvador and Roberto among the crowd, Samara said, "We have to stop them, or they'll keep beating them until they're dead!"

Salvador's and Roberto's hands shook on their spears.

Catching the attention of a dozen others, Samara said, "Come on! Let's go!"

She took a determined stride, but no one followed.

"Neena and Kai helped us when we needed it!" she pleaded. "It's our turn to help them!"

After another step, a handful of men and women broke from the rest.

Before they could second-guess their bravery, Samara led the small group down the ledge, wielding their spears. They kept away from the treacherous drop, paying no attention to the faraway, marching line.

Samara's heart pumped furiously, but the footfalls of her companions gave her the strength to push on.

Ahead, a cluster of women and children drifted from the Center Cave, trying to get a better view of the spectacle, or perhaps thinking of joining it.

Before they could turn thoughts into action, Samara screamed, "Stay back!"

Her followers screamed with her.

Their shouts startled the Center Cavers, who retreated into their cave, thinking better of entering the fray.

Samara pointed her spear in front of her, hurtling past the Center Cave with Salvador and Roberto and reaching the area where her friends were surrounded, creating a frontal offensive line.

Hearing a new source of commotion, a few people at the edge of Sherry's circle turned. Surprise struck them when they saw Samara, Roberto, Salvador, and a dozen others charging at them. They skirted away, avoiding the ends of their spears. A few dropped the rocks they still held in their hands, retreating.

"Get away from them!" Samara snarled, waving her spear from side to side.

She, Salvador, Roberto, and the others thrust their weapons. The less tenacious of the women quickly dispersed, like children caught sipping the family soup. Others backed against the cliff wall. Only half a dozen underlings scooted behind Sherry, refusing to yield. Sherry's eyes blazed with triumph as she stood in place, admiring her handiwork.

Samara gasped as she saw Neena and Kai's fallen figures.

Blood and dirt covered their bodies. Their clothes were ripped and torn. Neena lay on her stomach, motionless, while Kai lay on his back, his limp hands over his face.

Neither moved.

"What did you do?" Samara yelled, her anger mounting.

Sherry smirked. "I gave them what they deserved."

"Get back, or I'll stab you," Samara snarled, without hesitation.

Sherry pulled her knife. Her gaze flicked from Samara, to Roberto, to Salvador, and the dozen armed men and women behind. Instead of stepping back, she stepped forward.

To the women behind her, she said, "Come on!"

She arched her shoulders, making it clear she was ready to fight, until she realized not everyone followed.

One or two of her women stood united behind her, but the others had stepped backward. They glanced at the cave, where their children watched.

These were mothers, not fighters.

Begrudgingly, Sherry retreated, keeping a hateful eye on Samara. "This isn't over."

Getting the attention of her followers, Samara pointed at Neena and Kai. "Come on, let's carry them back!"

A few Right Cavers moved forward, carefully picking up Neena and Kai's limp bodies and shuffling them back along the ledge toward the Right Cave, while Samara, Roberto, and Salvador guarded.

When she was far enough away that no one could attack them, Samara gave Sherry a hard stare, before turning and retreating with the rest of her group.

CHAPTER 5: Samara

"**W**E NEED A HEALER!" SAMARA yelled through the gaping crowd, while her helpers carried Neena and Kai's lifeless bodies through the entrance.

She immediately realized the pointlessness of her cries. The healers were all deep inside the Center Cave, inaccessible. For all she knew, Sherry had twisted those people against them, too.

Samara hurried next to Neena and Kai. All around them, the Right Cavers gasped and pointed, reluctantly moving out of the way for the people carrying their fallen comrades. Children fought for a space alongside their parents. Their faces showed their helplessness. They wrung their hands, or shuffled nervously.

Samara felt a wave of regret. She knew the risks of moving injured people, but at the time, she knew that she needed to get Neena and Kai away from Sherry.

Finding a spot where she could pull two bedrolls close together, Samara said, "Over here!"

When the bedrolls were adjusted, the helpers gently set Neena and Kai down. Neither had their eyes open. Neither stirred.

"Are they breathing?" Samara asked frantically.

She leaned down to Kai first, but she heard and felt nothing.

The crowd murmured and leaned closer.

"Get back!" she yelled.

She put two fingers on Kai's neck, checking for the beat of his heart, the way she'd seen healers do, but she couldn't tell if she did it right. She searched for his breathing, but the commotion made it hard to hear anything. Finding a rag and a flask, she dabbed at Kai's bloodied face. He surprised her with a cough.

"He's still with us!" she cried, to the gasps of some people around her. "Kai? Can you hear me?"

He answered in a rasp. Rather than demanding an answer, she instructed, "Stay still! Don't move!" Samara looked sideways, where Amos had taken a spot over Neena.

"How's she doing?"

"I can't tell if she's breathing!" Amos shouted. Standing up, looking more nervous than she'd ever seen him, he said, "Everybody back! We need more room!"

CHAPTER 6: Bryan

PRIDE FILLED BRYAN'S HEART AS he led his two hundred people down the cliffs, approaching the empty patch of desert leading to the colony's northern edge. Earlier, through a break in the wall in the path's border, he'd seen the Right Cavers scooting away with their fallen companions. Whatever happened was over.

No more distractions.

It was time to fight.

Clutching his weapon, he scanned the colony's remains. Pride mixed with his courage. Rather than dwelling on the devastation, as too many did, he envisioned a stronger line of buildings, and the new regime he'd put in place. He envisioned the fresh construction of hovels they'd build once the monster's blood was taken and its holes were backfilled with dirt and sand. He imagined a slew of new homes so well put-together that they'd withstand even the harshest storms.

The creature's scales would be their walls.

The beast's jagged protrusions would rise from the roofs like trophies.

Its meat would fill their bellies.

That last idea was a good one.

If the beast were made of flesh, killing it would solve more than one problem. Its dried meat would feed plenty of hungry colonists. Those who survived — his heroes — would have a buffet fit for The Heads of Colony. Maybe they'd even consume it at the building's large table, overlooking Gideon's round, rusted relic.

The New Generation.

A confident smile spread across his face as he glanced behind him at his line.

His people walked in a steady progression, curving with the trail, neither stopping nor slowing. Most were already thinking past the skirmish on the cliffs.

They were ready to fight.

Catching the eyes of Isaiah, Boyle, Rodney, Clark, and Nicholas, he felt another surge of pride. The Watchers were well trained, and they'd spread their knowledge to the others behind them, so that all might succeed.

No one—not even Gideon—had led a march as united, or as strong. In fact, this might be the biggest force anyone had ever seen. What the colonists lacked in experience, they made up for in numbers.

If anyone had a chance at defeating the monster, they did.

Conversation behind him drew his attention. Louie hurried alongside the closest marchers, making last-second preparations and drilling them. His face was confident as he strode the last few paces to reach Bryan, adjusting his sling.

Louie was injured, but he was still useful.

"How are they feeling?" Bryan asked.

"The people are ready," Louie said with a firm nod. "A few are nervous, but none questioned what we are about to do."

"None of them turned back?" Bryan asked.

"Not that I can see," Louie affirmed.

Bryan nodded gratefully.

Louie's gaze wandered to the device in Bryan's hands, and Bryan's eyes roamed there, too. In the earliest hours of the morning, before the sun had crested the eastern cliffs, he'd tested it. The device was incredible. The small spears it shot had penetrated stone, just as Raj had showed him. He'd even instructed some of his closest Watchers to carve a small, extra stash, using Darius's spear as a template. He looked at the bag on his back, where the tips of those sharp, extra weapons stuck out.

"The weapon will definitely pierce a monster's flesh," Bryan said assuredly.

"I believe it," Louie agreed.

"Still, its power is limited," Bryan admitted. "It can only fire one small spear at a time. And it will take time to wind the crank, like Raj showed us." He looked down at his pocket, where he had stashed Darius's constructed tool. He looked back at the line. "Is Raj still with the others?"

Looking back along the marchers, Louie found a group of ragtag men and middle-aged, childless women in the center, whom had volunteered to join them. "Yes. He's ready for his duty, along with the other horn blowers." Louie's smile stayed on his face. "They are excited for their roles. I have prepared them to become heroes."

"Disposable heroes," Bryan corrected with a smile.

Louie's smirk matched his own. "May the heavens bless them."

CHAPTER 7: Samel

T EARS FLOWED DOWN SAMEL'S FACE. Leaning as close as he dared to Neena, he said, "Neena! Wake up!"

Next to her, Amos looked on in panic. Shaking, he put two old fingers on Neena's neck, before turning his ear toward her lips. He switched his attention to her chest, searching, but not finding anything.

About half the cave had fled their positions at the cave's entrance, switching their attention to the new spectacle. The smell of so many sweaty bodies in a confined space made Samel feel like he was going to gag. People spoke loudly, reeking of rat meat and soup. But he wouldn't leave his sister.

He felt sick to his stomach.

Neena's face was caked with blood and sand; her clothes were ripped and torn. Her hair was sweaty and splayed at all angles. Scrapes and cuts littered her arms and legs.

Snaking a hand past Amos, Samel found his sister's fingers and squeezed.

"Give me some room, Samel," Amos said. "I'm going to try to get her breathing."

Reluctantly, Samel scooted away, while Amos bent toward her mouth, pressing his lips against hers. After a few, rigorous exhalations, he used his weathered hands to push on her chest. He repeated the procedure numerous times, while Samara fought to keep back the ogling crowd.

"Nothing's happening," Amos said helplessly, as if someone might have another idea. "I can't revive her."

"We need a healer!" Samara yelled.

They looked around, as if someone might help, but no one stepped forward. Even if Samel were instructed to run for someone, he wouldn't know where to go. The Center and Left Caves felt as ominous and dreaded as the Comm Building.

The other cavers would never help his sister.

They'd done this to her.

A realization older than his years washed over him: this might be a tragic moment that would change his life, like Mom or Dad's death.

Neena was dead.

Samel was alone.

Samel laid his head on Neena's chest, tears blurring his vision. Sobs wracked his small body. Neena was one of the last people he had, and now she was gone.

A gasp drew his attention upward.

Neena's eyes fluttered.

A surge of hope sparked in him, so fast and so unexpectedly that he shot upright, looking at his sister.

"Neena?" he cried. "Are you awake?"

"I—" Neena's eyes rolled back and forth for a moment, before appearing to focus. "I hear you. Is that you, Samel?"

Neena's voice was weak and strained, but she was alive!
Alive!

Samel's tears turned hopeful. He leaned over, hugging her, telling her how much he had missed her, and how he had thought she was gone. Neena smiled through her obvious pain, dripping blood from her lips.

"Give her some room!" Amos called.

Neena groaned loudly, losing her strength. "I have to—"

"Have to what?" Samel asked.

She didn't answer.

She closed her eyes, and then she was under again.

CHAPTER 8: Raj

R AJ SWALLOWED AS THE PATH took its final curve. Far ahead, dozens of Watchers took their first steps onto soft sand, stepping out from the last of the cliff's shadows. All walked in the careful manner that Bryan had explained, heel to toe. The baking sun showed no mercy, beading their heads with sweat and scorching the sand.

Soon, it was more people's turn to leave the cliff path. Raj steeled his nerves as one pair of men after another entered the desert patch leading to the colony.

One marching step.

Then another.

That's all he had to do, for now.

He had to be strong. A hero.

He felt as if he was heading for the edge of the cliff, rather than a flat patch of land. And then he was upon it. Raj glanced at his boot, as if the ground might disappear beneath it, and a gaping mouth might swallow him whole.

His heart slammed against his ribcage.

He took the step.

Raj walked the way Bryan had demonstrated, soundlessly, deliberately. It felt as if he were traveling to some strange, foreign land, rather than back to his colony.

When he was far enough away that retreating wouldn't be easy, he turned and glanced behind him.

All conversation in the line had ceased.

People looked straight ahead, holding their horns, or

toting their spears. Raj turned and glanced at Eddie, who met his eyes. Their time was almost here.

They waded through the desert until they reached the edge of the trail at the eastern corner of the colony, passing the tithing and storage buildings. The structures looked dirtier than before, but mostly familiar.

The smell of death invaded his nostrils.

It was impossible to ignore the odor of decay consuming Red Rock when it was all around Raj, nor could he ignore the destroyed hovels. Gaping holes scarred the ground between them, where the colonists used to carry their buckets.

The line's leaders wove north up the hunter's path, between the tall rock spires that bordered the trail. The gigantic, reddish formations rose straight into the air, towering high above the line on either side, a few hundred feet apart. The first formations were about the width of a few people, but as they moved on, the spires grew wide enough to fill the foundation of a hovel. Raj looked up their smooth sides, remembering how he'd fantasized about climbing up them, back when he was young and foolish enough to believe that were possible.

To do that, he'd *have* to be a giant.

Or a spider, with long, sticky legs.

Now, those formations would help them defeat the monster.

They passed between a dozen pairs of spires — a tiny line of men, dwarfed by the heavens' creations.

And then The Watchers assumed the positions that Bryan had instructed.

Bryan and his Watchers fanned in two directions, twenty in each group. One group positioned themselves to the left of the western spire near the path, creating a horizontal line at a buffer from the stone, while the other stood near the eastern spire, forming a similar pattern.

Raj and the eleven other horn blowers split into two

teams of six, standing thirty feet in front of their respective spires.

The rest of the marchers divided themselves between Bryan's teams.

When they were finished, nearly a hundred men were in place in long, single lines near each of the spires with Bryan's Watchers. Bryan stood in the left group.

Raj scanned the desert with a growing unease as he waited. His hands shook on his horn.

The wind stirred, kicking up the top layer of sand and whistling around the rock spires in front of him. His comrades on either side of him shifted. No one was safe from the monster, but standing where they were now — about to blow their horns — Raj realized the horn blowers' peril. It felt as if he and his companions were on the other side of a wide, bottomless chasm.

But this was their important duty.

That's what Bryan had told them.

He looked over at Bryan, waiting for a signal.

The sun disappeared behind the clouds, turning the sky charcoal grey, dulling the silhouettes of the twin moons and sharpening his fear. Next to him, Eddie looked as if he might soil his shorts. The other four people in their group — two men and two women — waited with wide eyes, their horns quivering.

Bryan raised a hand.

As one, the six people in his group put their horns to their lips.

Raj and his group steadied their breaths.

Bryan's hand came down.

Raj blew with all his might.

CHAPTER 9: Samel

L ONG, SONOROUS NOTES ECHOED FROM somewhere outside, filling the Right Cave with their single-pitch song. The crowd at the entrance riled up even more, speaking in frantic tones. Slowly, the sound faded, as the horns dropped off one by one. A forgotten fear struck Samel's heart.

His brother was outside.

Getting to his feet, he started for the crowd.

"Samel! Where are you going? It's not safe!" Samara cried after him.

He didn't look back, nor did he heed Amos's cautionary cries. Neena was unconscious, but at least she was breathing.

No one was looking after Raj.

Samel ran until he was at the back of the gathering, standing on his toes. Too many bulky bodies blocked his view. Using his small size to his advantage, he scooted wherever he found an opening, weaving past fearful mothers, frightened children, and sweaty men. Eventually he found the open ledge, taking up next to two older boys. The scrawny kids watched the desert with awe, and more than a little fear.

"What's happening?" Samel asked them.

Neither answered.

He followed their eyes to the desert.

Far below, in the middle of the hunter's trail, north of the colony, two long lines of people stood on either side of a pair of spires. A small group of people was tucked into the shadows in front of the enormous structures. He watched the group on the left raise something to their faces. *Horns.*

The same, melodious noise filled the air again.

The people around Samel stared.

No one could look away, because everyone knew what was coming.

"They're calling the monster!" came a whisper.

Samel's heart pounded with empathetic fear. He felt as if he were among those in the desert, luring the beast, instead of safe on the ledge. From up so high, he couldn't tell men from women, and he didn't see Raj, but he knew his brother must be down there. The marchers stood rigid in the desert. Slowly, the horn notes faded.

He looked along the rest of the ledge. Even if he were courageous enough to take the path to the cliffs, the people in the other caves would hurt him, like they'd done to Neena and Kai. Frustrated tears fell down his cheeks.

Holding a hand to his heart, Samel said a silent prayer.

Maybe Raj would get lucky, and the monster wouldn't come.

Maybe the beast was far enough away that it wouldn't hear, or it had left for some other part of the planet.

His hope died.

A few hundred feet past the spires, a seam split the desert, veering toward the waiting people.

No...

CHAPTER 10: Raj

R AJ LOWERED HIS HORN.
Silence greeted him.
And then something happened.

About fifty feet away, Bryan shifted in the desert, reacting to a growing rumble.

Two hundred waiting people tensed.

Panicked murmurs filled the air.

Raj looked out into the desert.

What he saw made his knees buckle.

Two hundred feet away, the sand creased.

In the time they'd blown their horns, the sun had returned, shimmering the desert with its heat, revealing the true horror of what they faced.

The ground caved and fell inward in front of them.

It felt as if some strange lightning was splitting it open.

But this was much worse than lightning, and everyone knew it.

Raj's heart hammered. His roiling stomach made him feel like he might vomit, or collapse. Instead, he waited, repeating Bryan's instructions in his head.

"Stay in place. Do not move until the last moment."

It was easy to imagine bravery, when standing in a cave full of others. But it was another to stand in front of horror and face it with two rigid feet.

The rumble increased to a deafening pitch.

Raj's heart and mind shrieked at him to flee — to get far

away from the caving sand and retreat — but he couldn't fail Bryan. They had to keep their courage, until the last bit of time, when they'd...

"Run!" someone screamed.

Raj didn't need to be told twice.

He and his group turned and dashed over the sand, heading for the rock spire. Raj kept his eyes on the distant stone. He didn't need stories of heroism to motivate him.

Move, or die!

The five horn blowers around him huffed and sweated, stuffing their boots in and out of the sand, racing against certain death. The rumble was loud enough that for a moment, Raj thought he might go deaf, or keel over from fear. Someone's shoulders grazed his. Someone else shouted something he couldn't hear. The world became a frantic mess of screaming and panic. Raj kept his eye on the smooth, red stone, praying to the heavens that he made it.

Twenty feet.

Fifteen.

He was almost there.

He was about to curve around it when something distracted him.

Raj turned in time to see Eddie stumble and fall.

Eddie's horn flew from his fingers as he landed hard, turning over and over, coming to rest ten feet behind the others. He regained his footing, but panicked, and ran toward the line of Watchers instead of the spire.

"Eddie!" Raj cried.

If Eddie kept going that way, he'd ruin the plan. Not only that, he'd die. He was moving in the wrong direction.

Defying his good sense — just for a moment — Raj stopped and took a single step back, calling his name.

The sand exploded.

Raj hurtled through the air, his arms and legs flailing.

His face stung from the blinding, pelting sand. The world turned black and chaotic.

A last agony hit him, so hard and so fast that he couldn't help his cry.

He'd made a mistake, and now he and Eddie would die together.

CHAPTER 11: Bryan

"**F**ALL BACK!" BRYAN YELLED.

Instead of emerging and leaping toward the rock spire, the creature diverted, following the path of the dim-witted horn blower and erupting from underneath the surface in another direction.

Now it was rising over the line.

Dammit!

The monster's rising body blocked out the sun, casting a long, ominous shadow. Blood and bile spewed from something it chewed. Its protrusions unfolded from its side, piercing the air, promising death to all who came near. If they didn't flee, dozens of people would be crushed or impaled.

"This way!" Bryan shouted over the beast's primordial sounds, hoping someone might hear him.

A few foolhardy men took aim, throwing their spears even though the plan was fouled, but too many people veered farther west into the desert, descending into chaos.

Their agonizing cries were cut short as the beast landed, driving them into the ground.

Shouting at the hundred or so in his group, trying to reorganize, Bryan said, "Get to the spire! Follow me!"

The screams of the injured echoed through the air, but there was nothing anyone could do for them at the moment. He and the survivors fled in the direction of the spire, hoping to put it between themselves and the monster, and he clenched his powerful weapon, running.

The beast soared in and out of the ground again, prompting a chorus of new screams, catching the slowest runners.

Sand sprayed Bryan's back. An ear-splitting boom rang out behind him. Sucking in a winded breath, he looked over his shoulder, in time to see another caving hole. A hopeless feeling shook his boots and his heart.

Still, he didn't quit.

He ran, heaving, until he and the other survivors of the western line reached the back of the spire — the only point of relative safety.

A few dozen people stood around him, stock-still.

Looking across the desert, he surveyed the eastern horn blowers and Watchers, who hadn't moved. Panic gripped them.

Letting one hand off the weapon, he cupped his mouth and shouted, "Blow your horns!"

The scared people did nothing. They were terrified, and the sight of so many crushed, or eaten, froze them.

"Do it!" he insisted.

Putting their fear into their lips, the second group finally obeyed, blowing long and hard. A rising tide of sand lifted near the beast's last hole as it changed direction, heading southeast and toward them.

The second line of spear-throwers readied themselves, moving north to compensate for the beast's incoming angle. The horn blowers adjusted, too.

From his new position — out of range — Bryan watched the beast break the surface and soar into the air. Its massive, circular body reminded him of some of the cave grubs, only on a grander scale. In a strange, abstract way, the beast was majestic.

But it needed to die.

The horn blowers blew their note again, waiting for the moment to run.

The creature reached its peak height, arcing over the horn blowers, who took the cue and fled.

Its angle changed.

Changed?

No!

The beast's body twisted and convulsed; its scales shifted. Instead of crashing directly into the rock, it grazed the side of it, creating a small avalanche of rock. The horn blowers had dispersed too late. The monster slammed back into the ground, taking four with it.

A few of The Watchers in the eastern group chased behind, hurling their spears at its back, but they plunked uselessly off its scales.

Two surviving horn blowers screamed, running across the desert in the direction of the cliffs.

The beast followed underground.

Bryan looked at his decimated followers, and those fleeing toward the eastern formation. The second diversion had failed.

The strategy was lost.

Worse, the horn blowers had blocked off their retreat.

Finding Louie's face among the survivors, he traded a panicked look. They could stay, reform, and cobble together a plan. Or they could accept a temporary loss.

"What are we doing?" Louie yelled.

Bryan looked at the horn blowers and the monster, and then over his shoulder.

Motioning toward the survivors in his group, and those farther away, he shouted, "Grab whom you can among the injured and follow me to the colony!"

Together, they fled.

CHAPTER 12: Samel

HANDS TUGGED SAMEL BACK FROM his new perch on the ledge, leading him back toward the Right Cave.

"We have to get back inside, Samel!"

Samel resisted Samara's pulling.

All around him, people stared anxiously at the scene below. The area near the spires had turned to chaos. Bodies lay everywhere. Holes filled the desert around the spires, marring the landscape like enormous, monstrous eye sockets.

Addressing the crowd, Samara said, "It's too dangerous to be out here! Everyone get back inside!"

She raised a hand, pointing to the mouths of the other caves, where their enemies still lingered, watching. Slowly, the crowd headed inside.

But not Samel.

He couldn't move.

He was riveted.

Choking on his tears, he raised a shaky finger.

"Raj is still out there!" he cried. "He might be hurt, or... or..."

"I know, Sam!" she said. "But it's too dangerous to get to him right now!"

The last of the people bumped Samel's shoulders, while heading for the relative safety of the cave.

Samel dug his heels in the ground, ignoring Samara's

pulling hands. "We can't leave him!" he protested. "He'll die out there! He needs our help!"

Samara looked over the ledge. Her face formed an expression he had seen too many times. It was the same face people wore at the processions, after a loved one had been buried. "We can't do anything now, but we will, Sam, later. I promise."

Samel fought for several moments, but finally, he let Samara guide him, tears flowing down his face. The sight of those people lined up in the desert gave him a cold, dark feeling he remembered from the first day of the monster's attack. He'd been terrified. But that day, he'd had his brother with him, and now Raj was out in the desert with the awful beast.

Samel couldn't allow himself to think of his brother's death. He hardly felt his legs moving, or Samara's tight grip on his arm as she led him inside. He felt numb, as if someone had dipped him in the river before the first rays of morning sunshine.

In front of them, men, women, and children bustled deeper into the cave, looking over their shoulders with fright. Samara stopped at the cave entrance, calling out instructions.

To Salvador and Roberto, she said, "Get as many guards at the front and rear entrances as you can! The rest of you keep in the middle with the children, away from the tunnel's ends!"

Salvador and Roberto obeyed, shoring up men or women, who guarded the entrance and the rear of the cave, clutching their spears and knives. The rest hung in the cave's middle, speaking worriedly. Samel caught the eyes of a younger child, who peered out from behind his mother. Too many kids didn't know what was happening, and that translated to panic. Fear's grasp was contagious.

Smearing fresh tears away, he looked up at Samara.

"Where's Neena?" he asked.

"We moved her and Kai to a safe spot by the wall."

"Is she okay?"

"She's fine." Samara hesitated. "She's asleep again."

Samel couldn't stop his thoughts from racing. Was Neena going to die? And where was Raj?

"It's going to be all right, Samel," Samara said, grabbing his arms. "I promise we'll figure all this out. We just need some time."

He looked into her eyes, wanting to believe her.

Despite her reassurances, Samel didn't see how it could ever be all right again.

CHAPTER 13: Bryan

"To the Comm Building!" Bryan mouthed, keeping the remainder of his followers quietly moving.

Men and women hurried, or hobbled, soundlessly down the center path of the colony. The looks on their faces were much different than the line he'd led down from the cliffs. Courageous postures had turned to panicked slumps. Chatter had turned to silence. A few people carried broken spears, or bags, but many had lost them. None of that mattered now, as much as survival.

He directed them faster, past the tithing and supply buildings and between the broken houses in the alleys on either side. A mass of people followed, creeping over the ground.

They passed by some of the wreckage he recognized from earlier trips to the colony. Piles of mud brick littered the former alleyways. More bones were dragged out and picked over. The smell of rancid death clung to his nose, reminding him of their fate, if they didn't find cover.

A lone, circular roof towered in the distance.

Bryan and his people veered toward it.

Soon they approached the back of the annex, and the wide, circular path that looped left and right around the Comm Building. Making another split-second decision, Bryan swerved right, avoiding a few piles of scattered mud-brick. Soon they rounded the corner of the towering structure, glimpsing the threshold.

And then they were at the front entrance.

"Open the doors!" Bryan mouthed.

Louie, Clark, Nicholas, and Isaiah stepped ahead of him, approaching the large, shuttered doors that led into the Comm Building. The enormous group of people behind them waited, shoulders slumped, faces painted with fear. No one spoke, or moved.

Slowly, The Watchers inched open the doors, releasing a whiff of stale air from the building.

The structure smelled of weeks of dust and disuse, and the last few meals that The Heads of Colony must've eaten. Bryan held his breath and moved through the threshold, verifying that no predators had gotten inside, before waving for the others to enter.

Two by two, the survivors advanced through the entrance. A few women limped with tears in their eyes, carrying their spears. Bryan glanced at a man with a bloodstained stomach, who winced as two others ushered him through. And then they were all inside, closing the doors, putting the braces in position, and shutting out the carnage outside.

Bryan looked around the dimly lit Comm Building. All around him, men — and the few women who had marched with them — held torches, quietly tending to the wounded, or sipping their flasks nervously. Some lay in pained heaps on the floor, while others situated themselves in the rooms formerly occupied by the veteran Watchers. More guarded the doors, lurking among the shadowy, yellowed animal skeletons hanging on the wall.

The rumbling and the screaming had stopped.

Still, no one spoke.

They were safe, for the moment, but Bryan wasn't foolish enough to believe the creature was gone.

Walking through the structure, he located a few of his men gathered near the center table. Bags, supplies, and spears lay haphazardly on its surface. Under the glow of the torchlight, Louie, Clark, Nicholas, and Isaiah awaited his instructions.

Leaning close to Louie, Bryan whispered, "Where are Rodney and Boyle?"

Louie shook his head.

Bryan blinked hard, feeling a pang of despair that he hadn't expected. "How many of our group survived?"

"I'm not sure," Louie answered quietly, looking around. "We grabbed whom we could among the injured. Most of the casualties were the horn blowers, of course. But we lost some Watchers and some others in the line. I think Rodney and Boyle were among them."

Bryan blew a slow breath. Ever since they'd reached the Comm Building and safety, all he could do was review what had gone wrong. The monster was savage and unpredictable, operating on primal instincts. But his people should have listened more closely.

The *horn blowers* should have listened more closely.

He couldn't accuse the dead, but that didn't stop his rage. He kept remembering the moment that first horn blower had strayed off course. Everything had gone to pandemonium after that.

"Our thought to use the unintelligent ones as bait failed us," he said with an angry sigh. "We'll have to retool our plan."

His failure stung. They were supposed to be using this room as a victory chamber, not another squalid cave. A few of his men looked at the strange device he held. He'd never even had a chance to use it.

"At least you kept hold of the device," Louie said, with a grateful nod.

It was a small miracle.

Louie fell silent, looking around the room at the men and women, and Bryan followed his gaze. A few of the injured agonized quietly, afraid to make noise. Others paced nervously. A few women cried, or held onto one another. The man with the bloodstained stomach suffered in a corner, lying prone on the floor.

Death hung over the room like a vaporous cloud.

The irrational part of Bryan wanted to rush outside, lure the monster, and try killing it again. But that would certainly lead to more deaths. Instead, he looked toward the door, where his Watchers stood nervously, holding their spears. Another row of people behind them looked from wall to wall, listening for rumbling. Bryan glanced up at the ceiling, tracing the rounded contours of the dome. He'd been in here on numerous occasions—always during the meetings of The Heads of Colony—but never for an extended period of time. Only the unmarried Watchers lived here. Still, the structure had always struck him as impenetrable. More than one time during a storm, he'd wished he'd been here, riding it out.

If only he could be assured that the walls could withstand the monster.

Seeing the frustration on his face, Louie walked closer. "What's our next move?"

Looking around the room at all the tired and the wounded, Bryan grew resolved.

"We'll stay here so our people can rest and recover. We'll mend our weapons. And then we'll figure out another plan." His voice grew hard. "One thing is for certain. We're not heading back to the cliffs until the monster is dead."

CHAPTER 14: Sherry

S HERRY FOUGHT HER WAY THROUGH the cave's dark shadows, her heart slamming against her chest. She couldn't forget the things she'd seen in the desert: the monster, the screaming, and the chaos. Nor could she forget the skirmish on the cliffs, which had filled her body with adrenaline.

She glanced behind her, listening to the voices behind her fade. Soon, the quietness of the cave swallowed up everything but her footsteps.

Winding with the cave's turns, she found her way past the first cove, shining her torch into that first, empty recess. The injured people once staying there no longer convalesced.

Only the second cove was occupied.

Sherry approached quietly, greeting Jameson, before stepping into the foul-smelling room. The oppressive air reminded her of the important man inside.

"Gideon," she whispered, taking up by his bedside.

Turning his disfigured face toward her, he adjusted his blankets and said, "Sherry."

Sherry swallowed. Of course, he had expected Bryan. But she had to prove to him that she was an ally, and not just the woman behind the man he trusted. "I came to update you on what has happened."

Gideon's eye rolled on her. He opened and closed his chapped lips, awaiting more details. If she'd been in an alley in Red Rock, he might've ignored her, but now she had his full attention.

"Is the beast dead?" he asked.

Sherry felt a sting of failure for Bryan. Hoping to compensate for what might be considered disappointing news, she said, "Our people fought the monster bravely. They lured it with their horns, threw their spears, and tried killing it, but the beast was unpredictable. It crashed into the side of the rock spire, killing some and wounding others. It caused an avalanche that forced them to flee."

"Where's Bryan?"

"Alive," Sherry said with relief.

"How do you know?"

"His weapon made him easy to spot. I followed him with my eyes after the monster attacked, and saw him valiantly leading the others to safety in the Comm Building. They regrouped."

"A blessing," Gideon said, nodding. "And where is the monster now?"

"No one has seen it since the attack," Sherry said, "But I fear even the people it consumed did not sate it."

Anger welled up in Gideon's expression. "It will not leave easily, after tasting more Red Rock flesh. The Red Rock traitors have caused more bloodshed."

"We have begun punishing them," Sherry reported.

"You have?"

Gideon listened intently, while she detailed the attack she'd led on Neena and Kai. Pride took over her face as she told how their people carried their limp bodies away.

"The Right Cavers are scared," Sherry affirmed. "Especially now that Darius is dead."

A smile wrinkled Gideon's scars.

Feeding off his satisfaction, she said, "I think we've taught them a lesson that words never could."

Gideon reveled in the news, before his smile faded.

"They are weak, but ultimately, we want the rest of the Right Cavers on our side. Do not forget that. A colony is no colony without people to fill it."

Sherry refrained from a response.

"What are Neena's and Kai's injuries?"

"I am not sure," Sherry said. "Though I would like to find out, so I can finish what I started."

"Perhaps they are dead," Gideon said, a strange expression taking over his face.

Impatience made Sherry scratch the scars on her skin. "I do not know for sure, but I will find out, so I can end them, if possible."

Gideon thought on it for a long moment. "Leave them alone, while we wait for things to settle. All things will come in time." Gideon watched her for a moment, ensuring she understood. "How are the people in the Left and Center Caves doing?"

"We've consolidated the women, children, and elderly into the Center Cave."

"A good idea. All are safe?"

"All are safe."

"Another boon." Clearing phlegm from his throat and swallowing it, Gideon said, "Keep your guards posted, and keep an eye on the Right Cave, just in case. In the meantime, I have faith that Bryan will do what he promised. Where one plan fails, another will arise. He will kill the monster and lead us to victory. I am sure of it."

Sherry nodded. An unexpected tear fell down her cheek. Too many emotions had followed the monster's most recent attack. It felt as if she and the Left and Center Cavers lived in some dark, primal hell, waiting for the last jab from misery's knife.

But soon, they'd be through the suffering and into the light.

"Leave Bryan to his work," Gideon told her, watching

her dab her tear away. "Once the monster is dead, he will take care of everything, and our colony will return to glory."

Sherry nodded, moving for the entrance.

She had no arguments, but her mind was already running new scenarios. She couldn't help her burgeoning anger. She was through sitting around and waiting. She was ready to take action. Gideon had his goals and plans.

She had hers.

CHAPTER 15: Raj

P AIN BURNED THROUGHOUT RAJ'S BODY.

He blinked and groaned, certain that he was dead, or food for a foul creature.

It felt as if someone had flung him from the top of the cliffs.

Or dropped him from the top of a spire.

Dead.

I must be dead and dreaming.

It wasn't until he felt the sand in the corners of his eyes, and the taste of it in his mouth, that he thought he might be alive. The hot sun beat down on his back, sticking his shirt to his skin. A light wind blew up and over him.

He was on his stomach, near where the attack happened, covered in sand.

Raj lifted his head, dripping stringy drool. Slowly, he wiggled his fingers and toes. His body was stiff, sore, and swollen, but his appendages worked. He raised a hand and wiped away his spit, ridding himself of some of the dirty paste. Raj squinted, but the glare of the sun prevented him from seeing clearly.

Slowly, he pulled himself into a crawling position.

And froze.

Where was the monster?

He paused, lifting an achy hand to shield his eyes. Long shadows stretched between the mammoth rock spires, crisscrossing the desert. The stone structures rose like giant's legs. About a dozen feet away from Raj, a cavernous hole plunged to darkness.

He saw no sign of the hideous creature.

No sign of *anyone*.

He shuddered.

Memories of his comrades' screams, and their hasty, running feet, rushed back to him with such clarity that he instinctively backed away. The last thing he remembered was trying to help Eddie, before he flew through the air, assumedly to his death. His eyes riveted to the hole again, watching for signs of teeth or scaled skin. He crawled about ten feet and stopped, his knees and palms stinging from the friction of the sand. He held his gasping breath.

The world was silent save the wind.

Raj turned east, spotting another hole in the distance. A person's broken spear lay near it. On another side lay an abandoned bag. A desire struck him, so hard and so fast that it overtook his thoughts.

Water.

Choking on the pasty sand, he crawled in the direction of the bag, praying it contained a flask. Thirst consumed him. He could think of nothing more than liquid.

Praying the monster didn't detect him, he moved quietly and quickly. Soon his hands were fumbling with the bag. He kept an eye on the hole while he rummaged through it.

A few rags.

A spare shirt.

There had to be water. There had to be —

A flask.

Raj held it up, gently shaking it. *Half full.* Thank the heavens! He uncapped it and drank, using a little to clean out his mouth, spitting quietly before drinking some more. He blinked again, relieved, but weak.

The quiet bothered him.

Two hundred people had marched down to the colony.

Was he the last one alive? He looked past the hole and around him, certain he'd find his comrades searching for him, but he saw only more broken spears. Raj fought the glare and looked up to the cliffs. It felt like late afternoon, maybe evening. In a few shadows by the entrance of the Right Cave, he thought he saw silhouettes, but he couldn't be sure.

Maybe he was the last person alive on the planet.

Whatever the case, he needed to get away from here.

Carrying the flask, he crawled away from the hole. He needed to find The Watchers.

Something brushed his hand. Raj cried out and spun, facing whatever reached out for him.

A severed arm, half-covered in sand.

Crooked fingers reached out from the body-less appendage. The rest of the person was nowhere in sight.

Raj stifled his panic and backed farther away, spinning and looking around. More body parts lay in his path of travel. A bitten-off leg. An unraveled string of intestines. Ten feet away, a severed head appraised him with glassy eyes.

In horror, Raj recognized the person.

Eddie.

Raj couldn't control his emotion.

Smearing frightened tears, he stumbled to his feet and found the strength to walk. Fear and adrenaline carried his legs. He hurried away from the holes and the bodies, searching for someone — *anyone* — who could help him, using the spires to hide, in case the monster was near. He looked up to the cliffs again, but this time the shadows only looked like crevices in the rocks.

What if all the others were really dead, and this was his hell?

A few dozen steps later, the soreness in Raj's legs worsened. He stumbled, weak and thirsty. It felt as if the sun had dried out his body and his mind, sapping him of strength and clarity. He held up the flask, sipping greedily, but stopped. His survival instincts kicked in.

He knew it was dangerous to drink too much, too fast.

Dehydrated or not, he needed to be careful. Blinking against the sun's dying glare, he maneuvered around a few more scattered bodies, heading in the direction of the colony.

One man lay on his back, his body flattened, his tongue lolling from his crushed face. Another man's jawbone protruded through his cheek. With a shudder, Raj recognized Boyle, one of Bryan's men.

Be quiet, or you'll be next.

If this wasn't a dream, or hell, then the monster might lurk nearby.

Shielding his eyes, he weaved between the spires, walking heel to toe, passing in and out of the shadows of the rock formations. Every so often, he rested. More than once, his legs threatened to crumple. He was starting to think he might collapse when he saw something.

Boot prints.

Lots of them.

The prints were obscured, partially covered in sand, but he could just make them out. He studied them through his weakness. More than likely they led to the cliffs, which he'd never reach.

To his surprise — and his hope — they headed in a single direction: to the center of the colony.

Steadying himself, Raj followed them.

CHAPTER 16: Bryan

SOMETHING CRASHED AGAINST THE DOORS.

Heads turned. The Watchers jolted, holding up their spears. A few of the men put their weight against the braces. Bryan had been right to question the integrity of the building.

The monster was here again.

"Hold still!" he mouthed.

All around the room, men and women stifled gasps, or held on to one another. The wounded looked frantically from where they lay, to the entrance, probably praying for their ancestors to save them. They wouldn't make it more than a few steps before the monster devoured them.

The noise ceased.

Bryan held his weapon, aiming it at the middle of the doors, where no men stood.

The clatter came again. Harder this time.

The people in the room jolted once again.

It wasn't until they heard a thin voice on the other side of the door that a few in the room exhaled.

"Bryan? Louie? Are you there?"

The survivors looked from the door, to Bryan, and back again. The bang came again—not the shudder of an incoming monster, but the bang of a person.

Making a decision, Bryan raised his chin. "Open the doors."

Two of his Watchers lifted away the braces, carrying

them a few steps back, while others slowly opened them. Dust floated near the entrance, shrouding the person who stood there in the dying light, panting.

Raj's face was cut up and scratched; his clothes were torn. He reached out, stumbling for someone to support him.

Bryan traded a look with Louie, before directing The Watchers. "Help him inside. Quickly."

CHAPTER 17: Neena

NEENA WALKED AIMLESSLY THROUGH A long cave, feeling her way through the infinite blackness. Voices surrounded her, speaking quiet, indecipherable words. Sometimes she recognized Samel. Other times she recognized Amos, or Samara. No matter how far she traveled, it seemed she could never reach them. Every so often, she bumped a jagged wall, injuring a hidden bruise. Her head throbbed. Occasionally she collapsed, before finding her footing again.

She was doomed to wander her lightless prison, a prisoner of the darkness.

She followed the cave for what felt like an eternity, fearing monsters at every crevice, until the wall disappeared underneath her touch. Neena reached and grabbed, but found nothing.

The tunnel around her spun, so fast and so wildly that she almost fell.

And then she was awake from her confusing dream.

Neena's gaze solidified on a face. Amos stood above her bedroll with worry.

"Neena?" he asked, seemingly not for the first time. "Can you hear me?"

Neena tried to answer, but her lips were dry, stuck together. He offered her the flask of water in his hands. She gripped it, but her fingers were stiff and sore, and her head hurt even worse.

"Let me help," he said, assisting her.

Water dribbled down her chin and onto her neck. With a cloth, Amos wiped it away.

"How are you feeling?"

"Better," she said, reflexively.

A spear of guilt worked through her. She wanted to sit up, shake off her injuries, and resume her life, even though she could barely keep her eyes open.

"Take it easy," Amos said. "You need your rest."

"I—"

"Neena, please."

All at once, she remembered waking up several other times and asking Amos the same question. He'd given her herbs and drink. She'd tried getting up, but he'd stopped her, saying that she needed to take it easy. Light flashed behind her eyes, making her dizzy again.

"How long have I been out?"

"A few days," Amos said. "Your head was injured. I think you'll be all right, but you need to rest, or you'll never recover."

Hearing his voice reminded her of the others.

"Where are Kai, Raj and Samel?"

"Samel's across the cave. And Kai has been here most of the time, keeping watch over you."

"Raj?"

Amos didn't answer.

"I'm not resting, if he's not here," Neena refused. "I'm getting up and I'm—"

She sat up quickly—too quickly—and the room spun. Her vertigo reminded her of that dark tunnel where she was endlessly walking, and then she was back in it.

CHAPTER 18: Kai

DAYS AFTER THE BRUTAL ATTACK on the cliffs, Kai huddled in the back of the Right Cave on his haunches, sharpening his spear. Every so often, he turned the weapon, working on a new side. He paid little attention to the sharp edge, or the rock he slid it against.

The bruises on his arms and legs were a constant reminder of the attack he and Neena had suffered. Every ache and scab reminded him that the culprits had suffered no consequence.

They also reminded him of Neena's condition. While Neena had been rendered unconscious, he'd awoken the next night, injured and angry. For the past few days, he'd kept an eye over her, along with Amos.

Now he was taking a rare moment alone.

He couldn't stop thinking of Neena, Darius, and Raj.

Every so often, Kai glanced down the long tunnel he guarded. The light of several torches beat back the shadows, but too much of the area beyond them was as dark as his thoughts.

He was nervous, and he was angry.

He wanted revenge for everything that was done to him, and his comrades. He wanted to charge down to the Left Cave—or to the colony—and pay Bryan's people back for what they did.

Footsteps from behind ripped him from his thoughts.

"Are you okay?" Samara asked, approaching him.

The question was rhetorical.

"I'm tired of feeling angry," Kai spat. "I'm tired of feeling like we failed."

Samara sighed, sinking down to the floor next to him. "I understand."

"I want to take revenge on those pieces of waste."

Samara bit her lip, feeling similar frustration. "I know you feel guilty for not finding Raj."

Kai lowered his head to the bloodied bag by his feet. Shortly after he'd woken up—against the other Right Cavers' warnings—Kai had slipped down to the colony alone, searching for the missing boy. At the time, he had insisted the others stayed put and safe. Even if he had a larger group with him, it wouldn't have mattered. All he had found were bodies.

Bodies, and the bloodied bag by his feet.

Raj's bag.

Noticing his gaze, Samara reached over and touched his arm. "I'm sorry."

"For all we know, he's alive," Kai insisted.

Samara was quiet a long moment, before she spoke. "We all saw the devastation from the monster's attack. Too many on the ledges saw the horn blowers fall. And you said you saw Raj carrying one of the horns, when he marched down from the cliffs."

He didn't need her to make the logical assumption.

Kai gritted his teeth. He'd already heard about how the monster had savaged the people by the spires, killing the horn blowers and others. He'd heard about the people fleeing through the desert, seeking shelter.

All that had happened after he was attacked and unconscious.

The Right Cavers had seen nearly two-dozen people die before Samara had ushered them inside, and of course, he'd seen the bodies, when he'd been down there. The guards had kept an eye out for Raj and reported back to him, but they'd been preoccupied. They couldn't have seen everything.

"Someone's in that Comm Building. I saw some people going in and out when I was down there," Kai said. "There are people who escaped the monster's attack."

"But even more people could've been eaten without a trace..." Samara said, trailing off.

"I won't believe Raj is dead until I have proof. And neither will Neena, when she wakes up. I won't give up on him."

Samara sighed. "So what are you proposing? Even if you convince more people to go down there with you, the Left and Center Cavers outnumber us. I said I'd go with you, and I will, if that's what you want, but there needs to be a reason."

"Isn't Darius's death enough?" Kai threw down his spear and knife. "We haven't even buried him. We put his body in a crevice several tunnels away, afraid that someone might creep up and attack us. He deserves better. No one gave him a ceremony. And Neena had no time to grieve."

"Maybe when things settle down, we'll give him a proper burial..." Samara touched his arm.

"I don't want a meaningless procession," Kai argued. "I want Raj back, and I want to pay Bryan back for what he's done." He ripped his arm away from her and slammed his fist on the cave floor.

Samara fell silent. For a long while, they sat without speaking, until Kai turned toward her, ashamed.

"I'm sorry, Samara," he apologized, reaching for her. "It's not your fault."

"I understand how you feel, because I feel the same way, too." Samara shook her head. "I want to charge down there myself and pay them back for the hurt they caused. I want to teach them that they can't get away with this. I want to make sure they never do it again."

Kai's eyes blazed. "Every time I check on Neena, I get furious all over again. I can't take another day of looking at her like that. We should've been ready for Sherry's attack."

"You were focused on Raj," Samara reminded him. "The attack was underhanded."

"And yet it doesn't matter, because now we're trapped in here, and Raj is missing or dead, and Darius's body is stuffed in a crevice in a cave." Kai clenched and unclenched his hands. "Maybe Bryan was right. If I'd never come back here, all of this could've been avoided."

Another silence fell over them. This time it was Samara's turn to break it. "You helped all of us, when we needed it. No one has forgotten what you, Neena, and Darius did."

"But we couldn't help Raj."

"Maybe you still can."

Kai turned toward her, feeling a glimmer of hope in his dark mood.

Samara looked as if she was working through a suggestion. "Let's say you are right, and Raj is alive. If so, he's in no immediate danger. He's safe in the Comm Building, along with the others."

"With Bryan, you mean," Kai said angrily.

Samara considered that. "If Bryan didn't hurt him before, there's no reason to think he'd hurt him now. Raj marched down with Bryan and his men of his own volition. That means we still have time. Maybe we can still get him back safely."

Kai picked up his knife and his spear and stood up, ready to turn hope into action.

"Wait," Samara said, stopping him with her hand. "Not now."

"When, then?"

Kai took a step away, but Samara leapt up and elaborated. "Let's plan something better than charging down there. Let's figure out a way to determine the truth without throwing our lives away."

Kai shook her off, but she watched him in earnest.

"Neena would want both you and Raj to be safe. She wouldn't want you to end up like Darius."

Kai opened and closed his eyes. He sighed.

"Give us some time to think of a better plan," Samara pleaded. "Together, we'll come up with something."

Reluctantly, Kai settled back down. "Okay, but I'm not waiting much longer."

CHAPTER 19: Neena

"**N**EENA?"

Neena's eyes fluttered and came into focus. Slowly, she processed the person leaning over her.

Kai.

Kai's eyes were filled with concern as he bent down and asked, "Are you okay?"

He reached over, tucking a strand of her hair behind her ear. Perspiration dotted the strange markings on his forehead. Those once-foreign marks gave her a familiar sense of home.

"Kai?" she whispered.

"Yes, it's me." His concern turned into a smile, when he heard her recognition.

"Are we still in the caves?" Neena asked.

It felt like she'd been underwater, and was just surfacing.

"Yes, we're still here," Kai confirmed.

"Why do I feel so tired, even though I just woke up?"

"It's because of the medicines Amos has been giving you," Kai explained. "That, and the head injury you sustained."

"They pelted me with rocks..." Neena's confusion found its way to anger, as she looked around at the groups of people sitting near the middle of the cave. "They pelted you, too."

"I'm fine," Kai assured her, waving a hand up and down

his body to prove it. "But I was worried about you. You took the brunt of the attack. For a while, I thought you might be…"

"Dead?" Neena asked, sitting up. "I'm fine."

"Careful," Kai warned, gently settling her back down. "You don't want to rush things. The last thing you need is to aggravate your injuries."

Slowly, Neena moved her arms and legs. They were stiff, but not broken. That gave her the resolve to sit up again. A sudden, dull ache in her side made her reconsider.

"It's your rib," Kai said, noticing her wincing. "I think it's bruised. Amos has been watching you carefully. Can you breathe all right?"

Neena tested a breath. The sensation was a little shallower than normal, but she could take air. Telling another lie, she said, "I'm fine."

Neena gently removed the blanket from her body, looking down at her ripped clothes. Holes in her shirt and pants revealed the scabs and bruises she'd felt, but hadn't seen, until now. Her pain reminded her of the conversation she'd had with Amos, during her lucid moments.

"Where's Samel?" she said, looking around for him.

"He's with Adriana, across the cave." Kai motioned to a circle of people about fifty feet away. "He's safe."

"But Raj is gone," she remembered.

Kai didn't answer. His expression jarred her fully awake.

"I tried to find him, Neena," he said. "I searched for him, after the monster attacked. I didn't find him, not yet."

Neena refused to believe those words. "Where is he?"

"My hope is that he's in the Comm Building."

"The Comm Building?"

"That's where Bryan and most of his followers ended up," Kai said. "I'm sorry, Neena."

In a gentle voice, Kai explained the events that had happened while she was out. Neena listened with growing concern as Kai told of the Abomination's appearance, Bryan's men scattering, and how they'd sequestered in the Comm Building. He elaborated on his attempts to find Raj.

When he was finished, he went quiet.

"Raj is still with Bryan," Neena repeated blankly.

"That's what we hope," Kai said, looking away. His expression gave her more worry, instead of reassuring her.

"Do you believe that?"

"I want to," Kai said, clenching and unclenching his fists. "I feel awful that I didn't find him, Neena. But if he's alive, we're going to get him back. I swear by the twin moons."

"You're damn right we are," Neena said, pulling past her pain. "And we're going to do it now."

CHAPTER 20: Neena

"**N**EENA, WAIT!" KAI CALLED, TRYING to stop her from standing.

Instead of listening, she rose, scanning the cave floor next to her blanket. On the ground were her bag, her flask, and her spear. Ignoring Kai's protests, she bent down and retrieved her things. She'd been lying down for too long.

"What are you doing?" Kai asked.

"What do you think I'm doing?"

A few of the Right Cavers looked up from the circles where they stood or sat, startled to see her on her feet.

Maybe they'd counted her dead.

It felt as if she *had* been dead.

But now she was alive, and she was going to make everything right. She was going to find Raj and pay these people back for what they'd done. Ripping open her bag angrily, Neena searched for her knife, which was no longer at her side, and had presumably been taken off her while she healed.

"You can't do this," Kai protested.

"Why not?" Neena asked, eyes blazing. "Am I supposed to leave Raj down there to die?"

"Of course not," Kai said, battling his own emotions.

"Should I wait until they stab my brother and leave him in the desert for us to find, along with the rest of the bodies? Just like they did to Darius?"

"No, but we're in the middle of coming up with a plan," Kai said.

Neena looked up to find Samara coming toward her, an empathetic expression on her face.

"Neena!" she exclaimed. "You're awake!"

"I am," Neena said, "and I'm going to get my brother. Are you going with me, or are you staying here?"

A voice from across the cave interrupted her. She looked up to find Samel rushing toward her, his eyes wide with disbelief. Without a word, he crashed into her, squeezing her tightly. His quiet crying dampened some of her anger, but not enough of it. Behind him, Amos was already shuffling as fast as his old legs would allow, narrowing the gap. Looking at his creased, worried face, Neena remembered his vigil over her.

Slowly, more people in the Right Cave surrounded her. Some people patted her back gently, or said encouraging words. Their expressions showed their relief. A few women whispered to one another, thanking the heavens that she was alert and alive.

"Samara and I have been working on a plan," Kai said, taking her arm again. "Let's figure this out, before we rush to our deaths. These people need us. All of them."

Neena opened and closed her eyes.

"Okay," she said. "But I don't want to waste any time."

CHAPTER 21: Sherry

S HERRY STARED AT THE CIRCLE of dirty-faced women who sat on their haunches, untangling the snarls from their hair, or picking the grime from beneath their fingernails. A few sipped gently from their flasks, while others looked at the ground.

Studying their faces, she recalled how some of them had fled, after that first altercation. Their weakness sickened her.

Sherry was tired of feeling as if she'd performed half a job. Every night when she closed her eyes, she saw the wrinkled smile on Gideon's face, after she'd told him what they'd done to Neena and Kai. Despite his satisfaction, he'd told her to leave the fighting to the men.

That inflamed her.

Unable to contain her anger any longer, Sherry said, "For the past few days, we've wasted time in our cave, when we should be acting. We need to show our men that we can take care of our duties. We need to make them proud."

A few women nodded, but no one responded verbally. Ever since the attack on Neena and Kai, Sherry had had trouble convincing her women to do anything more than keep an eye on the Right Cavers from a distance. The altercation on the cliffs had scared them. It was easy to cast away fear when it was a dozen against two, but it was another to face a row spears.

They were mothers, worried about their children and their men.

"Bryan and the rest of our men are down there, preparing for another battle, while we huddle in our cave," she said in frustration. "We need to prove our worthiness. We need to find out what happened to Neena and Kai."

"What can we do?" A woman shrugged. "The Right Cavers are tucked safely away with guards at the entrances. It is not as if we can barge in and confirm that Neena and Kai are dead."

Sherry's face curdled. "So we should stay and do nothing?"

The woman furrowed her brow. "The men instructed us to protect them while they marched. We've already done that."

"And that is good enough for you?" Sherry snapped.

She looked around at all the nervous, tentative faces in the room. A raven-haired woman, Jodi, spoke out. "I'm sorry, Sherry, but we're worried about our men. For all we know, they were wounded in the desert. It's hard to think about much else."

A few women closed their eyes, wiping away emotional tears.

"For all we know, our husbands are dead," whispered another woman.

"And that is exactly why you should be furious at Neena and Kai," Sherry snapped. "They are responsible for all of this. We can't let them get away with it."

The group quieted.

"I'd rather check on our men," said Jodi.

"We can't go down to Red Rock," Sherry reminded her. "Bryan was very clear about that. We need to stay up here and protect our children."

"So you're suggesting we stir up more trouble and get them killed?" Jodi rebuked.

A murmur of agreement echoed through the group.

"It's been days since we've seen anyone but the guards

at the Right Cave," Jodi went on. "The Right Cavers are keeping to themselves. They aren't bothering us, even after what we did to Neena and Kai. And that means we shouldn't bother them."

A blonde-haired woman named Tanya agreed. "The monster is a bigger priority than the Right Cavers. It's down there, killing and wounding our men, while we're up here. How can you expect us to focus on your vendetta?"

"Vendetta?" Sherry's eyes blazed, as she drilled the women with a stare. "You think I am only doing this for Gary?"

Tanya quickly averted her eyes.

"Neena and Kai are the reason for our emotional pain." Sherry shook her head. "First, they bring the monster here. And now *our* men are down there fighting it, while they hide in their cave. Your husbands might die, because of what they've done. And yet, you do nothing."

The women fidgeted guiltily.

"Once our men return, they'll deal with the Right Cavers," Jodi said resolutely.

"What if our children are dead by then?" Sherry asked.

Silence met her ominous statement.

Gathering everyone' attention, preparing the lie she'd saved for this moment, Sherry said, "Apparently you haven't heard the rumors." She lowered her eyes.

"What rumors?" Jodi asked.

The women glanced at one another, their unrest growing.

Building on their fears, Sherry continued, "The Right Cavers planned to rob us after the scavenging trip they took with Bryan."

Nervous conversations grew among the women, who looked wildly around, as if someone else might be in the cave.

"They planned to sneak into our caves while we were sleeping, and ferret away our rations," Sherry continued, over the commotion. "Of course, our feud happened first. But it could easily happen now."

"Where did you hear that?" Jodi asked.

"One of The Watchers told me." Sherry shrugged. "He wasn't completely sure, but he was pretty certain. He saw them sneaking around a few times. And we all saw the way they looked around, when they supposedly came to reconcile with us in the Left Cave."

The women's eyes grew wide.

"They were clearly staking us out."

"Are you sure?" asked Tanya.

"Perhaps you've forgotten who lives in the Right Cave," Sherry said. "Kai is a criminal. For years, he lived in a jail cell, before escaping. And now Neena shares his bedroll. They are both untrustworthy. And now we've attacked *them*. Who knows what other plans they're making?"

Watching the women squirm and wring their hands, Sherry knew her lies were working.

"Think about it," Sherry said. "We're alone up here, without our men. We're hungry. So are they. There are more of them than us. What happens when they realize our food can be theirs? How long until they take advantage of that?"

Loud, panicked side conversations started among the women.

Feeding their worry, Sherry said, "Did you see the way the Right Cavers looked at us on the cliffs? They shook their spears at us as if we were rats, crawling along the ledge. They treated us like the dung beneath their boots. They were angry then, and I imagine they're even angrier now. It won't take much for them to hurt us or our children."

Biting her lip, Tanya looked around at the others. "Let's say you're right, and they plan on attacking us. What can we do? They have a hundred and fifty people, while we only have a hundred. We aren't practiced with spears."

"We won't be any use to our children, if we die," said another woman.

"We might not be able to fight them head on, but we can let them know we won't be victimized," Sherry said. "We can strike first, and give them a warning."

"We already did that on the ledge," Tanya argued.

"But that didn't stop them, did it?" Sherry asked, looking around at everyone. "They had no trouble running down here with their spears, did they?"

The din of unrest in the cave grew.

Silencing everyone, Sherry asked, "Have you ever seen a wounded animal in the desert?" She looked around, ensuring that she met every eye. "It only takes time before a predatory animal descends on it, pulling its flesh from its bones. If we do nothing, we'll suffer the same fate. We need to prove we're strong. We need to stay one step ahead of them."

Fear cemented in the women's eyes.

"The Right Cavers know our numbers," Sherry persisted. "They know the layout of our cave. We need to prove that we are the wolves, worthy of snapping back. We need to ward them away before they come for us and our children."

For the first time, no one argued. Fright was a powerful motivator.

Sherry tucked her hair behind her ears, before solidifying her appeal. "I know that you are worried for your lives and your children's lives. But we need to warn away the Right Cavers. Maybe we can find a way to do it without risking ourselves physically. Maybe we can send them a clear message to stay away."

The women nodded, hanging on her words.

"What do you propose?" Jodi asked.

"I'm not sure, but we'll figure it out together." Meeting the eyes of each of the people in the group, Sherry let her gaze linger on Tanya and Jodi. "I'll need all of your help to do that. Are you with me?"

Feeling the pressure of the others, Jodi and Tanya exchanged a glance, before nodding and agreeing.

"It's settled, then." Sherry smiled proudly. "Let's make our plans."

A warm feeling spread from her heart to her extremities.

Her words were effective, just like Bryan's had been. She was a leader.

A person worthy of respect.

Sherry's revenge was in motion. She'd break down the Right Cavers until they had no spirit left. Once their misery was at its peak, she'd get her hands on Neena and Kai, and give them what they deserved.

She could already feel the look of adoration on Bryan's face, when she told him that Neena and Kai were dead. He would praise her. Exalt her.

Love her.

CHAPTER 22: Raj

RAJ WALKED THROUGH THE COMM Building, weaving around the groups of people on the floor, who spoke quietly, or catered to the wounded. His shoulders sagged. Occasionally he felt a sting of pain, but most of those aches were minor, compared to the pain in his heart.

Ever since he'd arrived back at the Comm Building, the marchers had treated him strangely. A few times, Raj struck up conversations with them, but most of those conversations ended in awkward silences. More than once, his approach triggered a whisper or a look of disdain. It took him a while to realize what was going on.

They blamed him for the attack's failure.

They didn't accuse him outright—perhaps because he was a child—but they'd outcast him. He had tried to help Eddie, but since Eddie had died and he had survived, he had therefore become the face of their loss. The fact that he was Neena's brother didn't help his case.

Even the leaders barely glanced at him.

Raj had gone from a hero to a fraud.

Weaving around his comrades, none of whom looked at him, he blinked back tears. Memories of the mangled bodies and limbs in the desert plagued him.

A few times in the past few nights, he'd awoken from nightmares, searching the torch-lit room. More than once, he'd stifled a cry, certain that the monster rose above him. Whenever he thought about seeking comfort in another marcher, embarrassment made him crawl back to the ratty bedroll someone had given him.

The Left and Center Cavers weren't talking to him. Eddie was gone. And of course, Raj's family was still up on the cliffs.

Raj was alone.

Hanging his head, he walked past one of the Comm Building walls, staring up at the strange, ancient animal skeletons, his only friends. He traced the yellowed edges of their skulls, fighting another tear.

Staring at those old remains, he recalled Darius, telling him stories about the carcass in the tunnels.

Where was Darius now? Was he awake, and thinking of him?

The last time he'd seen the old man, it'd been from the shadows while Darius tested the weapon. That was before Bryan stole it, and brought it back to the Left Cave. According to Bryan, stealing the weapon had been easy—Darius hadn't been there.

Thinking of Darius brought needles of nostalgia to Raj's heart.

For a moment, he considered leaving the Comm Building, heading back to the cliffs, and reuniting with him, as well as Neena, Kai, and Samel, but they probably hated him, too.

Nobody had looked for him.

They probably thought he was dead.

Wandering aimlessly around the main room of the Comm Building, he scanned the Watchers' quarters, which extended off the main chamber. Inside one of them, Bryan sat on the edge of a bed, thinking through something.

Bryan hadn't spoken to him in days.

Still, watching him, Raj couldn't forget all those nights they'd spent together in the caves, discussing the relic, or making plans to kill the monster. He recalled the look of respect Bryan had given him when he'd shown him the weapon, or how he'd complimented him for sneaking out with Adriana. Raj had never felt so important.

Better memories drove Raj toward Bryan. He held his breath, praying he'd find a way to return to the leader's good graces.

Entering Bryan's room, Raj stuffed his hands in his pockets, waiting to be noticed. Bryan said nothing.

After a long, awkward pause, Raj said, "Are you making new plans to kill the monster?"

Bryan nodded, scratching his stubbly chin. Bags ringed his eyes. Raj knew he'd been awake for long hours, contemplating things, usually behind closed doors. He'd seen him holding many private conversations with his important men.

"Our plans failed, because of you and Eddie," Bryan said bluntly.

Shame reddened Raj's cheeks. "I'm sorry about what happened in the desert. I tried stopping him…"

"But you failed."

"If I could make it up to you, I would." The words felt inadequate, even as he spoke them.

Bryan was silent.

Steering the conversation away from his failure, Raj asked, "Do you have any new plans to share with us?"

Bryan looked at him, perhaps deciding what to divulge. "My Watchers and I are considering ideas. When we solidify our plans, we'll inform everyone."

Raj waited, hoping Bryan might elaborate, but he didn't. Instead, Bryan's eyes roamed to the strange device on the bed next to him, and his bag.

Trying to regain his usefulness, Raj asked, "Do you have enough small spears for the device?"

Bryan's eyes stayed on his belongings. Inside the bag,

Raj saw a handful of the extra spears that The Watchers had carved the morning before they left.

"I think we have enough," Bryan said. "Darius's template was easy enough to follow."

"He's always been good at carving," Raj said. "He showed me how, you know. If you ever need anything, I can help you."

Bryan looked up. A strange expression crossed his face. In a sharp voice, he snapped, "Would you mind leaving?"

Raj looked around, startled by Bryan's change in tone. "I'm sorry. If you need anything, I'll be out with the others."

He walked from the room, his head hanging, leaving Bryan behind.

CHAPTER 23: Bryan

B RYAN'S MIND SNAPPED AWAY FROM the leaving boy. Watching him go, memories flooded back to him. All at once, he was back in Darius's cove, trying to take the weapon. Bryan's original intent had simply been to snatch the device.

Things had gone very differently.

Until now, he'd tried pushing those images from his mind.

Now they came flooding back.

He recalled how he, Louie, and Ed had advanced into the small tunnel, finding Darius alone, working on one of his small spears. The device was next to him on a rock. At first, Bryan had asked the old man for the weapon, but Darius had refused.

And so Bryan had stepped forward, asking more insistently.

A shout of defiance escaped Darius's lips.

That shout triggered a recollection.

All at once, Bryan had remembered being back outside that hovel in the colony, listening to Gary's final, agonizing screams. Thoughts and reality blurred together. Before Bryan knew it, he was pushing the old man to the ground and drawing his knife. Darius's kicking and flailing reminded him of Gary fighting the falling rubble. His cries reminded Bryan of Sherry's heaving sobs, when she found out about her husband's death.

Blind rage took over.

Unable to stop himself, Bryan had slashed Darius's throat.

Instead of raising his sympathy, each gurgled scream from Darius triggered more of Bryan's emotion, and more traumatic pain. The gushing blood from Darius reminded Bryan of the stone protruding from Gary's stomach when they finally pulled him out of the rubble. Darius's tattered clothing reminded him of Gary's.

All Bryan wanted was for the pain to stop.

A slew of tools on the surface of the rock in the cove beckoned him, and so Bryan had picked them up, using them one at a time, quelling his inner torment. Each stab hushed more of Darius's gurgles. And then all of Darius's tools were sticking out of him, and Bryan was kneeling over a dead man, panting.

Realizing what he'd done, he'd looked over at Ed and Louie.

They'd watched him with emotionless eyes.

Neither had condemned him.

Instead, they'd seemed satisfied.

"Let this be a lesson to the Right Cavers," Louie had said firmly. "Maybe they'll think twice before following us."

Ed had agreed.

Darius had forced Bryan's hand, or at least, that's what Bryan told himself, in those moments of self-doubt, or when memories of that bloodied night came back to him.

Blinking away those images, he forced himself back to the present. None of the marchers in the Comm Building knew what had happened that day, except for Louie, Ed, and Sherry, whom he'd told before he left, but Bryan couldn't think about that now. When the time was right, everyone would stand by his side.

They'd follow him, like they'd followed him down from the cliffs.

His gaze wandered elsewhere through his open doorway, where people huddled and spoke in low voices. About half of them sat cross-legged on their bedrolls, sharing their worries, or counting the supplies they didn't lose.

Walking over to the round, center table, he perused a stack of broken spears with Louie.

"The people are anxious," Louie reported.

Bryan sighed. No one needed to tell him about the growing feeling of unrest.

"They want to return to the cliffs," Louie continued. "They're worried about food and water. And they miss their relatives."

Bryan wrung his hands. Too many tears had been shed for the fallen, or the injured. The attack had sapped the marchers' courage. They, too, blamed the horn blowers, but that didn't stop people from their guilt, or their worry.

"They want to bury their dead, and report back to their women and children, who certainly miss them."

"It's too dangerous to bring a large group back to the cliffs," Bryan said. "We can't risk another march."

"If we stay quiet..." Louie started.

"It will only take one fool to do what that horn blower did and cause chaos," Bryan said, quietly, looking over at where Raj hovered near the other end of the table. For the past few days, the boy had been like a rat searching for table scraps, skulking around the others.

He'd outlived his usefulness.

Turning the other way with Louie, he lowered his voice.

"How many supplies do we have left?"

"We'll run out soon," Louie said. "As you know, we only brought enough for a few days. And we lost some during the monster's attack."

Bryan clenched his fists. They'd hoped to defeat the creature in short order, and therefore, had left most of their provisions on the cliffs for their women.

"Perhaps a few of us can return, inform our relatives of what is happening, and check in on them," Louie suggested. "Our scouts can bring back supplies."

For a moment, looking around at all the bedraggled people, Bryan considered it. But then he thought of his promise to Gideon, and the inspiring words he'd spoken to Sherry. He'd promised her a better life. He'd promised it to all of them. And now he'd spilled blood for their cause.

"What will we tell our women? That we failed?" A surge of anger washed over Bryan as he thought about admitting defeat. "That we marched down here, only to have more people killed for nothing? I won't do it."

"Surely, they already saw what happened down here," Louie said.

"They saw us fall, but next time, they will see a victory," Bryan promised. Gesturing at some Watchers stationed around the table, he said, "Arrange for a dozen of our most trusted men to go out into the colony to scavenge. Have a dozen others go down to the river, to collect water and any crops they can find."

Louie nodded.

"In the meantime, I will keep working on our next plan," Bryan said.

CHAPTER 24: Neena

NEENA GLANCED AT THE TWO-DOZEN people around her, who sat perched on rocks, or cross-legged. Kai, Samara, Amos, Roberto, and Salvador sat the closest. She flinched at a needle of pain from one of her many, crusted wounds. With some time to settle down from her initial, emotional outburst, other, buried pain had set in.

Looking around at all the faces around her, she kept expecting to find Darius among them. Of course, he was dead, and she'd never see him again.

Darius's loss was a pressing weight, hovering over all of them.

Blinking back some tears she hadn't had a chance to process, she wiped her face and asked, "Where did you put his body?"

"In a tunnel a ways from here," said a woman, beckoning toward the back of the tunnel. "Kai found a smaller cove for him. We covered him with rocks the best we could."

Neena blinked hard. Looking past the group and toward the rest of the cavers, she asked, "How did everyone take the news?"

"We protected the children from it, and whomever else we could," Kai lowered his eyes, through his emotional pain. "Of course, no one could stop talking about it for days."

"Nothing like this has ever happened in Red Rock." Samara blew a long breath. "Nobody could bear to keep his tools, after how they'd been used. So we laid them to rest with him, along with his cane. I cleaned up the cove where he worked."

"And I carved a circular marking on the wall of his resting place. " Kai's eyes welled up.

For a long while, they sat in silence, remembering their lost friend, blotting their eyes. Each quiet sob from the women was like a jab to Neena's heart. Thoughts of vengeance mixed with her sorrow. But of course, they had other things to consider.

"When the time is right, we'll give Darius a proper burial," she swore. "Or maybe even a procession. But right now, we need to focus on getting back Raj."

Those who were crying smeared away tears. Others nodded.

"If we don't act, Raj might be killed next," she added.

A tense silence returned. The others looked up, ready to listen.

Pushing away her sorrow, Neena put on a stern face. "What is your plan?"

Kai and Samara traded a glance, deciding who should speak first. Samara started.

"As we've discussed, rushing down to the Comm Building and looking for him would be a recipe for death," Samara said. "They have two hundred armed people. We have only a hundred that might be able to fight, out of our hundred and fifty. Too many of us are old, inexperienced, or have children to tend."

The others agreed.

"So, what are we thinking?" Neena asked.

"My guess is that Bryan's people are holed up and dressing their wounds, preparing for the next attack on the monster," Salvador said. "With a group that large, they'll need provisions. And that means they'll come out again soon. At least, some of them."

"That is our opportunity," Kai said. Taking the next

logical step, he added, "Assuming they don't all come out at once, we might be able to get a small group alone."

"We can leverage that," Samara said, tilting up her chin.

"How?" Neena asked.

Samara traded a glance with Kai. "Our thought was that we could ambush one or two people when they go out for supplies. If our logic holds, they'll split up, and we'll have an opportunity. We'll confront a few of them, pull them into a hovel, and find out if Raj is in the Comm Building."

"What about Sherry's women?" Neena frowned.

"We'll use the lower caves and sneak down at night, so they are less likely to see us," Kai elaborated. "We'll stick close to the hovels in the colony. We'll bring only a small group, so we'll be agile."

Neena fell silent. Thinking about the Left and Center Cavers brought back a slew of angry, painful memories. Neena couldn't forget Sherry's attack on the ledges. More than once, she'd entertained the notion of confronting Sherry and her women, but she forced the thought away. Raj was the important issue now.

Returning to the current matter, she said, "With any confrontation, we risk a disturbance. We might draw more people, or the monster."

"It is a risk," Kai admitted. "But if we confirm whether Raj is alive, it will be worth it."

Neena blew a breath. Of course, she'd do anything for her brother. "Let's make the hopeful assumption that Raj survived. What would our next step be?"

"That's where Samara's leverage comes in," Kai said. Looking around at the others, he continued, "If Raj is alive, we'll bring the ambushed people back to the Comm Building and offer a trade."

Sensing some hesitation among the others, Samara added, "Our intent is not to harm them, of course. We'll disarm them and avoid conflict. But that will give us bargaining power."

A small silence fell over the group.

"What if Bryan won't give Raj up?" asked a woman with short, dark hair. "Will we make good on our threats?"

Kai and Samara looked at one another, before Kai finally answered, "We'll do what we have to do to make sure Neena's brother is safe."

The woman breathed nervously. "So we'll do what they did to Darius."

"Or what they did to us," Kai said, looking at his bruises. "Hopefully, it won't come to that."

The woman chewed on her thoughts for a moment, looking around at the others. Not for the first time, Neena saw hesitation. Everyone was happy to see Neena alive, but they were worried. Thoughts of Darius's death were fresh on their minds. And, of course, everyone had witnessed what happened on the ledge.

"What if we trade our ambushed men for Raj, and Bryan's group attacks us afterward?" the woman with dark hair asked. "Who's to say he will honor our agreement?"

More silence.

"Perhaps we bring our kidnapped marchers with us," Samara suggested, after thinking about it. "We'll release them when we get to the top of the cliffs. They'll return, and we'll stay here with Raj. That will give us security."

"Or we'll provoke a battle with two hundred people that we can't win," the woman mumbled.

The people on the fringes of the circle shifted uncomfortably. A man with shaggy gray hair blew a long breath, looking around at the others, before saying, "I'm not disputing the importance of finding your brother, Neena. But we've already seen the way Bryan's people treat us. Everyone will reap the consequences of our actions. What if confronting them brings death to us all?"

A few people murmured, looking behind them at their relatives elsewhere in the tunnel, who tended the children.

"Anything we do carries a risk," Kai said. "But this is the safest plan we can think of."

The group sat in silence. Looking at their concerned faces, Neena couldn't help but think they were right.

What if they were discussing the very thing that would get them all killed?

"There is another thing no one has considered," Amos said, breaking the quiet. "What if Raj doesn't want to return?"

Everyone turned toward him, listening.

"Clearly, Raj made a choice to sneak out and leave us behind," Amos elaborated. "And obviously he told Bryan about the weapon. What if we go to the trouble of ambushing these people, and Raj refuses to go with us?"

The group looked at Neena. It seemed like her question to address.

"As much as I do not want to believe he would do that, it is possible," Neena said, hating her admission. "Clearly, Raj harbored deeper feelings of resentment than I realized. Maybe Raj is alive, and he doesn't want to come back. And if that's the case, I don't know our recourse."

Angry tears stung her eyes. She looked away from the concerned group to Samel, who sat elsewhere in the cave.

What if she died in the process of finding Raj, and left him alone?

Or what if Raj was already dead, and she was chasing a ghost?

Impossible questions.

Sitting forward in the dirt, the dark-haired woman said earnestly, "All I'm asking is that you consider your actions, Neena, before you make a rash move."

Neena blew a long sigh, before she conceded. "I'll mull it over tonight and commit to a plan in the morning."

CHAPTER 25: Bryan

"**B**RYAN," LOUIE CALLED.
Resting his uninjured arm on the jamb of the doorway, he peered into the quarters where Bryan sat ruminating.

"What is it?" Bryan asked.

"I've gathered a group of our stealthiest Watchers, like you asked," Louie said, motioning behind him. "A dozen will search for food, under my direction. A dozen will go with Ed to secure water and Green Crops."

Bryan nodded.

"I have concerns, though," Louie said. "It's getting dark. We're less likely to spot what we need under torch light. And if the monster arrives, it'll make for a dangerous scenario."

"Agreed," Bryan said. "Leave first thing at dawn. And return as soon as you have enough to fill your bags."

"Will do, sir."

CHAPTER 26: Neena

EENA SAT IN HER BEDROLL, staring at the ground. Conversations rose and faded around her, but she barely heard them, nor did she pay attention to the people bringing back rats from their traps.

"What are you thinking?" Kai asked.

Neena grappled with her thoughts. "I understand why people are so hesitant to act. I understand they think that we might be killed."

Kai sighed. "I understand it, too."

Neena shook her head. Breaking her gaze from the floor, she said, "We've already jeopardized everyone by bringing the monster here. How can I ask them to risk their lives again?"

Kai stroked his stubbly chin, just as conflicted.

"Something else is weighing on me," Neena said. "Something we only talked about a little bit."

Kai watched her carefully. "What is it?"

It took a moment for Neena to muster the words, and even longer to say them. "I keep thinking about what Amos suggested, about Raj not wanting to return. And that leads my thoughts to darker places. Obviously Raj told Bryan about the weapon. But what if he had a part in Darius's death?"

Her words felt like a betrayal to Raj.

"I don't think he did," Kai said, reaching over and touching her arm.

"How can we be sure?" Neena asked, not wanting to believe the words she spoke. "I had no idea that Raj was leaving. Who knows what other secrets he held?"

Kai considered it a moment, before answering. "I don't know your brother as well as you do, but I don't think he would hurt Darius."

"I want to believe that, too," Neena said, fighting back a tear. "But his actions shook me. It's hard to fathom that he would leave his family behind. He must really hate me. And that makes me wonder what else he could do."

Kai shook his head. "He's a boy, Neena. He's struggling to find his place on the planet. I know exactly how that feels." Kai trailed off, finding more words. "At one time, I was as young and as lost as he was. I made stupid mistakes, and even bigger mistakes later, when I went to jail. But now I am here, and those mistakes matter less. And that makes me think that Raj can get past this."

"I hope," Neena whispered, wiping her eyes.

Kai scooted closer to her, and she found his arms, holding him tight. Together, they surveyed the rest of the cave, watching people speak in smaller circles. Every so often, someone looked over at her and Kai, obviously worried.

An undeniable resolve washed over Neena.

"No matter what my doubts are about Raj, I won't leave him down there," she said, firmly. "If he is alive, I will get him back, even if I have to do it myself."

"I'm coming, too," Kai promised.

Neena squeezed him tighter. "I knew you'd say that."

They held each other tight.

"Bryan's anger is with us. It always has been," Kai said. Drawing a long, nervous breath, he added, "Perhaps this is the safest choice for our people."

"We brought the monster here," Neena agreed. "We

angered The Watchers. And my brother is the one missing. It is our problem to solve."

A strange calm washed over Neena. If this was the way their lives would end, then at least they'd do everything they could for Raj.

"Perhaps we are better off not telling the others," Neena said. "We don't need them feeling pressured to endanger themselves. We'll get a little rest. After we've slept a while, we'll tell the guard, and go."

CHAPTER 27: Raj

RAJ SAT IN A QUIET corner of the Comm Building, chewing his dried meat. After speaking with Bryan, he'd retreated to his bedroll, where he'd stayed. His hope was that if he blended in with the others, they'd forgive him. The shadows seemed like his only friends.

He couldn't stop replaying his conversation with Bryan in his head, or the way he'd dismissed him. Bryan clearly didn't want his help, nor would he discuss his plans.

And he certainly didn't want to talk about Darius.

Raj's eyes wandered the room miserably. For most of the day, he'd watched Louie and Ed counting their remaining supplies, sharpening their spears, and readying empty bags.

It didn't take a genius to see that they were preparing for a scavenging trip. One look at the tired, hungry faces around him supported that. Raj's eyes roamed to the other people in the room. Almost everyone was focused on the important men who spoke in curt, confident tones.

Unlike Raj, The Watchers were men of respect, worthy of looking up to.

Raj felt a pang of envy.

He wanted to feel the same way as before. He wanted to be strong and admired, not a castaway boy.

He'd give anything to walk among The Watchers again, or to feel as important as he had when he'd first crawled into that passage and discovered the strange device.

No one—not even they—could've done that.

A small sense of pride came over him.

An idea struck him, so hard and so fast that he had to stop himself from getting up.

Maybe that was it. Maybe this was a way he could redeem himself.

Gaining his courage, he tucked away his food pouch and slowly rose, finding Louie. At the moment, he was directing some Watchers.

Raj weaved around a few surprised people, who looked up, startled to see him leaving the shadows. He was halfway to Louie when the large man broke from conversation, heading toward Bryan's quarters.

Raj halted.

He stared inside the room where Bryan sat, looking as intimidating as he had earlier. He wasn't ready to go back in there.

Not again.

When he woke up, he'd find a quiet moment with Louie.

CHAPTER 28: Adriana

ADRIANA LAY IN HER BEDROLL in the Right Cave, drawing circles in the dirt. Guilt festered in her heart. Ever since Neena had regained consciousness, she and her closest comrades had been discussing things in quiet circles, always out of earshot, always away from the children. The few times Adriana had interjected herself, they'd dismissed her, shielding her from the conversation.

She felt useless. Frustrated.

Ever since Raj had taken that final march down to the colony, she could think of little else. She sensed his absence every time she looked over at his wrinkled bedroll, or in the pile of rocks that still remained. She felt it in every sad, vacant stare from Amos, or in the constant worry that rang in Neena's voice.

Adriana didn't know if Raj was alive, or dead.

She felt like it was her fault.

She hadn't known about Raj's plan to leave with The Watchers, but somehow, she felt responsible. She'd seen the gleam in his eyes after he met Bryan. She knew how Raj respected him. She should have pieced things together.

Puzzles were always easier to solve after the fact.

She heaved a long sigh and returned to her drawing in the dirt. Without thinking about it, she'd created two people: her and Raj. She couldn't stop thinking of the adventures they'd had together, their conversations, or their kiss.

She didn't think she'd miss him this much.

Raj could be stubborn, but he'd interested her in a way that few boys had. Sure, he'd kept a huge secret from her, but his last conversation felt like an apology. And she'd never forget the way he'd tried helping her grandmother.

Could he really be dead?

Adriana left her finger in one spot in the dirt, sick with grief. She thought of what she'd seen in the colony the other day—the gasps of the crowd, and the screams of Bryan's people in the desert. It certainly seemed that all the horn blowers were dead. And Raj had been carrying a horn.

That should've convinced her of the answer she feared.

But it hadn't.

Adriana couldn't stop thinking about Raj sneaking around the caves, avoiding the guard's detection, keeping his weapon a secret. She couldn't stop thinking about how he'd outwitted them all.

If he was that resourceful, there was a chance Raj was still alive.

And if he was alive, Adriana would find him.

CHAPTER 29: Adriana

DRIANA LOOKED ACROSS THE CAVE at her sleeping parents, watching their stomachs softly rise and fall under the glow of a nearby torch. At the moment, they were deep in slumber.

She looked to the end of the cave, where the guard leaned against the wall, scratching his beard.

Adriana wasn't stupid. She paid attention.

She studied things.

Like Raj, Adriana knew some of the tunnels, and where they led. Whenever Darius or the water collectors travelled their routes, she'd listened carefully, and asked tactful questions. She knew of a tunnel that carried people out to the desert patch, close to the river. That path was longer and more circuitous than the ledge, but of course, she couldn't take the shorter route, without running into more guards and Sherry's people.

If this guard spotted her, she had an excuse.

Bladder shy.

That's what an old woman had once said, when heading to a more private section of the cave to do her business.

Waiting until the guard was occupied, Adriana rose quietly and snuck toward the interior tunnel. Her heart bounded. She followed the wall, sticking to the shadows, until she reached the curve in the tunnel.

She passed the guard.

Nobody yelled, or noticed her.

She kept on, waiting until the tunnel was pitch black before sparking her torch.

And then Adriana was alone.

Lizards and rats skittered away from her. The smell of their droppings filled her nose. It seemed the small critters had gotten even more curious, with so much human activity. Her boots disturbed their waste, or accidentally kicked a few rotten carcasses. She stuck to the middle of the passage, avoiding dark crevices that made her nervous.

Halfway down the tunnel, she realized that the air had gotten thicker.

Adriana held her hand to her mouth, stifling a cough.

Holding her torch high, she spotted a splash of light around the upcoming bend. Not a light.

A fire!

Panic struck her as billowing smoke headed in her direction. The smoke curled down the tunnel, getting worse. This wasn't a campfire, but something worse. This time Adriana was unable to refrain from coughing. Something bad was happening.

Something more urgent than her mission.

She had to warn the others!

Turning, Adriana raced back to her cave.

CHAPTER 30: Neena

"FIRE! FIRE!"

Neena opened her eyes to smoke. Glancing upward, she saw a thick, gray cloud floating above her. Her heart pounded frantically. She looked over to find Adriana and a guard racing into view, cupping their mouths and screaming.

"Everyone out!"

Their words were like Watchers' horns, creating instant alarm.

A hundred people sprang from their bedrolls, casting aside blankets and fumbling for their children. They coughed, batting away the thickening smoke while heading for the exit. Neena looked left, frantically finding Samel, Kai, and Amos, who were already on their feet.

"What's happening?" Samel cried.

"I'm not sure, but we need to go!" Neena said. Grabbing Samel's hand, she yelled, "Cover your mouth and stay close!"

Samel pressed his other hand over his mouth, stumbling after her, while Kai and Amos followed, bleary-eyed and confused. Neena pulled her shawl over her face, fearing that the smoke would invade her lungs and stop her beating heart. All around them, people raced through the haze, bumping into one another. The cave felt like a place of death that no one would escape. Too many people rushed in the same direction, and their panic was causing them to get in each other's way.

Smoke stung Neena's eyes.

Dizziness overtook her.

With a cry, she stubbed her foot on a bag, nearly tripping. In their haste to leave, they'd had no time to pull on boots. Neena could no longer see more than tumbling bodies and thickening smoke.

Looking over her shoulder, she found Adriana and the guard through the haze, shouting at a few disoriented people.

"The fire is further down the tunnel! You need to go outside, on the ledge!"

Passing a few dying embers, Neena had a moment to confirm that their cooking fires weren't the source of the smoke, before reaching the cave's threshold.

A hundred people poured out of its mouth, clasping shawls or shirts over their mouths, gasping for air. They grabbed their children close, keeping them away from the ledge. The night sky illuminated their silhouettes. Only a few were quick-witted enough to bring torches, or spears.

The rest were barefoot and unarmed.

Finding a place near Kai, Amos, and Samara, Neena huddled under the light of a neighbor's torch. Shouts and cries filled the air, as people searched for their missing relatives. The pouring smoke blotted out most of the light from inside the cave, making it difficult to see. Neena folded her arms, fighting off the nighttime cold.

Spotting the shouting guard, Neena grabbed him and asked, "Where's the fire?"

Red-faced and sweating, the man huffed, "Adriana saw smoke coming from the other direction of the tunnel! She alerted me!"

"Adriana told you?"

"Yes. She was going to the bathroom," the guard said,

obviously angry with himself for not finding it first. "I should've spotted it."

Neena nodded, listening to more.

"When I went around the corner to check what she found, I saw a huge fire burning, and people fanning the flames toward our cave! Someone started it on purpose!"

"What?" Neena asked incredulously. "Who?"

The guard didn't answer.

He didn't need to.

Neena's gaze roamed along the ledge. Through breaks in her people, she spotted a group of women with torches standing at the mouth of the Center Cave. Neena couldn't make out everything, but she saw enough. At the forefront of the women, holding her head high, was Sherry.

CHAPTER 31: Sherry

HERRY'S ALLEGIANT WOMEN CLUSTERED AROUND her, hugging one another, or patting each other's backs, congratulating each other. Sherry's eyes riveted far along the ledge and to the two people at the front of the crowd.

Satisfaction made her temporarily forget her emotional pain.

Neena and Kai were alive, but they were miserable. Their postures showed their confusion, and their terror. Staring at the scattered, panicked Right Cavers, she couldn't help her elation.

"We did it!" cried a few of the women, squeezing one another.

Wiping some soot from her face, Jodi said, "Everything worked exactly as you planned, Sherry. We drove them out!"

Sherry rubbed her stomach. Her only regret was that she couldn't join her women in that tunnel, lighting the fire and fanning the flames.

She wanted nothing more than to see Neena's anguished face up close.

Soon.

"What now?" asked Jodi, when some of the celebration had died down.

"Hopefully our warning is clear," Sherry answered. "Even still, we'll keep a close eye on them. We'll ensure that they are not a threat."

Jodi nodded with satisfaction.

Sherry's revenge wasn't a hope, but a certainty.

She'd beat Neena and Kai down, the way they had done to her. She'd strip them of the safety they took for granted. She'd make them feel the piercing pain of loss and guilt that she felt each night, before she went to sleep, thinking of Gary. The Right Caver's misery would become a venomous poison, taking root inside them and spreading to one another. Soon, they'd hand them over to her.

And then she'd kill them.

A small discomfort made Sherry look down at her small, growing belly. She rubbed it in a circle.

"What's wrong?" Jodi asked, noticing.

"Nothing," she said with a smile. "The baby must be kicking. Apparently, it is as excited as I am."

CHAPTER 32: Neena

BELCHING SMOKE POURED FROM THE cave, filling the air with its odorous fumes. Through the haze, Neena watched Sherry and her cohort file back inside the Center Cave, until no one was left. Despite their absence, the light of their torches showed they were still near the entrance, watching.

"Do you think they're going to attack us?" Kai asked.

"If they wanted to attack, they would've it already." Neena seethed. "They're toying with us."

"Ignorant pieces of waste," spat the guard.

He stepped forward, prepared for a fight, probably still upset about his perceived failings. A few Right Cavers who had managed to grab spears gripped them more tightly, anticipating trouble, but no one emerged from the Center Cave, nor did they emerge from the Left, which seemed to have been vacated.

After a while of watching the ledge, the Right Cavers relaxed, but only slightly. Neena turned her attention to the cave, watching smoke fill the air and sky, and then to the other end of the ledge, which ended in just a few feet. The only way down from the cliffs was past the Center Cave, or through their own, smoke-infested home.

"What are we going to do?" Kai asked, eyeing the rattled Right Cavers.

Half-dressed and shivering, they looked at each other for answers. Only the guard and a few of his comrades seemed ready to battle. Most of the Right Cavers were weaponless. The children were crying and cold. And the elderly — and a bunch of others — were already wheezing from the smoke they'd inhaled.

Neena gritted her teeth. The illogical part of her wanted to join the guards, rush down the ledge, and reclaim the last of their dignity. But her instincts told her that would be a bad idea.

"They've smoked us out of our home," Neena reiterated. "All our possessions — our bedrolls and our bags — are inside. And so are most of our torches. Most of us don't even have spears, or boots."

"They probably counted on that," Kai said.

"We should pay them back," the guard persisted, clenching and unclenching his fists. "We should make sure this never happens again."

"I'm not sure we're in the condition to march down and confront them," said Salvador, clutching his spear.

Looking down the ledge, Neena pictured herself and her people inching along it, sharing a few torches, and even fewer spears. Some might fall to their deaths. Others might retreat, or perish in a pointless battle. Could they really fight Sherry and her women?

Neena questioned her fantasy of revenge.

How many children were in that cave? Three dozen? Four? And most of the women were mothers. Sherry's people had clearly incited an attack, but how could she and the Right Cavers kill a slew of women in front of their offspring? Would any of her people actually do it?

Neena couldn't imagine it, as much as she wanted to believe she could.

Nor could she imagine leaving their own children and infirm unprotected.

More anger settled in her heart.

Sherry knew what she was doing.

Neena shook her head in frustration. Whatever game this was, the Right Cavers had clearly lost.

With no other logical options, Neena said, "Let's wait until the fire burns out, and then we'll go inside and assess the damage."

CHAPTER 33: Neena

NEENA PEERED INTO THE MURKY tunnel. Most of the small cooking fires by the entrance had died out, leaving the rest of the Right Cave to smoky shadow. Through the gloom, she saw a few of their scattered bags, bedrolls, and flasks.

Sherry and her women were nowhere in sight.

Holding up a torch and a spear, she beckoned for the dozen people behind her to follow. Kai, Roberto, Salvador, Samara, and eight others walked in slowly, shawls tied around their mouths, spears pointed in front of them.

The odor of fire and smoke was pungent enough that they could smell it even through their fabric barriers. Every so often, one of them coughed, drawing the nervous attention of the others. It appeared that the inciting fire had died out. Turning behind her, Neena checked on the people on the ledge, who waited with hesitation, and more than a little fear. Every now and then, they shone their lights in the direction of Sherry's cave, making sure no one followed.

Treading softly, Neena's group continued, skirting around their loose possessions. Blankets lay tangled in messy heaps. Clothes were scattered everywhere. It felt as if they walked into a ruined colony, as tattered and destroyed as the one down in the desert.

Avoiding flasks that could turn an ankle, and bags that could cause a fall, Neena and the others traveled deeper into the cave, reaching the curve where the guard had been stationed, before heading toward the source of the fire.

Wispy smoke hovered near the ceiling.

Neena led with her spear, half-expecting Sherry and her cohorts to leap out, but she saw and heard nothing.

"Where was the fire?" Neena asked the guard.

"Farther down, I think," he said, his voice muffled through his shawl.

Keeping a tight formation, they continued with the turn, until someone cried out, noticing something. On the ground ahead, charred and melded, lay a heap of broken spears and rags. Digging through the embers, Neena found a few pieces of kindling that had escaped the flames, and some larger sticks. Further down the tunnel, they found some discarded blankets that were used to direct the fire.

Other than those scorched remnants, the tunnel was empty.

CHAPTER 34: Neena

THE HUNDRED AND FIFTY RIGHT Cavers shifted on the ledge, clinging to one another, nervously watching the children. A few of the injured people coughed, while others dusted dirt from their clothes, or rubbed their eyes.

Voicing the question on all of their minds, Samara asked, "What now?"

Neena looked around at her people. Almost the entire night had been spent fleeing the fire, standing on the ledge, or inspecting the cave. They were chilly, they were miserable, and when the sun came up, they'd bake. Succumbing to fatigue, some already crouched on the ledge, or leaned against the wall.

Looking toward the Center Cave, Neena saw only a few faint lights. She couldn't see anyone, but she sensed Sherry's people watching. Always watching.

Anger roiled inside her.

"The cave is dangerous, with so much smoke," Neena said. "The fire's fumes will linger for a long while, making people sick. We can't stay there now."

As if on cue, someone coughed.

Beckoning to a few people behind him, still struggling for air, Kai worried, "We have about a dozen or so people with issues. They need a place to lie down and rest."

"And obviously, we can't stay here on the ledge," Neena said.

"So, should we move?" Samara asked.

Neena thought on it. "I don't see that we have another choice."

"Where will we go?" asked Roberto.

Kai scratched his chin, working through something. After a while, he recalled something. "When we were first settling in the caves, Darius told me about a few other tunnels, farther back in the formation. One of them had a small spring. It is a bit of a journey, but we could stay there temporarily until our cave completely airs out. And we'll eliminate the risk of running into Sherry's people at the spring."

"That'd be a blessing," mumbled another woman.

"Are you sure you can find it?" Neena asked Kai.

"Darius told me the way to get there," Kai said. "His marks are still on the walls, from his days of exploring."

Neena blew a breath. "We'll have to keep the smoke of our torches to a minimum, since we won't have an entrance."

"And we won't want to attract Sherry's people," Kai added. "That means we should avoid cooking fires. We'll have to rely on our dried rations."

Neena shook her head. Those rations were already running low. But what else could they do?

She sighed. "I don't see another option."

CHAPTER 35: Neena

S TRAPPED WITH THEIR BAGS AND belongings, the hundred and fifty Right Cavers marched behind Neena, Kai, Samara, Roberto, and Salvador. They'd stationed their strongest men and women in front and behind, who kept an eye on any branching tunnels. Despite leaving the location of the fire, the smell of smoke came with them, in their bedrolls, blankets, and clothing. Each whiff fueled Neena's anger.

Just as they'd suspected, about a dozen people had inhaled an unhealthy amount of it. Their coughs carried throughout the line, reminding everyone else of the fire's toll. The thought of Sherry's people being so close, undetected, fueled a flame in Neena's belly that scorched worse than anything their enemies had burned.

She put her anger into her steps, hoping to leave those people behind.

Walking in a tight group, they curved through the tunnels, deserting the place where they'd spent the last few weeks. The Right Cave wasn't home, but it was the closest thing they had. And now it was violated. Ruined.

Neena couldn't imagine ever going back.

The children wiped their faces, smearing frightened tears and keeping close to their parents. The elderly hobbled along. For a while, coughing was the only sound, as they followed Darius's marks. Each of those etchings on the wall reminded Neena of her dead friend. One day, she swore, she'd bury him.

After traveling a long while—and hearing no signs of danger—they allowed themselves to speak in whispers.

"Our plans to find Raj will have to wait," Kai hissed, leaning close to Neena's ear.

Neena fought the sick feeling in her gut. "Each step brings us farther from the Comm Building. If anyone comes out, we won't be able to see them."

"Unfortunately, true," Kai agreed.

"As much as that angers me, I can't imagine leaving these people behind right now—especially Samel. We have to take care of our injured and make sure they are protected, before we can leave."

Kai nodded.

Too many obstacles.

Neena blinked her tired eyes. A night of anxiety and missed sleep was already taking its toll. Thoughts clouded in her mind, taunting her with a lack of answers.

After a while of thinking and walking, she asked, "How far do we have left to travel?"

"Only a half a klick, I think," Kai said. "Once we settle everyone down, we'll figure out our next steps. It's all I can think to do."

For a while longer, they followed the caves, traveling deeper into the formation's bowels. Neena recognized a few tunnels from when she, Kai, and Darius had fled. Others were new and decidedly ominous. They followed the faded marks—some that were easy to spot, others that required keen observation—without pause. Once they walked single-file, squeezing through a passage that was barely wide enough to admit one person.

They didn't stop, or rest.

After journeying for some undeterminable length of time, they came upon the large chamber that Kai had decided on. Neena scanned it from wall to wall. The tunnel was wide enough that they could fit most of them in a large area, while keeping in view of each other. Long, crooked rocks hung from the ceiling, which stood at the height of a few people standing on top of one another.

But too many crevices worried Neena.

High in some of them, she heard the flap of bat's wings, as they reacted to the intruders. A few, skulking rats skittered away, not used to seeing humans. Neena shuddered.

She felt the same way she had when they'd first entered the caves. They were new, and that made them feel more dangerous.

"I don't like this," she said to Kai, unslinging her bag and setting it down.

"I don't, either," Kai admitted. "But we have water here." He pointed at the small spring, which was located near one of the walls. "Hopefully, our stay here will be temporary."

After situating Samel in a spot near the middle of the room, Neena walked to the sides of the cave, shining her torch around. Some parts of the wall were as black as the darkest sky; others were reddish, or brown. In a few places, Neena saw cracks on which they'd have to keep an eye. Thankfully, this section of tunnel had only two ends to guard, with no nearby branching tunnels. In that way, it was similar to the Right Cave.

When she was done with her walk-through, she returned to Samel and Kai, helping Samel unfold his bedroll.

"Amos is tending the people who suffered from the smoke," Kai reported.

Neena looked over toward the center of the chamber, where Amos shuffled around tiredly.

Noticing her gaze, Kai said, "He's exhausted, like we all are. A night of fleeing, standing on the cliffs, and traveling has depleted everyone's strength. Regardless of what happens afterwards, we need rest."

Neena couldn't imagine sleeping, after what had transpired. And she couldn't stop thinking about Raj. Still, she felt her eyes closing, and her muscles aching. She looked nearby, where Samel laid down on his bedroll, unsettled.

Instinctively, Neena's eyes went over to the guards.

"They'll let us know if they see anything," Kai said, urging her to her bedroll. "Let's sleep. If we don't, we'll be no good to anyone."

Neena reluctantly agreed.

CHAPTER 36: Neena

EENA LAY IN HER BEDROLL, fitfully turning. This chamber was decidedly bumpier than the Right Cave. Every so often, she reached underneath her, removing a rock, or smoothing out her bedroll. Whenever sleep gently tugged at her, her mind resisted, luring her back.

For a long while, she tried to turn off her tumbling thoughts, until something made her abandon them.

A voice, hissing her name.

She looked up to find Adriana crouched near her.

Studying the girl's grimy face under the light of several hanging torches, Neena whispered, "Is everything okay?"

Adriana bit her lip.

"What's wrong?"

Adriana looked sheepishly over to where Kai and Samel quietly slept. "Can we talk?"

Neena rose from her bedding, motioning Adriana over to the cave wall, where they could whisper. Adriana followed guiltily.

"What's going on?" Neena asked.

Adriana fumbled for words. "I was just thinking about the fire. Every time I close my eyes, I imagine the thick smoke."

"That was a brave thing you did, alerting us to it," Neena complemented. "We would've suffered greater tragedies, if you hadn't been so alert."

"Thanks," Adriana said, averting her eyes. "I can't forget about those women, wafting the fire in our direction. The image of what the guard told me won't leave my mind."

"I understand," Neena said, and she did.

"Too many children are sleeping restlessly." Adriana looked over at Samel, who slept clutching a fist-sized rock that Neena had seen him take from Raj's bedroll, before they left. She was worried about him. Hell, she was worried about all of them. Sensing that Adriana had something else on her mind, she said, "You look as if you have something else to tell me."

Adriana hesitated, glancing back at her sleeping parents. "Yes."

Whether it was the guilty look on Adriana's face, or her wavering tone, Neena could tell it was something private. "Whatever it is, I will not repeat it, if you don't want me to."

Leaning closer, ensuring that no one else heard, Adriana asked, "You promise you won't tell my folks?"

Neena watched her. "I swear."

"I wasn't going to the bathroom when I saw the fire. I was looking for Raj."

Neena felt a jab of emotion.

Adriana looked at her boots in shame. "I snuck past the guard, thinking I might head down to Red Rock and find him. It was a foolish idea. I don't even know if he's alive… but I can't stop thinking about him. I feel guilty that he left."

Neena watched her a long moment, fighting off tears. She reached over, squeezing Adriana's arm.

"You had nothing to do with it."

"But I did…" Adriana's voice trailed off.

"What do you mean?"

After some coaxing, Adriana relayed the story she'd obviously come to tell. Surprise hit Neena as she heard about Adriana's trip with Raj to see the weapon, their run-in with Bryan, and Raj's distant behavior. "I had no idea about his plans. If I had known he would march down with Bryan, I would've stopped him."

Tears welled up in Adriana's eyes. Reaching over, Neena pulled her into a hug. "It's not your fault, Adriana. There's nothing you could've done."

Adriana resisted the hug. "Maybe if I had told you, we could've figured out Raj's plan and stopped him together."

For a moment, Neena considered that possibility. But obviously, they couldn't change anything now. Thinking about what Kai had said earlier, she said, "Raj was going to make his own choices. There was nothing we could've done to stop him. I'm convinced of that."

"Do you really believe it?" Adriana asked.

"I do." Neena paused. "When I was talking to Kai earlier, he said some things that made sense. Everybody makes mistakes. I just hope we can help Raj, before it's too late."

"You're not mad at me?"

"No," Neena said. She hugged her again, holding her longer. "As soon as we settle in here, we'll figure out a plan to get Raj back. I promise."

Adriana nodded. "I'm worried about Sherry, too."

"We all are," Neena admitted. "We might have to tackle that issue first, before we get Raj. But we'll figure it all out when we wake up. I swear."

Adriana closed her eyes hard, reopening them. Watching the pain in her face, Neena fought the lump in her throat.

"Just promise me you won't do anything foolish like that again. Okay?"

"I promise," Adriana said.

"Now get some rest, and I'll do the same."

Adriana scooted back to her bedroll near her parents, while Neena returned to her sleeping area.

Neither noticed the two women who secretly watched them through a crevice in the cave.

CHAPTER 37: Raj

R AJ WOKE AND RUBBED HIS eyes, looking up at the hard, domed ceiling. All around the Comm Building, people groaned, rousing from another difficult night's sleep. They were achy, and they were tired. Their stomachs were empty. Of course, no one had expected to be in the same place for so long.

They'd hoped for their hovels.

Looking over at the braced doors, Raj wished he could see the sun, the silhouette of the twin moons, or the cliffs, towering high above them. He couldn't tell the time of day in here.

In any case, he was glad to be awake.

Looking over to the round table, he noticed a group of Watchers talking and collecting their bags.

His intentions from the night before came hurtling back.

He needed to find Louie.

He scanned the enormous main room. Luck was with him—the door to the large man's quarters was closed. He could position himself in such a way that he could have a quick discussion, before the man became otherwise engaged.

Wiping the last of his sleep from his eyes, Raj rose to his feet, weaving around blankets, bags, and sleeping people, headed for Louie's quarters. A few people watched him with disdain, but he ignored them.

If his plan worked, they wouldn't look at him that way for long.

124

Raj had just reached Louie's quarters when the door swung open, revealing the large, lumbering man. Louie's face was creased with tiredness. His clothes were rumpled. He winced and adjusted his cast, surprised to find Raj standing in front of him.

"What are you doing here?" he grunted.

Raj swallowed his apprehension. This was his moment.

Waving a skinny arm at the gathering men, who flanked the Comm Building table, Raj said, "I was hoping I could go to the colony with you."

Louie looked at him. He looked at the men. "You want to go on the scavenging trip?"

Putting on his bravest face, Raj said, "Yes."

He waited for the rejection he knew was coming. He had an argument prepared. Louie looked Raj up and down, scowling at his appearance, as if he might've stepped on some rat dung. Or maybe he'd stained his clothes. Nope. Raj's clothes were clean. To his surprise, Louie laughed.

"What is it?" Raj asked, after an awkward pause.

"You want to go out with the men?"

"Yes, sir."

"Your place is here, among the others," Louie said, gesturing toward a group of scraggly women.

"I can be of much greater help out there than in here," Raj insisted. "I can get into crevices no one can reach, like I did when I found the weapon."

"We need people who can lift up heavy stone, not horn blowers who run the wrong way."

Raj forced away tears. "I'm quiet. You know that I am."

"Our best men are going, not our weakest."

"And I can be one of them. I swear." Raj swallowed the lump in his throat and stared up at Louie. "I can be just as brave as all the others."

He searched for the kindness he'd seen in Louie's face, back in the chambers when they'd tested the weapon, but the large man looked away, uncomfortable. A voice distracted them both.

"Louie!"

The big man turned, seemingly grateful for the interruption. Bryan came their way, giving orders to a few passing men.

"What's the problem?" he asked in a stern voice as he approached.

"No problem, sir," Louie said. He waved a dismissive hand. "The boy was just asking me a question."

"What?" Bryan inquired.

Feeling the pressure to answer, Raj said, "I want to go on the scavenging trip." All at once, his arguments crawled back in his throat. His mouth felt dry and pasty. He forced himself through it. He couldn't give up. Not now.

Putting on an earnest face, Raj regained his courage. "I'm small. I can reach things that others can't. I won't get in anyone's way, but if you need me to crawl in after something, I'll retrieve it. I'll find rations no one else will. If you let me go on the scavenging trip, neither of you will regret it."

With his case made, he waited. Louie barely looked at him, but to his surprise, Bryan seemed like he was considering. Raj capitalized on the silence for a final plea.

"Let me make up for what happened in the desert. I swear that I won't fail you again."

Bryan glanced over at the men in the center of the room. He looked back at Raj. For a long moment, he scratched his chin, wading through some thoughts. Instead of responding to Raj, he spoke to Louie.

"Keep the boy close. Don't let him wander. If you find you have no use for him, send him back here, and he'll clean our dung buckets."

"Yes, sir," Louie said.

CHAPTER 38: Raj

R AJ ADJUSTED THE EMPTY BAG on his back. Pride filled his belly. Two-dozen men walked around him, holding spears, following Louie's and Ed's directions as they walked away from the Comm Building. Raj's gaze wandered around the wide, dusty path that circled the enormous structure, and to the closest hovels and alleys, which sat at a large buffer.

In the weeks without the stomping boots of the colonists, the sand had taken over, piling in every corner, blurring the lines between paths and alleys. It dusted the tops of the intact buildings, coating the wreckage of the fallen hovels. It wormed its way into every crevice, covering most of the things they hoped to find.

Still, they couldn't fail.

Nearly two hundred hungry mouths counted on them.

Raj was nervous and scared, but he was excited, too. Once again, he was useful.

He had another chance to prove himself, and he wouldn't toss it away.

The men split into two groups—Ed and his followers traipsed down the main path, heading in the direction of the river, leaving Raj, Louie, and the others to search for rations.

Together with Louie, Raj's group curved around Comm Building on the wide path, heading north, passing the jutting annex and getting to where the path straightened. While they walked, Raj's eyes wandered up to the cliffs.

Squinting, he made out the openings for the three caves. He saw nobody at the mouth of the Left and Center Caves, nor did he spot the Right Cavers, as he'd secretly hoped.

He did see smoke drifting from the Right Cave entrance, though.

They must be cooking breakfast.

Not for the first time, he pictured his family inside, eating their rations. No one had come after him yet. A pang of sadness temporarily overrode Raj's pride.

He quickly pushed it away.

Movement drew his attention back to the group. For a moment, he feared it was the monster, coming to snag them, but it was six men breaking off down one of the alleys, contending with debris and scattered belongings. Louie beckoned Raj and the others left, toward another alley.

Raj followed them on quiet feet.

A few birds flapped their wings overhead, scaring them, but they meant the monster couldn't be close.

Sticking near Louie, Raj followed the large man into the first hovel in the alley, while the others broke off. To both of their surprise, they found a few pouches of dried meat, untouched. That finding inspired them to continue. They scanned the next hovels, locating a few spears, passing them to the other men.

After a while of scavenging, they fell into a rhythm: Louie pointed out things, and Raj grabbed them, filling their packs. Once they completed their alley, they returned to the main path, where a few Watchers rummaged through a collapsed hovel.

The broken stones were piled as high as a man. It took a moment for Raj to determine the men's goal: in the center of the rubble, beneath a crevice, protruded several pieces of fabric.

Raj looked at Louie, and back at The Watchers.

Catching the glimmer in Raj's eyes, Louie nodded.

This was his chance.

The men stepped back, allowing Raj to crawl into the small space. Despite his fear, he kept on, uncovering blankets and cookware, handing them to the men so they could appraise them. Buried deeper were a pouch of meat and another spear. Raj tugged them free and brought them out, handing them to the grateful group.

Pride surged through Raj, as he got to his feet and dusted himself off. The men nodded at him, respect in their eyes.

For the first time in days, Louie looked pleased.

Raj, Louie, and the rest of their group headed back down the path, carrying their bountiful loot. Every so often, they looked over their shoulders at the desert, listening, but the monster didn't come.

They met Ed and his men at the center of the colony. It seemed the second group had had equal luck. A few patted the flasks at their sides, or motioned to full bags. In another man's arms, Raj saw a handful of Green Crops.

Success.

They were approaching the end of the straight path, coming to the spot where it curved around the Comm Building annex, when Raj saw something else: an object, poking from the sand.

With Louie's approval, he headed toward it, keeping his footsteps even. Raj bent, brushing off two ends of a long, skinny object.

A sharp tip graced one end.

The rest of it was long and smooth.

Pulling back, he avoided a dangerous prick from the creature's quill.

For a long moment, he and Louie studied their incredible discovery. Raj had never seen anything so strange, or so fascinating. The piece of the beast looked as if it was made of some combination of muscle and bone. One side was definitely sharp, but the other side—where it had broken off—was jagged. Leaning down, Raj imagined it protruding off the side of the incredible beast.

The quill was intriguing, but it was also fear inducing.

"Leave it," Louie mouthed, and the group moved on.

⟫✷⟪

Raj huffed a sigh of relief as he and the others returned to the Comm Building, laying out their spoils. The trip had been safe and expedient. Their combined provisions should last a few days, filling the stomachs of the hungry.

More importantly, no one had disturbed the monster.

Proudly, Raj spread his recovered items on the table, ensuring that everyone saw. Unlike before, the people in the room watched him with relief, perhaps even admiration. Looking over at Louie and Ed, who patted each other's backs, he joined them in a huddle.

"We did it," he said happily.

They nodded, congratulating each other before acknowledging him.

"It was a successful trip," Louie agreed.

"I'm glad I was able to fit in that collapsed hovel," he said, reminding them of his usefulness.

"You're a regular explorer," Ed said with a smirk. "Just like your old friend Darius."

They snickered and looked at each other, sharing some joke Raj didn't understand.

And then they turned away.

CHAPTER 39: Bryan

BRYAN STOOD IN HIS QUARTERS, cracking his neck. Footsteps drew his attention. He turned to find Louie coming toward him.

"The trip was successful?" Bryan asked.

"Yes," Louie reported with satisfaction. "We scavenged enough food for a few days. The water was no problem. But Ed's group had to dig deep for the Green Crops. It's probably the last time we'll find anything suitable for eating."

"I expected as much," Bryan said. "When this is over, we'll plant a bigger bounty than the last. We'll harvest so much that our bellies will be eternally full." He looked at Louie a moment. "But first, we must focus on today."

"Of course."

"I assume you didn't see the monster," Bryan surmised.

"We kept quiet and away from the area of attack, as you instructed," Louie said. "We didn't see it. But we did find one of the creature's quills on the way back, buried in the sand. The sharp end almost poked Raj."

Bryan listened to the details of the account, as well as the specifics of the recovered food. When Louie's report was concluded, he turned and headed back into the main room with the others. Bryan stared at the ceiling, the particulars of the mission swimming through his head.

He couldn't stop thinking of something Louie had said.

An idea was on the edges of his mind.

Hopefully soon, he'd solidify it.

CHAPTER 40: Sherry

SHERRY WALKED THROUGH THE CENTER Cave with her head held high, weaving around the clusters of women and children, all of whom paid attention to her. A few awaited her directions, as if she might pass along a task, or an important message.

It felt as if she were born for this role.

She smiled.

Earlier, she'd seen Bryan's men far below on the ground, making a scavenging trip. She didn't recognize many of them, but one figure had stuck out: a small, identifiable person. Apparently Raj was still alive. The fact that Neena's brother had survived was a minor irritation. She'd deal with it later.

Still, the sight of the men brought a much-needed burst of morale. It kept her women going in their times of doubt.

Reaching the back end of the cave, she moved toward two approaching women. Tanya and Jodi's faces were lit with excitement, as they hurried over. Her two biggest doubters had turned into her biggest supporters.

Ironic.

"What did you find?" she asked.

"We followed the Right Cavers, like you asked," Jodi said, huffing for breath. "We reached the new chamber where they are located."

Describing it, Tanya added, "They can no longer see the

daylight. They have no access to open air, or visibility to the Comm Building."

Sherry smiled, as she pictured them living like rats, nestled in their decrepit burrow. Everything was going perfectly.

"How far away is this cave?" Sherry asked.

"It is a ways travel," Jodi said. "They are deep underground. They have a spring, however."

She listened to Jodi and Tanya describing the path to get there, and the crevices in the walls through which they'd spied.

"What are they doing?" Sherry asked.

"Most are clustered in the center of the chamber. Some are sick from smoke. Others are resting. It didn't seem as if they were doing much, other than recuperating."

Sherry felt a burst of vindication. But vigilance was needed. "As a precaution, I'm going to have some of the women block off one of the passages further down, in between our tunnel and theirs, so they cannot easily access us."

"A good idea," Tanya agreed.

"In the meantime, keep an eye on them," Sherry said. "Report back to me if you see or hear anything. I'll arrange for some other women to relieve your shift before evening."

Jodi and Tanya nodded, their heads held high.

A young, brown-haired boy rushed over, hugging Jodi. "Mom?"

"Yes, honey?"

"Are you coming back to play with me soon?"

"I'll be there soon," Jodi said. "Mommy has to take care of some duties first."

The child nodded, disappointment in his eyes, and then the women started back to their post.

CHAPTER 41: Neena

WITH THEIR BACKS TO THE spring, Neena, Kai, Samara, Salvador, and Roberto faced the Right Cavers, who sat in nervous circles, watching them. A few held their children, while others tended to the injured. Every so often, a cough punctuated the room, as someone dealt with the residual effects of the smoke. Looking out among them, watching Amos move from one wounded person to the next, Neena bit her lip.

"What should we do now?" Roberto asked.

The people in the audience shook their heads in dismay.

Surveying the tired and the pained, Neena said, "It seems as if we are fighting a war on two ends. We have Sherry's women to contend with, and we have Bryan's marchers. And of course, we have the problem of Raj."

"Obviously, Bryan's people aren't here at the moment," Kai reminded her. "But Sherry's people are."

Unable to contain her frustration any longer, a woman called out, "First Sherry attacks you on the ledge, and now she does this. Who knows what else she'll do?"

Motioning toward a coughing woman, a man spat, "Look at what the fire did to my wife! She can barely breathe."

Commiseration rippled through the crowd.

"Sherry deserves punishment for what she's done!" someone yelled.

More time in the dank cave had deepened their misery, just as it had deepened Neena's. Looking around at her people, who voiced their anger to their neighbors, she felt a pit of resolve.

"Maybe it is time we show her she can't do it again," Neena suggested.

Those with injured relatives nodded vehemently, clenching their fists.

Looking around at her upset people, Neena said, "I agree with you. Sherry has no intention of stopping. She has driven us to a choice." She paused for emphasis. "We can sit here and wait for things to get better, or we can take the upper hand. We can show them we'll no longer tolerate what they are doing to us."

"What are you suggesting?" asked one woman.

"We confront them."

Samara lifted the spear in her hand, showing her solidarity.

"We attack?" a man questioned.

"A coordinated threat might be all we need," Neena said. "But yes, we should be ready to fight, if it comes to that."

The people in the circle looked at one another, gauging each other's reactions.

Sharing their confliction, Roberto said, "I can't picture stabbing a cave full of mothers in front of their children."

"Neither can I," Neena said. "But we have to do *something*. If we don't take a stand, they'll continue this treatment of us, and then our children will pay. We have to stop what they are doing."

The group turned to one another, contemplating the ramifications of her suggestion. Uncertainty had ahold of them.

"Even a few dozen of us, armed with spears or knives, will make them reconsider their actions," Neena continued. "Who knows? Perhaps this will be the moment that staves off later violence. It is time we stood up for ourselves."

Some of the hesitant people regained their courage.

"We've seen the price of our inaction, in Darius's blood," Neena said. "We've seen it in the attack on me and Kai. And we've seen it in the way they smoked out our cave. The more we accept this treatment, the more we will receive it."

A few nervous breaths drifted across the cave.

A woman spoke up. "Let's say we confront them and succeed. What happens when Bryan and his marchers return? We might pay for our decision later." She clutched her children.

Neena sucked in a stale, damp breath. The odor of smoke from her clothing and the stench of bat droppings revived her anger. "Let's say Bryan's people aren't killed by the monster, and they return. How long do you think it will take for them to find us in this cave, if they want to? A day? A week? Sooner or later, they'll come across us, and then we'll no longer have a decision. We've seen what they did to Darius. What makes you think that won't happen to us? Why not surprise them now, when the choice is in our hands?"

A few people rose to their feet, ready to take a stand.

Inspired, Neena pressed on. "We'll show them that we are more than weak people, waiting for their next hurled rock, or torch. We'll show them that we'll defend ourselves."

A murmur of excitement went through the room.

"How many are with me?" Neena shouted.

She looked around the room. A dozen hands went up, and then a few more. So did Kai's, Roberto's, Salvador's, and Samara's, until almost fifty hands were in the air. Their unity brought warmth to her heart. It was certainly better than fear.

It was time to turn bravery into action.

"It's settled then," she said, before anyone could disagree. "Let's sharpen our spears and knives. When we're ready, we'll march to the Center Cave."

CHAPTER 42: Samel

SAMEL LOOKED AROUND AT ALL the people in his cave, who readied their spears and knives, their torches, and their bags. Neena seemed to be everywhere at once, giving directions, speaking with Kai, or preparing her weapons. At the tunnel's ends, a few guards relayed instructions to their replacements.

Neena's meeting increased Samel's anxiety. He understood her reasons. Sherry was a vile woman, capable of unspeakable violence. And the rest of Bryan's people were just as dangerous.

Still, he couldn't help but think that Neena might be marching off to her death.

He couldn't stop thinking that he might end up alone.

No more Neena.

No more Raj.

What would he do?

Fighting off tears, he reached inside his bedroll, retrieving the rock that he'd salvaged from Raj's bedroll, before leaving the Right Cave. The fist-sized stone was a small memory of his brother. Thankfully, Neena hadn't hassled him over it.

Turning the rock in his hand, he pictured himself and his family back in their hovel, sharing a nice, happy meal. One day, this would all be over, like Neena had promised, and he and his brother would be reunited.

The more he tried believing that, the more his wishes turned to awful memories.

Monsters. Fire. *Screams.*

Samel's breath heaved.

His heart beat frantically. Panic took over.

Roaming to the nearest wall, he leaned his head against it and squeezed the rock, hoping to calm down.

When would this ever be over?

CHAPTER 43: Raj

R AJ SWIGGED FROM HIS FLASK, looking across the room. Unlike before, he no longer lowered his head, or wished to be invisible. After returning from his trip, he'd helped The Watchers pass out the new rations to Bryan's grateful men and women. No one had turned away from him while receiving a dried piece of meat, or a flask full of water. A few times, he'd even received a pleasant smile, or a thank you.

Raj felt helpful again.

Important.

Setting down his flask, his gaze roamed to the circular table, where The Watchers congregated. Riding his newfound acceptance, he walked across the room and joined them. Ed was among them, sliding a particularly large blade against a rock.

"Would you like me to help?" he asked Ed.

"Do you know how to sharpen a spear?" Ed asked curiously.

"I've done it before," Raj said. "They say I'm pretty good at it."

With a shrug and a smile, Ed conceded, "It's better than standing there staring at me." He handed Raj a spear. "Here. Take it."

Raj took the spear, finding a sharpening rock and getting to work, while Ed and some Watchers did the same. For a while, they worked together, grunting and smiling, speaking of the successful trip, or the enormous procession they'd hold once the monster was dead. Every once in a while, Raj added a joke, to a chuckle.

Despite the men's apparent friendliness, something bothered him.

He couldn't stop thinking of the smirks on Louie and Ed's faces when they jested about Darius. Something dark lurked beneath those smiles. Everyone knew they didn't get along with the Right Cavers, but it seemed like they held a secret.

And that reminded him of Bryan's odd behavior while they talked about the device, and the spears.

More and more, Raj's thoughts were growing uneasy. It felt as if something was buried beneath the surface of Bryan and his closest men, some subtext he didn't understand. Raj wasn't sure what it was yet, but he was going to figure it out.

Finished with his spear, he handed it back to Ed.

"Should I sharpen another?" he asked.

"Sure, kid," Ed said.

Raj took the next weapon, working on it.

"What are Bryan's plans for the monster?" he asked, hoping to get more information.

Ed cracked his neck, sharpening his own weapon. "He had an idea he said he'd share with Louie soon."

"Do you think we're almost ready to fight?"

"If we're lucky," Ed said. With a grunt, he added, "I hope this is over soon. I've got a few women I wouldn't mind seeing back in the caves."

A man nearby laughed.

Raj turned the spear in a circular pattern, performing his duty efficiently.

"You weren't lying," Ed said. "You are pretty proficient. Who taught you to do that?"

"Neena, originally," Raj said. "But Darius taught me a better method."

Immediately, Ed looked away. The same, strange feeling filled Raj's stomach.

Swallowing—doing his best to keep an even tone—he tested his awful theory. "I'm not as good as him, though. Maybe someday Darius can teach you, too."

Ed glanced over from his spear, his smile fading. The look in his eyes solidified everything that Raj had feared.

"I don't think he'll be teaching anything to anyone, soon."

CHAPTER 44: Neena

NEENA WALKED THROUGH THE CHAMBER, overseeing the Right Caver's final preparations. Since the meeting, they'd sharpened their weapons, filled their flasks, and packed enough rations to make the trek. They'd prepared their fill-in guards, instructing them to stay vigilant.

Still, too many uncertainties lived in her heart.

Would they take Sherry's people by surprise? Would the women fight, or would they stand down? Looking around at the people with whom she'd travel, she wished she could see the end of this day.

But worse things would happen, if they did nothing.

She was convinced of that.

Instinctively, Neena looked toward the ceiling, wishing she could see the sky. This deep in the formation, she had no idea whether the sun was full, or the twin moons were visible. That added to her unease.

Looking past the people who spoke with their relatives, or adjusted their bags, she found Kai.

"All our marchers have at least one weapon," he reported. "And we have enough to arm those we leave behind."

Neena nodded gratefully. "Has anyone backed out?"

"They are nervous, but they are ready," Kai said.

Neena nodded. "Soon, this will be over."

"I hope," Kai said.

"I'll do a last check with the guards, and then we'll leave." Neena completed her last task, ensuring they were prepared, before returning to her sleeping area.

It was time to start the conversation with Samel that she dreaded. She sighed and closed her eyes, mentally preparing herself for an emotional talk.

Samel wasn't at his bedroll, nor was he near the wall where she'd last seen him, holding the rock.

Panic struck her heart.

Racing over to the spot where he'd been, she shined her torch into a deep, dark crevice.

The rock he'd taken from Raj's bedroll lay on the ground.

Samel was gone.

CHAPTER 45: Samel

S AMEL KICKED AND FLAILED AGAINST the people who held him, to no avail. One person carried him backward, arms snug under his shoulders, hand clamped over his mouth, while the other carried his legs. It felt as if they'd pulled him away some time ago, though he couldn't be sure. All he knew was that he could no longer hear the Right Cavers, and of course, he couldn't see Neena, Kai, or Amos.

His heart slammed against his ribcage.

One moment he'd been leaning against the cave wall, the next these people's hands were on him, stifling his cries and pulling him through a dark crevice.

Who were they?

Why wouldn't they let him go?

At first, he thought two monsters had grabbed him, rather than two humans. If not for their ragged breathing, whistling past their teeth, or their sweaty clothing pressed against him, he might've believed that.

His captors wound through more caves than he could count, bumping into walls. The world around them was dark. Samel couldn't tell where he was headed, or how far he'd gone. Of course, he couldn't ask through the hand pressed against his mouth. After a while, they set him down.

One of them restrained him, while the other lit a torch.

Samel blinked, his eyes adjusting to the sudden light.

A scraggly, blonde-haired woman leaned close, holding

a knife under his chin. Her lips curled back into a sneer. "Do anything stupid, and we'll cut you. Understand?"

"Yes," Samel whispered.

He recognized the dirty woman standing in front of him. She was from the Left Cave, though he didn't know her name. He blinked, as if she might realize she'd made a horrible mistake, but her eyes held no sympathy.

"No screaming, no fighting," whispered the woman holding him. "Got it?"

He said he understood.

"I'm going to walk next to you while Jodi leads you along, so we can go faster," the knife-wielding blonde said, motioning to the other woman, Jodi. "Try anything, and we'll stab you."

And then the hand was off his mouth, and Jodi was next to him, tugging his arm. He glanced over, catching a glimpse of her dark hair and her nervous, darting eyes.

They walked forward—Jodi herding him, the blonde lighting the way beside them. Thoughts catapulted around Samel's head. He desperately wanted to run, or scream, but the thought of a knife piercing his flesh filled him with terror. Instead, he followed his strange captors through the winding tunnels, praying at every fork that Neena would arrive with her spear and rescue him.

No one came.

They traveled for what felt like a good part of the night, taking several branching tunnels, as if they were trying to lose someone.

Maybe Neena? he thought.

Every so often, his captors peered nervously over their shoulders, searching for pursuers. And then they came upon on a tunnel that was long and narrow.

Risking a whisper, Samel asked the women, "Where are we going?"

"You'll see soon enough," the blonde lady hissed.

CHAPTER 46: Neena

"**S**AMEL!" NEENA SCREAMED INTO THE crevice.

Fear snaked around her heart. With a knife in one hand and a torch in the other, she stepped inside the narrow passage, frantically leading with her torch. For the first ten feet, the twisty, jagged rock opening was barely wide enough to fit her, but farther down, it widened.

"Samel!" she yelled again, peering into the darkness.

In the time she'd discovered Samel missing, a handful of people had congregated behind her, hurriedly searching. Almost everyone had heard her panicked cries. Those who hadn't had quickly been alerted.

"Do you see him?" Kai asked from her heels.

"No!" Neena said desperately.

Her awful feeling worsened as she squeezed through the crevice, hurrying toward the wider portion of the passage, where the air smelled even staler. Something squished under her boot. Neena looked down to find a half-rotten rat carcass, crawling with insects.

The sight of the dead animal intensified her fear for Samel.

How long had it been since she'd last noticed him? Amidst her preparations, she hadn't paid close enough attention. The only thing of which she was positive was that he wasn't in the chamber.

The others stuck close to her heels. Their solidarity would've impressed her, if she had time to acknowledge it.

Neena moved faster. The passage curved for a while, thinning and widening, before emptying out into a larger cave. Entering the new tunnel, she looked left and right, but could only see as far as the edge of her torchlight.

She'd warned Samel not to stray. She'd warned him to stay close. Why had he come here? Nothing about his disappearance made sense.

"Samel!"

She took another step, but quickly stopped. Had he gone left or right? She studied the ground in both directions for any indication he had been here, but she saw no boot prints or scuffed gravel. The floor was too hard.

This part of the cave system was foreign to her.

A few dozen Right Cavers emptied out around her, calling her brother's name, joining the search, while the others hung back in the main chamber with the children.

Standing among those in the cave, Kai said, "Let's split up! Neena and I will take a group left. Samara, you lead a group right!"

They agreed, splitting their parties into a dozen each and continuing.

Neena and Kai led their group left down the unfamiliar passage. Those with torches shone them in all directions, illuminating the cave's ruddy walls, its craggy ceiling, and its firm ground. With more space to maneuver, they moved at a faster clip, getting farther from where they'd entered.

They traveled for a while into uncharted territory, with no sign of Samel, until they reached another fork.

Dammit.

Neena shone her light in the direction of each new tunnel, searching for clues. Nothing. Each moment without her brother deepened her fear.

What if something else lurked in these tunnels, and had taken him?

Her knowledge of the Abomination made anything seem possible.

"A few of us will go this way," Kai suggested, pointing left down one of the new tunnels. "Why don't you go the other?"

Neena hated the idea of dividing the group further, but what choice did they have? She rushed ahead with three men at her side, searching the new tunnel's fissures and shadows, alert for threats, combing the passage.

And then she saw something.

Just ahead, wedged between some craggy rocks on the wall, was a thin piece of fabric. Neena's heart leapt in her chest as she rushed over and removed it, finding a knife jabbed through the center. She took out the blade and held up what looked like the sleeve of a shirt. Not just any shirt.

A boy's shirt.

Samel's.

CHAPTER 47: Neena

WITHIN MOMENTS, THE OTHERS HAD heard Neena's cries of discovery and come running. Those who hadn't were quickly rounded up and summoned. They stood rigid and close, clutching their torches and their spears, their eyes reflecting her panic.

"She has him," Neena said in a quivering voice, holding up the sliced piece of Samel's shirt. "Sherry is sending us a message. She wants us to know what she's done."

She glanced around at the shifting crowd, who looked anxiously in front of them and behind.

"What if this is a trap?" Kai asked. "She might be leading us this way for a reason."

A murmur of panic went through the crowd.

"For all we know, they left this here and went in another direction," Samara piped up.

Despite the possibility of that statement, Neena couldn't shake the idea that Samel might be just up ahead.

"If Samel is alive, I have to reach him," she insisted. "If something happens to him, I'll never forgive myself. Let's keep going!"

Rallying her people, she led them in a tight formation down the cave, holding their weapons. They called Samel's name, scanning the crooks and crevices, checking behind them. Every so often, a Right Caver bumped into a neighbor, causing a brief, panicked stir. The sweat and footsteps of a few dozen people in such a small area gave Neena a claustrophobic feeling. She wanted nothing more than to get out.

Too many horrific possibilities plagued her mind.

What if Samel's kidnappers had hurt him?

What if the shirt sleeve wasn't a message, but a taunt, and they'd killed him instead of doing whatever else they planned?

If Sherry had harmed him in any way, Neena would make her pay. She'd ram her spear into her throat and make sure she never hurt anyone again. Her wrath wouldn't end until the woman was dead.

They scoured the tunnel for a long while, moving as quickly and quietly as possible, reaching another fork. This time, Neena couldn't help herself. A frustrated cry escaped her lips.

Another branch. Another choice.

Neena took a step, ready to divide everyone and plunge down another tunnel, until Kai stopped her.

"Neena, wait!" he said, grabbing on to her.

"We have to hurry!" she shouted. "We have to—"

"We don't even know where we're going," Kai said, doing his best to restrain her. "What if this is a trap?"

Neena tried ripping her arm away, but Kai kept hold of her.

"For all we know, they didn't come this way at all, like Samara said," Kai warned. "We might get lost."

"These tunnels aren't marked, like the ones we took to get to our chamber," added a man. "We could die before we ever find Samel."

Neena's frustration was at a boiling point. The group waited, looking at her.

"What do you want to do?" a woman asked finally, fright in her voice.

Kai let go of Neena's arm.

Silence permeated the tunnel.

All eyes remained on her.

Looking at all the people around her, Neena resolved, "We're heading back to our chamber, taking the tunnels to the Center Cave, and marching on Sherry. We're getting Samel back."

CHAPTER 48: Raj

R AJ LAY IN HIS BEDROLL, clutching his knife in his shaky hands. Ever since his conversation with Ed, he'd been unable to concentrate on anything. He hadn't eaten. He'd barely slept. The Comm Building felt like a place of monsters, rather than a place of friends. His eyes darted around the torch lit room, where most of Bryan's people slept. Every so often, a cough punctuated the silence, startling him, or someone's conversation disturbed him. Each hushed whisper made him paranoid. It took every effort to finish the spears he'd started sharpening, say goodnight to Ed, and hurry back to his bedroll. The times he'd tried sleeping, he'd failed.

His heart thudded wildly.

He couldn't believe what he thought he heard.

It didn't take a fool to understand Ed's implication. The more he thought on it, the more Raj was certain that Darius was dead. Flashes of memory circled through his brain—Ed's smug expression, Bryan's strange demeanor, and Ed and Louie's private joking. Those clues felt even more obvious now.

Bryan had told him Darius wasn't in that cove when he retrieved the weapon, and he'd believed it.

Or maybe he'd wanted to.

An angry, confused tear fell down Raj's cheek. Bryan had lied to him. Of course, he had. He hated Darius as much as he hated Neena, Kai, or the rest of the Right Cavers.

As much as he hates me, Raj thought miserably.

If Bryan came across Darius, things would've gone really badly.

He couldn't stop thinking of the old man's kind face, sharing stories of his travels, or the way he'd helped Raj and the other Right Cavers to safety.

Whatever had happened to Darius, it was Raj's fault.

Raj let his tears flow. He deserved to feel the pain. Peering around the room at what felt like strangers, regrets flooded him. If he'd never marched down here, Darius might be safe and asleep in the Right Cave. And Raj might be there, too, next to his friends and family, instead of lying in a den of people who'd never quite accepted him anyway.

His anger toward Neena was a consuming, blinding rage.

He shouldn't have succumbed to it.

Those memories led him to think of another.

All at once, he was back on the ledge outside the Right Cave with Neena, after he had lashed out at her. Despite his foolish behavior, Neena had apologized to *him*.

She'd never treated him poorly like these others. She'd always been there at the end of the day, smoothing out their arguments, ending their disputes with a hug or a kind word. She'd never condemned him, like these people had.

To Bryan and his people, Raj was an annoying rodent, constantly proving his worth.

His family loved him.

Maybe living in the Right Cave hadn't been so bad, after all.

Unable to dam his falling tears, Raj shook under his blankets.

This is my fault, he thought. *I've made an awful mistake, and now I'll never be able to take it back.*

The question was, what would he do about it now?

CHAPTER 49: Bryan

"Louie," Bryan whispered, motioning quietly through the doorway of the large man's quarters.

Louie immediately sat up from bed, looking over at him.

"Were you sleeping?" Bryan asked.

"No, I was just dozing." Louie wiped his eyes. Whether it was the look on Bryan's face, or the time they'd spent together, he deduced something important was on his mind. "What is it you need?"

Bryan couldn't hide his enthusiasm. "I need you to arrange another trip out to the colony."

Louie rose. "Of course."

In a confident voice, Bryan gave his orders. "I need you to go to the edge of the desert, to the place where the rock spires crumbled from the monster's body. If my hope is correct, you will find more of the creature's quills, just like the one you located the other day."

Louie refrained from voicing a question.

Continuing his instructions, Bryan added, "I'll also need some tools from the blacksmith's shops." Bryan informed him of which tools they'd require, making Louie repeat them back.

"Is that all, sir?"

Looking at Louie's arm, Bryan made a decision. "Perhaps Ed and a few Watchers are best suited for the task. Let's keep the group small. We don't need any unnecessary risks."

Louie nodded. "I understand. I'll relay your instructions to Ed, so he can prepare his men for the morning." Watching Bryan at the doorway, he finally voiced his question. "Are we almost ready to fight the monster?"

"We are close," Bryan said with a smile.

CHAPTER 50: Louie

"**E**d." Louie peered down over Ed's bedroll, stirring him.

"What do you need?" Ed asked, grunting awake.

"Bryan needs you to go back out into the colony first thing in the morning. He has a job for you."

Ed watched Louie with curiosity and trepidation.

"Remember the quill we found in the colony, near one of the broken dwellings?" Louie asked.

"Yes," Ed replied.

In a hushed voice, Louie passed along Bryan's requests.

Ed furrowed his brow. "We only saw one quill."

"Bryan has an idea where you can find some others," Louie said, telling him the location.

"Okay," Ed affirmed. "I'll do my best."

CHAPTER 51: Sherry

S HERRY PACED THE DARK, EMPTY section of the cave. Her thoughts tumbled over one another. Each glance at the walls brought her back to happier memories in the shadows with Bryan, falling into his arms, venting their frustrations. When she closed her eyes, she could still feel his touch, hear his whispers, and imagine his embrace. She yearned for those tingles of pleasures and pain.

Their trysts felt as if they'd happened months ago, instead of days.

Digging her nails into her hand, she tried replicating those feelings, to no avail. Frustrated, she grabbed the torch and thought about scalding herself, until she saw a light in the distance.

Immediately, Sherry pulled her knife.

Voices and boot steps echoed off the walls.

A flickering torch moved closer.

Sherry headed in the direction of the noise, walking until she saw three silhouettes coming around a corner. Tanya and Jodi's faces were covered in dirt and grime. In between them was a child.

"What's going on?" Sherry called.

She moved toward them at a hectic speed, stopping short as she recognized whom they herded. Sherry blinked, as if she might be imagining a miracle.

But Samel's whimpering proved that he was real.

The boy's face was dirty and scratched. One shirt sleeve

looked as if it had been cut, or torn. He looked at Sherry as if she were a ghost, or a monster, coming to torment him. All at once, Sherry's pining for Bryan was forgotten. Relishing in the boy's panicked expression, she slowly held out her knife, resting it beside his nose.

"Please don't hurt me," he whispered.

Ignoring his pleading, Sherry asked Tanya and Jodi incredulously, "How did you get him?"

"We found him by a crevice in his cave," Tanya said, prodding the boy's bare arm with a knife. "We grabbed him while no one was looking. We had to."

"What do you mean?" Sherry asked.

Tanya exchanged a glance with Jodi. "The Right Cavers are planning to march on us."

"They had a meeting," Jodi continued. "We couldn't hear everything, but we heard enough. They're coming for us." Jodi swallowed. "We were worried about what might happen to our children. And then we saw Neena's brother, lingering near a crevice. We saw an opportunity. We grabbed him and ferried him back here, so we can stave off their attack."

"If we hold him among us, perhaps we can keep our children safe." Tanya looked wildly over her shoulder. "We left a piece of his shirt tucked in the wall with a knife through it, so they will know we are serious."

Silence overtook the cave. Sherry looked from Tanya to Jodi, to the quivering boy. If not for the gravity of their discovery, she might've been angry.

"If they are coming, we need to get ready," Sherry said resolutely, pulling her knife away from Samel's face.

A prickle of fear and excitement coursed through her. She looked past Jodi and Tanya, prepared for a barrage of incoming lights and people, but the tunnel was dark.

Jodi's face wrinkled with emotion. "They're going to hurt us," she worried.

"No, they won't," Sherry said with a grin. "Now that we have Samel, we're in a far better position. You have done good work."

CHAPTER 52: Sherry

COMMOTION RIPPLED THROUGH THE CENTER Cave. One by one, heads turned, ceasing their private conversations and turning in the direction of the rear passage. Whispering turned to exclamations. Children tugged at their mother's shirt sleeves.

No one could miss the coming spectacle.

Sherry proudly marched Samel through the middle of the cave, stopping when she'd reached the middle of the crowd. All around her, people gasped and pointed, looking between her and the frightened, bedraggled boy. Tanya and Jodi stood a few steps behind, looking hastily around.

There was no point in holding anything back.

"The Right Cavers are on their way here," Sherry announced, to the Center Caver's startled reactions. "They are coming to face us. We must prepare."

A few handfuls of women rose to their feet, grabbing their spears or their children. Others leapt up, ready to flee.

"What is he doing here?" asked a mother, frantically pointing at Samel.

"Jodi and Tanya took him from their cave," Sherry said. "They did it so we would have leverage when the Right Cavers arrived."

"Leverage?" another woman asked. "We were supposed to ward them away, not lure them here!"

"What have you done?" cried another woman.

"They were already coming to face us," Jodi defended. "We had no choice."

"Your comrades have done us a service," Sherry said, lifting her voice over the crowd's protests. "Confrontation was inevitable. Sooner or later, they were going to attack us. We have no choice but to defend ourselves."

More women stood up, fear in their eyes. A few children burst into tears. The commotion in the cave was quickly descending into chaos.

In a shrill, commanding voice, Sherry yelled, "Quiet! We must plan our defense!"

Some of the din lessened.

"I have told you this day was coming," Sherry said loudly, raising a hand to keep the cave in order. "It is not a surprise."

A few guards at the door scrambled to raise their weapons. Before the disorder could get out of hand, Sherry barked out orders. Pointing to a cluster of women on the left-hand side of the tunnel, she said, "You women over there! Guard the front entrance of the cave!" To the women gathered on the right-hand side, she said, "You others, watch the rear entrance of the cave, past Gideon's cove! The rest of you stay in the center, protecting the children!"

A stream of women poured past her, heading down the long, rear portion of the tunnel and following her orders, while more went to the front. Others stayed in the center, gathering up the children.

"What about us?" Jodi asked, her voice shaking.

"You and Tanya follow me," Sherry said. "We're taking Samel with us."

"What about our children?" Jodi asked, looking toward a brown-haired boy in the middle of the room.

"Have them go to the middle of the tunnel with the others. I need you by my side."

Jodi paused, unconvinced, until she saw Sherry's

unrelenting stare. "Now!" Sherry dragged Samel past a few hesitant women. Looking down at them in disgust, she said, "To your feet and defend yourselves, women! Defend yourselves, or die!"

The women looked around wildly, before obeying.

They would fight, because they had no choice.

CHAPTER 53: Sherry

"**W**HERE ARE WE TAKING HIM?" Jodi asked.

"To a place where we can hide him, for now," Sherry spat.

She wrenched the boy's arm, pulling him down the long, dark tunnel, while Tanya and Jodi kept an observant eye out. Up ahead, she heard the voices of the women headed to keep guard in the far end of the tunnel. Samel yanked against her grip.

Finding courage through his fright, he cried, "Let me go!"

Sherry looked down at the distraught boy. Fresh tears tracked his cheeks. Fear glazed his eyes. Despite his obvious terror, she saw a defiance she didn't like.

Stopping, she pulled out her knife and poked him. "Shut your filthy mouth!"

Samel quickly silenced.

She kept going.

Rounding the next bend, they came upon the entrances to two familiar coves. The healer stood at the mouth of the second.

"What's going on?" he asked. "Gideon wants to know!"

"I'll tell him later," Sherry snarled.

Sherry pulled Samel into the first cove, instructing Tanya to stuff her torch into a crevice on the wall. The added light gave her a better view of the whimpering boy, and the empty place where they'd kept the ill and the injured.

Bedrolls and kitchenware littered the floor. A few lizards scuttled into crevices.

Sherry surveyed the abandoned room, looking for something she couldn't find.

"Go get something to tie him up with!" she told Tanya.

Tanya nodded through the fear on her face, hurrying from the cove and out of sight.

Sherry pushed Samel toward Jodi. "Hold him."

Jodi obeyed, turning him around.

"What is Neena planning?" Sherry demanded of the boy.

"I'm not sure," Samel said. "Please don't hurt me."

Advancing, Sherry held out her knife, tracing his features with its sharp blade. The boy flinched under its touch. His eyes widened. His tan skin and his rounded nose reminded her of Neena. She wanted nothing more than to carve him up. Tilting up the blade, she kept it near his eye, contemplating a slice that would ease her own pain. Samel's eyes darted around the cove, looking for an escape he'd never find.

"You knew they were planning on coming here, didn't you?" Sherry insisted.

Swallowing, Samel said, "I don't know anything. I swear."

Sherry's eyes fixated on Samel. Rather than seeing a harmless, frightened boy, she saw an enemy, whose existence tainted Gary's memory.

He deserved to pay for what his sister had done.

All of the Right Cavers did.

"Please, don't hurt me," he whispered.

Sherry kept moving her knife along his cheek, unable to quell the aching, hollow pit in her stomach. Hurting herself made the emptiness go away.

But hurting Samel... That might be even better.

"What are you doing?" Jodi asked.

Ignoring Jodi, she pressed gently, just deep enough that a single drop of blood escaped the boy's skin. Jodi pulled Samel away.

"He's just a child," Jodi said. "We need him intact, so that we can use him."

Startled, Sherry looked at the knife in her grasp. Anger coursed through her. Before she could scold the woman, a voice interrupted.

"Sherry!"

She spun to find Tanya returning.

"I found some shreds of clothing we can use," she said, holding them up. "Want me to tie him up?"

Sherry returned her knife to her sheath. "Do it."

Tanya moved in, coordinating her efforts with Jodi's and binding Samel's wrists and ankles.

When the chore was done, Sherry instructed, "Stay here and keep guard. Don't leave."

"Okay," Jodi said.

Sherry's stomach churned. She looked down, startled by another of the baby's unexpected, early kicks.

"Is everything all right?" Tanya asked.

"Yes. I'm going to check on the rest of the women. Whenever the Right Cavers get here, we'll be ready."

CHAPTER 54: Neena

S IXTY PEOPLE'S BOOTS HIT THE ground behind Neena, keeping pace, their harried breathing filling the air. Neena's knuckles were white from clutching her spear. Thoughts swirled through her head. How long had Sherry and her people known the location of their chamber? More urgently, what were they doing with Samel?

She couldn't stop thinking of the last time she saw him, or the precise moment he might've been snatched. Perhaps the fire had all been a ploy, leading up to this.

Filthy vermin. That's what they were.

Horror mixed with her rage.

She envisioned Darius's bloodied body, stabbed with tools. Kai's description had haunted too many of her dreams, and her waking hours. Each panicked thought drove her feet faster. She couldn't let the same thing happen to Samel.

Reaching a split in the tunnel, she asked Kai, "Which way is the quickest?"

Kai scanned between the two passages, locating one of Darius's faded marks. "If I remember correctly, the right passage will lead us to the Center Cave. That will be the quickest way, but it is less familiar. Which way do you want to go?"

It wasn't a question. Not really.

They were going right.

Neena stormed up the right-hand tunnel, inspiring the others to follow. Her people moved without whispers or protest. No one argued with her, especially those with children, because they understood her pain.

Neena's brow beaded with sweat. It already felt like they'd been traveling forever. Or maybe it was the urgency of getting to Samel, which made her feel as if she couldn't walk fast enough, or far enough.

She concentrated on the path ahead. At any moment, she might find a mob of dastardly women, or a screaming boy. Watching the darkness at the edge of her torchlight, she felt frustrated.

Each tunnel looked the same.

None of them yielded Samel.

What if they had already chosen an incorrect path?

Not for the first time, she asked Kai, "Are you sure about our direction?"

"Pretty sure," Kai said, forging ahead. A little way farther, Kai noticed a jagged section of the wall, where part of the rock had crumbled away. "That's familiar! Darius and I came here once in the first few days, catching rats. We're making progress."

The Right Cavers trekked on, passing a few more tunnels, eventually squeezing through an area where a passage grew tight. They shuffled in rows of three, while Neena called out for her brother.

"Samel?"

Her voice no longer echoed.

Strange...

She thrust out her spear, taking a few more steps, until she found the reason for the dampening sound. In front of her, blocking the tunnel from floor to ceiling, was a wall of piled rock. Shock overtook her group.

"I don't remember this being here," Kai murmured.

"What's going on?" someone asked.

Neena clawed at the rubble with her hands, but there

was too much of it, and it was stacked so high that she saw nothing around it.

Frantically scanning the wall of rock, Kai said, "They must've put this here to block us!"

"Dammit!" Neena threw down her spear, frantically removing pieces of the obstruction.

A few others leapt in, doing the same, but the narrow passage prevented too many people from working at once. Grunting, Neena tugged at larger rocks, hoping to make quicker headway. A rumble startled her. She cleared the way just in time to avoid a few rolling, mid-sized stones tumbling to the floor. The noise frightened the people in back, who leapt away. When the dust settled, they looked at the area on which they'd worked. More stones stood behind the first blockade—enough that no one could see past them.

"Who knows how many rocks they've put here?" Kai said in frustration.

Neena shook her head, but it was quickly becoming clear that they were wasting time. Who knew how long the stones would take to move?

"We'll have to backtrack," Kai said in frustration. "It's all I can think to do."

Neena looked ahead. She looked behind. Every moment they remained here risked Samel's life. But what choice did they have?

"Let's go!" Neena said, turning around, trying not to think of the repeat distance they'd need to travel.

CHAPTER 55: Raj

R AJ CRANED HIS NECK UP from his bedroll, scanning the sleeping people. Earlier, he'd seen Louie waking Ed and speaking in a hushed whisper. His attempts to eavesdrop had been fruitless. He was too far away, and too scared to get closer.

Now, he watched Ed rouse from his bedroll, collecting a handful of Watchers.

The men gathered their spears and their bags, tiptoeing through the room. Only a few people woke, looking at them in confusion. Raj was contemplating getting up and asking them where they were going when one of the men glanced over at him.

Their eyes locked.

A sudden, paranoid fear made Raj wonder if they had figured out his suspicions.

The man looked away.

Intent on his mission, the man moved for the front doors, joining the other Watchers. One man quietly removed the wooden braces, while another opened the entrance.

The men filtered silently out.

CHAPTER 56: Ed

E D FOUGHT A PRICKLING CHILL as he crept over the wide, Comm Building path and curved north. In his short time away, more sand had piled over the area where they trekked, creating a bumpy, uneven journey. It felt like as if nature was trying to bury the colony.

Or maybe it was his imagination.

In any case, he couldn't wait to get the mission over with.

Following the path next to the annex, he brought his men past it, rejoining the main path and walking between the intact and shattered hovels. He crept along, reaching the area where they'd been with Louie's men the day before.

To his relief, the same quill still protruded from the ground.

Reaching the object, Ed carefully removed it from the sand, holding it up for his men to see. He waited until they nodded before lowering it.

It was their example.

Hopefully the horrid thing satisfied Bryan.

Ed kept on, leading his men up the path until they eventually reached the hunter's path.

And then they were in the desert.

Uneasiness crept over him as he and his men passed between the enormous spires, moving in and out of the long, ominous shadows. Caving holes covered the ground around them. Most of the horn blower's bodies were buried, but every so often they saw an irregular lump in the sand, or some unraveled, rotting intestines. Once, they came across a dusty, gore-stained shawl.

Death's fetid odor was a constant reminder to keep wary.

Soon, they reached the rock formation where the second group of horn blowers had fled. About halfway up the rock was the jagged stone where the creature had impacted. Below it were piles of stone, which had plummeted and stuck in the sand.

Following Louie's instructions, they sifted through the rubble.

"Careful," he mouthed, scanning the dark crevices.

He was starting to think Bryan's suggestion was a failure when someone waved their hands and pointed. The group turned their attention toward a long, sharp object, protruding from underneath a rock pile.

Success!

Ed's hope grew as The Watcher pulled out a second quill and held it in the air. A ripple of quiet enthusiasm went through the group. After more searching, his men found a few more of the long, smooth objects, covered in sand, or wedged between fragments of rock. They kept searching, until they had eight of the strange objects in their possession.

The wind gusted.

His men turned.

North, deep in the desert, a billowing cloud of sand moved in their direction.

A storm.

Making the best decision he could, he whispered, "To the tradesmen's buildings!"

The men followed his direction, hurrying to complete their mission and return to Bryan.

CHAPTER 57: Neena

NEENA TORE DOWN THE TUNNEL, ignoring the sweat dripping from her face. Her legs ached. Her clothing was drenched. It felt as if it'd been days since they'd found Samel's shirtsleeve. The backtracking they'd done had killed any hope she had at catching up to Samel's captors.

Now all they could do was confront Sherry when they arrived.

Neena kept a wary eye on the cracks in the walls around her, as they made their way back to the Right Cave. For all she knew, Sherry's women watched them from some hidden crevice. The Center Cave women were like snakes, slithering through the formation and finding cracks she didn't know existed. But their sneaking and plotting would end soon.

Finally, they came around the last bend leading to the Right Cave.

The faint scent of smoke reached Neena's nose. She forged ahead, thinking of the sick people they'd left behind, and of Samel—always Samel. Soon they stepped over the burned blankets and kindling that Sherry's women had used to start the fire. None of the ashes were disturbed, or bore the prints of vile women's boots.

They moved into the main cave.

The Right Cave reeked of stale sweat and old smoke. The abandoned tunnel no longer felt like home.

Neena's anger was a building dam, threatening to burst.

She let that drive her through the Right Cave, pushing toward the entrance.

And then they were almost on the ledge.

A gentle gust of wind blew, rifling through Neena's hair as she stepped out into the open. She instinctively looked to the horizon, where some ominous clouds gathered. A pit settled in her stomach.

"A storm is coming," Kai warned.

Neena gritted her teeth.

Even that wouldn't stop what she needed to do. She spun toward the Center Cave, where a few women suddenly scattered, or pointed.

"There they are!" Kai cried.

More of the women retreated back into the cave, presumably getting reinforcements, while others raised their spears. Neena's resolve stiffened.

"Let's go!" she yelled, driving her people forth.

Together, they charged down the ledge.

CHAPTER 58: Bryan

"**Y**OU FOUND THEM!" BRYAN SAID, wide-eyed and excited, looking from one Watcher to the next.

Ed stepped forward, holding up his quill as if it were a baby he had delivered. Bryan approached, running his fingers over the long, smooth object, marveling at its texture. The object was hard, but surprisingly flexible. He pushed it, watching it bend. He recalled the way the quills unfurled from the creature as it launched from the ground to the sky. It seemed as if they helped propel it through the ground, but they were clearly defensive, too. One prick from the jagged end of the quill would gore a man.

Or a beast.

Hopefully, his plan was good.

"What are we doing with them?" Ed asked, looking as if he had a guess.

"Our powerful weapon is an asset, but its use is limited," Bryan said. "Hopefully, these quills will supplement our arsenal."

The men looked at the quills, waiting for him to explain.

"Perhaps the best offense against the monster comes from its own body." A triumphant smile crossed Bryan's face, as he looked from one quill to the next. "We will use pieces of these quills to tip our spears. If my guess is correct, they will penetrate the creature's hide."

Understanding turned to hope in the men's eyes.

Focusing on Ed, Bryan asked, "Did you bring the tools?"

"Yes," Ed said, unslinging his bag. He revealed the selection of implements they'd grabbed. "We ferreted these from the tradesmen's shops. Are they sufficient?"

"Yes," Bryan confirmed. Staring intently at his men, he instructed, "We will use these tools to construct new tips for our spears. When they are ready, we will have stronger weapons than we had before."

Confidence rose in the men.

"Between these, the device, and careful planning, we will make sure that the Abomination never harms our people again," he concluded.

Bryan could already feel his faith reigniting.

The men arched their backs, regaining the courage they had possessed on the march.

With his proclamation made, Bryan raised a hand, signaling the end of their discussion.

"There is something else," Ed interrupted, pointing at the ceiling. "A storm is heading this way."

Bryan looked up, listening to a light wind keen over the top of the dome. The men in the room awaited his reaction.

After a moment of thought, he said, "A boon. We are in the safest place we can be for a storm. Besides, the noise will give us some better cover, while we create the weapons."

The men nodded, satisfied.

"Let's get to work," Bryan said.

CHAPTER 59: Sherry

" SHERRY! THEY'RE COMING!"

In the middle of the Center Cave, Sherry paused, surrounded by the huddles of women who protected their children with their spears, and waited for the woman who approached.

Cranking a thumb toward the entrance, the woman said, "They're heading down the ledge now!"

Sherry's eyes blazed. "How many are there?"

"Four or five dozen," the woman said, through gasping breaths. "I can't tell for sure."

Sherry looked past her at the mouth of the cave, where other women waited uneasily for her direction.

"What do you want us to do?" the woman asked.

"Hold them off!" Sherry ordered.

"How?"

"Do whatever you need until I return!"

The woman nodded, biting back her fear, before returning to the others. Shouts and boot steps resonated from the entrance. Sherry was already moving in the opposite direction, hurrying past the panicked mothers and children, who instinctively took a few steps back. Grasping her torch and knife, she returned to the winding tunnel leading to the coves, her heart pounding furiously.

The time was here.

She needed to get the rest of her women.

Revenge was coming.

A smile crept across her face, allaying some of her fear.

A sharp pain ripped that smile away.

Sherry's knife and torch fell. She clutched her stomach with two hands, stumbling. She staggered toward the wall, reaching it before sliding toward the floor. Another burst of pain caused Sherry to cry out in agony. Her eyes widened. Under the flickering light of her dropped torch, she noticed a blotch of blood on her pants where there shouldn't be one. She couldn't accept what that might mean.

She'd had this pain before.

Flashes of memory returned.

All at once, she was crouched in her hovel with Gary, suffering similar agony. But that awful event hadn't come without a warning. For weeks, she'd had cramps. This time, she hadn't—

All at once, she remembered the kicks.

Some of those had been harder than she'd felt before.

And they'd definitely come earlier.

Maybe those kicks hadn't been kicks, at all.

Sherry grabbed her torch, shining it on the growing splotch of blood on her pants. Fear and panic consumed her. She clasped her stomach with a hand, trying to stop something she knew was unstoppable. But her body was already acting out of nature.

Even a healer couldn't fix this.

Too many in similar situations had tried and failed.

No!

Not my baby!

A scream built up in Sherry's throat, so loud and so consuming that she couldn't contain it.

She let it out.

Her loud, agonizing wail reverberated up and down the cave, bouncing off the walls and echoing back to her. Sherry fell the rest of the way to the floor, grasping her stomach and her clothing. She stayed that way for some indeterminate length of time, clenching and unclenching her fingers, before boot steps interrupted her.

Looking up, she caught sight of six women pouring from the rear of the cave.

She sat up.

"What's happening?" a women yelled, immediately recognizing something was wrong.

Sherry looked up at them. Rage and disbelief overtook some of her pain. As one, the women looked to Sherry's stomach.

"What's going on? Are you hurt?"

"No," Sherry managed, gritting her teeth and hiding the splotch of blood.

"Did something happen to..."

"Nothing happened!" Sherry shrieked, startling the women. "Neena's people are here! Get to the front of the cave and fight!"

"Are you sure that—"

"Go! Now!"

The women traded a frightened glance, before running off in the other direction.

Anguish washed over Sherry as she watched them go. Slowly, she found her footing, continuing down the tunnel in a haze of grief. Staring at the splotch on her clothes, she pressed the folds together, making sure that no one saw the evidence of another awful event.

A thought echoed in her head, so loud and so persistent that it drowned out the others.

Revenge.

That thought drove her down the tunnel, strengthening in fervor, until she reached the first cove.

Tanya and Jodi's faces were filled with shock as she appeared.

"What's going on?" Jodi asked, fear in her eyes. "Are Neena's people here?"

"Untie Samel's legs!" she roared. "We're taking him with us outside!"

CHAPTER 60: Neena

NEENA RACED ALONG THE LEDGE, Kai at her side. The heaving breaths and stamping boot steps of The Right Cavers reminded them that they weren't alone.

But their presence was a small consolation.

Everyone knew the danger they were about to face.

It was evident in their wide eyes, the sweat rolling down their faces, and the way they stuck close together for courage. It was evident in the way their hands shook on their spears. Neena and Kai kept their eyes riveted and their weapons poised, leading Samara, Roberto, and Salvador, who ran in the row directly behind, among the fifty some-odd others.

More of a stir was happening at the cave.

A dozen women guarded the mouth of the Center Cave ahead, but more were quickly streaming out onto the ledge, blocking their path. The women lifted their spears with shaky hands, digging their heels into the ground and forming defensive rows, extending thirty feet past the mouth of the cave.

Neena continued getting closer, winding along the dangerous cliffside.

The clouds continued to grow on the distant horizon. A slow, menacing wind continued to blow. It felt as if the women weren't the only ones trying to stop her from reclaiming Samel. But no storm or spear would stop her.

With her teeth clenched together, Neena tore along the ledge until they reached the first row of dirty, frightened women.

A scared, blonde-haired woman blocked Neena's approach. A ruddy-faced woman next to her pointed a weapon at Kai. Those in the rows behind stared at Neena with a disdain she remembered, from too many recent encounters.

All at once, Neena was reliving a memory, trapped under the women's kicking boots and their hurled stones.

A burning, repressed anger spilled out of her. Scanning the women, she recognized a few more who had attacked her.

Neena wanted to ram her spear into their ugly faces. She wanted to ensure that they hurt no one else. Only fear for Samel's life stopped her.

"Where is he?" Neena's voice came out in a growl. "Where's my brother?"

She scanned from the blonde-haired woman to the ruddy-faced one.

For a moment, the ledge grew uncomfortably silent, save the whipping wind and the shifting pebbles. The two women in the front exchanged a nervous glance, deciding what to say. A few others behind them looked over their shoulders toward the cave entrance.

"Where is he?" Neena screamed.

In the time they'd faced off, the sun had disappeared beneath the storm sky, cloaking the Center Cave entrance in shadow. Following the women's gaze, Neena saw only silhouettes at the cave's mouth. Her eyes shot back to the blonde-haired woman.

"I don't know what you're talking about," the woman answered, nervously.

"The hell you don't," Neena snapped. "You left a piece of his shirt for us to find. You took him!"

The blonde and the ruddy-faced woman traded another glance.

They were unable to sell their lie, even to themselves.

"We know you have him," Neena spat. Trading words for actions, she reared back her spear. "Give him back, or I'll kill you!"

The two women cried out, lifting their spears to block. Neena eyes shot from the blonde to the ruddy-faced woman.

"You aren't the only ones with children to protect." The ruddy-faced woman lifted her chin.

"You've taken one of ours!" Neena countered. "My brother!"

"You are a threat," the woman said, her eyes flicking to the others for reinforcement. "You plotted against us. We've done what we had to do."

"Plotted against you?" Neena scoffed. It felt as if she was talking to a part of the cliff wall, instead of a person. "You attacked us on the ledge. You smoked us out of our home. And you *killed Darius!*"

"Darius?" asked the woman, confused. "I don't know what you're talking about."

"Neither do I," the blonde-haired woman insisted.

Neena was running out of patience. Maybe words were useless, and her spear was her answer. Movement interrupted her. Thirty feet away, shadows shifted at the Center Cave entrance.

"Step aside!" a voice snarled.

A woman plowed through the middle of the crowd, casting others aside, heading for the first few rows of the commotion.

Sherry's face was a mask of anger, as she drew up close enough that Neena could see the end of her jagged blade, and the fury in her eyes. Positioning herself between the two women and Neena, she took a defiant step forward.

"You despicable wench," she growled.

CHAPTER 61: Neena

NEENA'S BLOOD BOILED. HER PULSE pounded. She could hardly contain her anger as she laid eyes on the person responsible for her physical and emotional pain. Rage demanded that she forego talk and resort to action.

The only thing keeping her from an immediate attack was fear for Samel's safety.

Tightening her grip on her weapon, ready to stab Sherry, she yelled, "Give me Samel back!"

Sherry opened and closed her mouth on a thought she didn't voice.

Something wild and unnerving lurked behind her eyes, something that Neena hadn't noticed before. Maybe the caves had darkened her mind. Or perhaps she was more unhinged than Neena thought.

Surprising Neena with a coherent answer, Sherry said, "The next time you see your brother, you will both be with your ancestors."

"I will take him over your body, if I have to!" Neena warned.

"And we will help her," said a voice from behind Neena. She turned to find Samara, Salvador, and Roberto stepping forward, inspiring the other Right Cavers. "You've done enough, Sherry. This is the end."

Neena swallowed, her eyes moving back to Sherry. She appreciated her people's encouraging words, but she didn't need them. She'd gore all of the Center Cavers, if it meant getting to her brother.

Sherry motioned to the people behind her.

"My women are ready to fight and die, too," Sherry said, drilling them with a stare. "Right, ladies?"

Her words weren't a question, but a command.

The women closest to Sherry shored up to her. To Neena's surprise, even those in the farther rows behind seemed allegiant. Sherry's presence had a unifying effect on the crowd. Or maybe they were afraid of her.

"We have more people than you," Neena said, tilting up her chin. "Our people know how to use their spears. Do yours?"

A sneer crossed Sherry's face. For a moment, Neena thought she'd lost her sanity, until she motioned behind her again.

"I think you misunderstand your position." Spinning, Sherry waved a hand toward the dark shadows of the Center Cave. "Jodi! Tanya!"

The guards near the entrance shifted, allowing three more figures to pass. Two women emerged. The other— clutched between them and shivering with fear—was Samel.

"Samel!" Neena yelled, taking an instinctive step.

"Neena!" Samel cried back.

Sherry and her women put up their spears.

Neena craned her neck, trying to keep her brother in view.

"Move aside!" Sherry yelled over her shoulder. "Let her see him!"

Obediently, the people in the far back dispersed, creating an open circle around the three new sources of attention.

Tingles of fear coursed through Neena's body. Samel's shirt sleeve was missing. His face was covered in dirt. He tried breaking loose, yelling for his sister, but the two women held him tightly. Her stomach sank as she saw his bound wrists. Too many rows of women stood in Neena's way of getting him. She felt powerless.

"Let him go!" Neena cried, unable to stop the quiver in her voice.

With a smug expression, Sherry said, "Gideon should've killed you when he had the chance. And so should've Bryan. But I'm going to fix that."

Neena looked over at Kai, trading a desperate glance.

"It is time for you two to answer for everything you've done," Sherry continued triumphantly. "It is my turn to give the orders."

Sensing a motivation behind her display, Neena asked, "What do you want?"

"You and Kai in exchange for Samel." Sherry demanded, looking from Neena to the Right Cavers. "If you give yourselves up, the rest of your people can leave with Samel."

Neena looked desperately to the sixty people behind her. Indecisiveness plagued them, as they held their weapons.

"If you fight, some of your people will die, and so will ours," Sherry admitted. "But the first will be Samel."

She turned over her shoulder, instructing Tanya and Jodi to pull Samel a few steps toward the edge of the cliff. Neena panicked.

"Stop! Don't hurt him!"

Jodi and Tanya stopped, awaiting Sherry's next order.

"Toss your spears and come forward," Sherry said, smiling in victory. "Do it and this will all be over."

Neena looked down at the spear in her hands. She looked at Kai.

"She's lying!" Samara yelled. "Don't trust her!"

Kai blew a breath and relaxed his spear, ready to stand down, if that was what Neena wanted. His loyalty would've brought tears to her eyes, had the situation not been so dire.

"What do you want to do?" he asked her.

Despite his bravery, she sensed his fear.

Neena clenched the wood handle of her weapon. She wanted to lunge forward, jab Sherry in her venomous face, and take back her brother. She wanted to pay Sherry back for all the wicked things she'd done. But Neena wouldn't make it more than a few steps before Samel was killed.

Samara grabbed her arm, trying to stop her. "Don't do it. Don't give yourself up."

"Enough talk," Sherry said. "Jodi! Tanya! To the edge!"

The Right Cavers gasped, watching Tanya and Jodi drag the screaming, writhing boy. Even Sherry's women opened their mouths. They turned, torn between the impending battle and the riveting scene. Bringing Samel within a foot of the ledge, Tanya and Jodi halted, staring nervously between Sherry and the edge. A few pebbles rolled away from their boots.

Petrified by death's closeness, Samel went limp.

"My next order will be to toss him," Sherry warned.

Neena clenched her eyes shut. "Let him go now, and we'll give ourselves up."

"You will do things in the order I say, and when I say it," Sherry said matter-of-factly.

A hush fell over both crowds. Neena looked from her brother to Kai, and back again. If this were the end, she'd have no regrets in trying to save her brother.

With a last, fateful sigh, she lowered her spear.

"If she breaks her promise, kill her," she told Samara, making sure that Sherry heard. "Keep my brother safe."

Neena relaxed her gripped fingers, about to drop her spear.

A voice interrupted her.

"Mom?"

A child's cry rang out over the quiet.

The startled crowd turned.

A brown, curly-haired boy about Samel's age broke

from the dark shadows of the Center Cave, running away from some women who had been holding him.

He raced toward Jodi.

"What are you doing, Mom?" he asked her. "Are you going to kill that boy?"

His words were like a spear to Jodi's heart, unleashing some hidden emotion. Tears rolled down her face, but she didn't let go of Samel. She looked from the bewildered, brown-haired boy who had stopped five feet short of her, to the boy in her arms, and back again.

"Get him back inside!" Sherry screeched.

"Sherry's right. Go inside, William!" Jodi urged.

A few women called out to William from the shadows, but he didn't listen.

His arrival had caused a stir. A handful of women looked back at the mouth of the cave, where more children peered out from the shadows, intently watching. Seeing them caused a ripple of doubt. A few of Sherry's women grabbed hold of the loose child, herding him back inside, but others seemed torn in their allegiance. Tanya and Jodi looked around, suddenly unsure of what they were doing. A few women near them lowered their weapons.

Trying to regain control, Sherry demanded of Neena and Kai, "Drop your spears!"

Neither heeded her instructions. Sensing an opening, Neena said, "I'm not doing anything. And neither are your women. Are you?"

Sherry looked frantically from Neena to Jodi and Tanya. Jodi cried, while Tanya froze.

"You wouldn't harm an innocent child, would you?" Neena yelled louder. "Because I would never do that to you. Let Samel go. He has nothing to do with this. Release him, and we'll all figure this out."

Jodi and Tanya looked as if they were considering it.

Sherry's face twisted in frustration. Misdirecting her

anger, she raised her spear and took a step in Jodi's and Tanya's direction, but they didn't move. A relief spread through Neena, so hard and so fast that she thanked the heavens for her luck.

Sherry's next words ripped away that relief.

"Throw him!"

A gasp went through the crowd.

Tanya and Jodi tensed.

As one, all eyes turned toward them. Neena stepped forward, suddenly regretting her lack of compliance, while Samel screamed.

"Do it now!" Sherry insisted.

Jodi and Tanya looked over the ledge, and back toward Samel.

"I said, *now!*" Sherry shouted again.

The crowd shared a single, held breath.

Jodi and Tanya looked at Samel, who shook his head in a final panic.

And then Jodi lowered her head.

"I-I can't...." she said.

She let Samel go, and Tanya did, too.

In shock, Samel raced away from the edge, heading toward the cliff wall and away from harm.

Sherry turned around, stunned.

Neena blew a breath, sharing a look of relief with Kai. Her relief didn't last long.

"Watch out!" Kai yelled.

With a shrill cry, Sherry raised her spear and leapt at Neena.

CHAPTER 62: Neena

NEENA SKIRTED TO THE SIDE, narrowly missing the sharp end of Sherry's spear, as chaos took over the ledge. Women cried out, shocked, or frightened. Some ran toward the cave, hurrying for their children. But some of the allegiant women had started fighting. Out of the corner of her eye, Neena caught a glimpse of a few dozen women rushing at the Right Cavers, engaging them in battle. She had no time to help them, nor did she have time to locate Samel.

She was in a struggle for her life.

Sherry's snarls filled the air in front of her. She jabbed her spear at Neena, striking her shirt near the hip and cutting her skin. Neena cried out at a raw pain she hadn't expected. She had no time to survey the damage. Leaping backward, she swung her spear, striking Sherry with the wooden part of the shaft. Sherry fell to the ground on her knees, but sprang up just as fast. Somewhere nearby, Kai defended himself from a snarling woman.

A yell from Sherry kept Neena focused on the current battle.

"You wench!" Sherry shrieked.

Holding her spear sideways, Sherry charged Neena, knocking her spear up, pushing her backward across the ledge. Neena fought for balance, crashing into some others who fought around them. Venomous spit flew from Sherry's mouth. Her breath stank of dried rat and dirty water.

Neena dug her boots into the ground, frantically trying to disentangle from Sherry, but she was stuck in a defensive position.

With a cry, she found strength and pushed hard on her spear, hurling the woman away.

Sherry fell back a few steps, before lunging again, swinging her weapon sideways.

The blunt side of the spear hit Neena's head. She recoiled in shock as blood trickled down her temple and dripped into her eye. Sherry gave her no time to recover. The crazed woman reared back the spear's point, jabbing, forcing Neena to dodge. Neena avoided being gored, but not before knocking into someone else, pitching them both off-balance.

Neena and the other person fell in a heap.

Neena rolled.

With effort, she broke free from the person, recognizing Samara. Samara sprang up to help her, only to get pulled into another skirmish.

Sherry charged Neena.

Rage overpowered her lack of experience.

She thrust her spear mercilessly, screaming with bloodlust, forcing Neena to retreat while avoiding the ledge. Neena managed a few lucky parries before the spear slashed her arm. Neena shrieked as a fresh wound tore her skin. Sherry's eyes burned with hatred.

"I'll kill you for what you've done!" Sherry spat, thrusting her spear again.

Neena scooted sideways, trading a few more ineffective stabs, before ending up near the cliff face.

She dodged another jab, listening to the ping of metal against rock. The temporary reprieve allowed her to scan through the commotion toward the Center Cave. A few handfuls of women had fled inside, while others stood frozen. It looked like Jodi and Tanya had caught hold of

Samel again. What were they doing? Seeing Samel with them incited her rage. She lashed out with her spear, catching Sherry's arm. Fabric and skin tore.

Sherry wailed.

Her pained scream reminded Neena of how Darius might've screamed, or how Samel might've yelled while being dragged away. Those thoughts fueled her anger.

Neena reared back her spear, thrusting hard, grazing Sherry's leg. Her opponent howled. Instead of retreating, Neena fought harder, switching to the offensive. She plunged her spear forward repeatedly, missing Sherry several times, but forcing her backward.

Neena kept on attacking, trading positions with Sherry, until she forced the other women up against the cliff face. With little room to maneuver, Sherry frantically tried blocking. She raised her spear, but Neena batted it away.

Desperate, Sherry lashed out with a foot, catching Neena hard in the knee, sending her reeling.

Neena recovered, rearing back her spear and thrusting.

This time she caught Sherry unguarded.

Her aim was true.

Sherry screeched in rage as the spear pierced the meat of her thigh, and Neena pressed deeper. She turned the spear's handle, thinking of all those who had suffered, and all of Sherry's actions, before pulling it out.

Sherry dropped her spear and fell to the ground.

Her hands flew to the gaping wound, tamping the flow of blood.

She looked from the wound to Neena, as if this might be a dream, or a mistake.

Neena kicked Sherry's spear out of reach.

She moved directly in front of Sherry, holding her spear inches from Sherry's face.

Quiet reigned in the gentle breeze.

Quiet?

Looking around, Neena noticed that all the nearby battles had stopped. All eyes riveted to the spear in her hand, and Sherry's anguished face. Gasping for breath, Neena lifted her spear under Sherry's chin, trying to get a word out.

"I want my brother back," she finally hissed. The words came out in barely a whisper.

Sherry's eyes roamed from Neena's face to the spear.

She opened her mouth to speak, but groaned instead.

"That's enough!" someone shouted.

Neena looked past Sherry toward the mouth of the Center Cave, where Jodi and Tanya stood with Samel.

"She's pregnant!" Jodi cried. "You promised you wouldn't hurt any children!"

Neena looked from the woman to Sherry, who groaned again, letting one hand off her leg and grasping her stomach, which had a slight bulge that Neena hadn't noticed. Neena blinked hard, switching her focus to Jodi and Tanya.

"Let Samel go!" she yelled over to them.

The women hesitated only a moment before releasing Samel. His breath heaving, he dashed for the cliff's face, sticking close to it and finding his way back to Neena. None of the women on the ledge grabbed him, or impeded his path.

And then he was holding on to Neena, safe. Tears streamed down his face.

Neena blinked hard. It felt as if she'd dodged a strike of lightning.

"We only grabbed him again to protect him from the fighting!" Jodi explained.

Several Right Cavers released the breath they'd been holding. Looking around, Neena saw a few people holding spears on one another. A handful more — including Salvador — were on the ground, shaken, but not majorly wounded. Those women who had fled when the battle began congregated by the mouth of the Center Cave.

Even Kai seemed relieved.

Slowly, Neena withdrew her spear, stepping away from Sherry while Samel clung to her.

"This is over," she said.

Tears welled in Sherry's eyes. Reluctantly, she nodded.

Samel walked over to Kai, who started cutting the cloth from his wrists, while Neena took a step toward the Right Cavers.

A shout stopped her.

"Watch out!" Kai screamed.

Neena's head swiveled back to the wounded woman. In a moment's time, Sherry's face had turned from anguish to madness. She darted for Neena, hands groping, blood leaking from her leg. Neena scurried backward, but not in time to avoid the woman from crashing into her.

Still on their feet, they skidded backward, entangled.

With horror, Neena realized they'd ended up near the cliff's edge.

Sherry scratched and growled, tearing at Neena's clothes and her skin, filling the air with her rabid cries. Neena got up her arms, thrusting her backward.

And then Sherry was lunging, Neena was skirting sideways, and Sherry was barging toward a target that was no longer there.

A last, angry cry turned to realization, as Sherry's balance failed. One boot followed the other. Her arms pinwheeled. And then she was over the edge and out of sight. Her shriek echoed for a long while, off the lower faces of the cliff, up to where her women and the Right Cavers stood.

The long, fading scream ended in a thud.

And then all was quiet, save the wind.

CHAPTER 63: Neena

NEARLY A HUNDRED SHOCKED, BEDRAGGLED people hurried to the cliff's edge, while keeping a buffer from the enormous drop. Gasps punctuated the crowd as they looked down. A few women covered their mouths. Those who'd been hiding in the Center Cave slowly emerged, ordering their children to stay put before joining the others.

Shaking and in pain, Neena mimicked the gathering crowd, peering down. All at once, the fight was forgotten.

A new tragedy had taken center stage.

Neena scanned the rocky formation from side to side, searching for Sherry's body. Sherry's momentum had taken her to a different place than they expected, but the end result was the same.

The crazed woman's pulverized body lay at an ugly angle on an outcrop of stone. Her legs were folded beneath her, snapped below the knee, bone jutting from the ends. Her mouth was open in a ghastly expression of death. Neena couldn't see everything from here, but she saw enough. She immediately covered her mouth.

Sherry wasn't moving, and would never move again.

Sickness made Neena back away from the edge. A hand on her arm startled her, until she realized it was Kai, pulling her back and away from the dangerous drop. Samel grabbed her in a tight hug, while Roberto, Salvador, and Samara surrounded them, checking on their well-being. All around them, the Right Cavers stood in a stunned cluster, their faces scratched, their clothing torn. A few of the Center Cave women got up from where they'd fallen and hurried back to their peers, joining a cluster of their comrades about thirty feet away.

At a safe distance, Jody, Tanya, and the rest of the women gathered near the entrance of the Center Cave, watching Neena and Samel, crying, or in shock.

For a long, uneasy moment, the two groups stared at one another, listening to the whistling wind. Neena squeezed Samel tightly, as if someone might try to rip him away, even though she'd never let that happen again.

After what felt like a long time, Neena broke the silence and said, "I have no interest in fighting you."

The women looked at one another with tear-streaked faces, debating something. No one answered, but they weren't raising their spears, either.

Continuing Neena said, "I never intended for Sherry, or anyone else, to die today. All I wanted was my brother back."

Jodi and Tanya looked at each other, and then toward the mouth of the cave, where the brown-haired boy — William — and a few others trickled out, hugging their mothers. The women squeezed their children tight, looking back and forth from the ledge where Sherry had fallen to Neena's group.

"All we wanted was to keep our children safe, as well," Jodi said honestly, holding William.

"I'm not sure what lies Sherry told you, but we never intended anyone harm. It was your people who killed Darius. We only wanted to work together."

"I heard you mention that before," Jodi said, seemingly just as confused as the other woman. "We don't know what you're talking about."

Neena glanced at Kai. "Someone killed Darius in our cave. He was stabbed with his tools and left dead."

"We found him right before your men marched," Kai explained.

Jodi glanced over at Tanya, perplexed. "We don't know anything about that."

The other women looked around, just as bewildered.

"We discovered his body right before we discovered my other brother missing," Neena said, the words bringing back the emotion of that day. "Darius was brutally killed sometime before Raj went to the colony with Bryan and his men."

Jodi lowered her head. "I do not know what to say, other than I am sorry for your loss."

"And I am sorry for yours," Neena said, motioning toward the edge of the cliff where Sherry had fallen. "I am even sorrier for her baby."

An unexpected tear wet Neena's eye. As angry as she'd been with Sherry, she'd never wish harm upon a child. A long, emotional pause fell over the cliffs, while some women blotted their eyes, staring vacantly off the edge of the cliffs.

And then another woman stepped forward, addressing all of them.

"Sherry was no longer with child," she said, to the surprise of the others. "We saw her in the cave before we ran out here. She was clutching her stomach, trying to hide some blood on her clothes. I'm not sure if it was a sudden miscarriage, or if it had been happening awhile, but it sounds as if the worst of it occurred before you came."

The women at the cave looked from the cliff toward the Center Cave, covering their mouths, or shaking their heads in grief.

"It seems as if another tragedy has struck our cave," the woman said, squeezing her eyes shut.

"Too many losses have devastated us," Neena agreed, lowering her head. "But my hope is that we can prevent one more."

Jodi and Tanya watched her carefully.

"Samel isn't the only one I was trying to get back. I was trying to get Raj back, too," Neena said. "We are afraid he is dead. But we need to find out for certain."

Jodi looked at Tanya before speaking again. "Your brother is alive. We saw him scavenging with the men a day ago."

"Alive?" A surge of hope coursed through Neena.

"We saw him from the cliffs," Tanya said. "There were only two dozen men down there. He was the smallest. I assume it was him. They returned to the Comm Building when they were finished."

Neena glanced at Kai. She couldn't believe what she heard. "If that is true, we have to get to him."

The news invigorated the Right Cavers, who straightened their backs and gripped their spears. A few looked out over the colony, toward the Comm Building, while others shifted uneasily.

Their uneasiness spread to the Center Cave women. Neena immediately realized the reason.

Hoping to dampen their fears, Neena said, "Our intent is not to harm anyone else. But I need to get my brother back."

"More deaths might occur, if you confront our men," called out a woman with fright.

"Please." Another woman stepped forward. "Let us speak with them. Perhaps we can convince your brother to come back."

Neena exchanged another glance with Kai. She couldn't agree to that, even if she wanted to. "It is my duty to keep my brothers safe, just as it is your duty to protect your children. What happened to Darius might happen to Raj. I cannot risk it."

The woman squeezed her eyes shut. Others held their young ones, fear in their eyes.

"We will do our best to avoid bloodshed," Kai swore.

The women on the ledge wavered nervously. For a moment, Neena was certain they'd block their way, or stir up trouble. They looked at one another, whispering.

Eventually, all of their eyes landed on Tanya and Jodi.

A decision formed in Tanya's eyes.

"I'll go with you," Tanya said. Looking around at the other women, she continued, "I have no children of my own. I will help Neena and her people. Perhaps together, we can avoid more death."

"But Tanya!" Jodi objected. "It's too dangerous."

"I have decided," Tanya insisted. "The rest of you stay here and protect the children. I will return."

Neena traded a look with her people, none of whom objected. "Okay. We'll go together." Looking at the sky, she saw the clouds darkening. "But we should hurry, before the storm arrives."

CHAPTER 64: Neena

S TRONGER WIND RIFLED THROUGH NEENA'S clothes, making her shiver as she, Kai, Tanya, and the other sixty Right Cavers headed down the cliff side toward Red Rock. Now that the adrenaline of the attack was over, Neena could feel the sting of her injuries more sharply, and the dull aches of her body. But she had even more to consider. For all she knew, she was heading into a predicament from which she might not return.

The threat of the incoming storm didn't ease her worry. Looking at the horizon, she scanned the ominous clouds. The storm seemed to be moving slowly, and didn't seem too powerful at the moment, but who knew if that might change?

Looking over her shoulder, she searched up the craggy rocks, finding the entrance of the Right Cave, where she'd left Samel. A few others had promised to bring him back to their new chamber. If all went well, Neena would return with his sibling. Her family had experienced enough heartache.

It was time to put an end to it.

The path curved, winding behind a passage of tall, jutting rock on either side, as if the cliffs were trying to swallow them up. No one spoke, or made a sound. Fear consumed their thoughts.

A momentary flash of recollection reminded Neena of Raj walking this same path, heading off toward a precarious battle, like she was.

She had no idea what would happen when she reached the Comm Building.

Facing Sherry and her women was one thing.

Confronting Bryan was another.

She looked behind her at the sixty people who accompanied her. Most had only suffered minor injuries, but they might not be so lucky a second time. Neena wasn't deluded. She knew her people weren't as numerous or as experienced as Bryan's or Gideon's. And she had little faith that Tanya could reason with Bryan, when she'd already tried and failed.

A battle with The Watchers might prove disastrous.

But she was intent on her mission.

Noticing Neena glancing around, Samara met her eyes, giving her a determined nod. Roberto and Salvador matched her steps.

Regardless of what happened, she was glad to have them by her side. They weren't her family by blood, but they'd grown almost as close, in the short time they'd lived together.

After traveling a long while, Kai pointed at a familiar curve in the distance. "We're almost there."

Her shoulders brushed his. His touch reminded her of the moments they shared in their bedroll in the night, holding each other for warmth, caressing each other gently.

Without thinking about it, she reached over and squeezed his shoulder.

And then they reached the sandy desert below the cliffs.

They moved without pause, making quicker progress than their previous trip to the colony, passing the tithing and storage buildings.

When they reached the middle of the colony's northern border, they forged down the main path.

CHAPTER 65: Raj

A CTIVITY RIPPLED THROUGH THE COMM Building's main room. Watchers lined up on the edges of the circular table, hovering over the quills and spears, working carefully and diligently, constructing the new weapons that Bryan had ordered, while the wind keened against the building outside.

Those who weren't engaged in the work spoke in quiet, excited tones, hope lighting up their faces.

Not Raj.

Horror and guilt filled his stomach. No one had asked him to go on Ed's early trip. In fact, they hadn't even looked in his direction. If Raj hadn't realized his role before, he'd figured it out now: he was only as good as his last discovery. He'd never been good enough, at all.

The nightmarish bubble of reality had burst inside him.

He couldn't stop envisioning Darius's face, or dwelling on the way he had betrayed his old friend.

What should he do?

Looking at the doors, a part of him wanted to make a break for them, running back to the cliffs and his family. But fear held him back. For days, he'd lived among Bryan's men, fighting with them, eating with them, and sleeping among them. For all he knew, a move like that would be considered the ultimate betrayal.

If he were trapped here, he'd make it count.

Staring across the room, he located Bryan.

Instead of seeing the man he'd once called a friend, he now saw a beast, as ugly as the Abomination. Raj gritted his teeth, watching Bryan give his men orders. His eyes roamed to the quills and spears on which The Watchers worked. Every so often, one of the men put a finished one into a pile. He wanted to grab one of those new weapons, thrust it in Bryan's face, and demand answers.

Raj thought about that.

No matter what he did, he couldn't change what'd happened to Darius. But perhaps he could make it right in another way. Maybe he could atone for his decisions.

The more he sat on his bedroll, watching Bryan and thinking, the more his seething guilt turned to a different kind of thought.

When the time was right, he'd get revenge for what Bryan had done to Darius.

CHAPTER 66: Neena

A GUST OF BUILDING WIND SNAKED from behind, kicking up a billow of dust and startling Neena. For a moment, she questioned her decision to forge onward, but she already saw the back of the annex, and the enormous dome building. This was their time.

"Let's go!" she mouthed to the people behind her.

She kept a wary eye around her. Since walking the main path, she hadn't seen any sign of Bryan's people, nor had they glimpsed any activity from the cliffs. Their separating distance had cloaked their fight.

They passed by several dozen alleys of hovels — some ruined, some intact — and most of the tradesmen's buildings before reaching the cusp of the wide, circular path. Thirty feet of open path gave them plenty of room to spread out, but they stuck together, as more wind and sand swirled around them.

Passing by the annex, Neena had a moment to feel blistering anger for how Bryan had kept her and Kai there.

And then they were at their destination.

The Comm Building rose high above them, casting an ominous shadow. She saw no boot prints on the path. Assumedly, the blowing sand had covered them over.

That thought led to another.

Maybe Bryan's people were gone.

The thought scared and relieved her, but she knew it was the wrong hope.

She needed Raj back.

They circled the building and approached the main entrance.

A spike of fear coursed through Neena, as her people stopped at a twenty-foot buffer from the thick, wooden doors, staring at them.

She and Kai traded a look with Tanya, who nodded.

Slowly, Tanya crept toward the doors, reaching the threshold and putting an ear to one of the doors. She heard nothing. The gale had grown strong enough that it would mask any noise from inside. Neena and her people glanced from Tanya up to the sky, watching the approaching clouds.

Tanya raised a fist and knocked.

Neena, Kai, and the others maintained their position, holding their spears, riveted on the door. The next few moments took more courage than the thousands they'd already spent getting here.

And then those moments yielded something.

Something scraped against the other side of the doors.

CHAPTER 67: Neena

ATHUD FOLLOWED THE SCRAPE.

Neena held her position with Kai at the front of their group, twenty feet away, watching Tanya, while sand continued swirling up around the path. All around Neena, sixty Right Cavers steadied their spears, prepared for whatever came next.

It was a stand, as well as a statement.

Neena swallowed. She'd guessed this scene so many times in her head that she knew all the outcomes. All that was left was to live one of them.

The door cracked open, revealing a sliver of torchlight, and a face.

Louie.

The large man stood in the cracked doorway, scanning over them. Surprise lit his face when he saw Tanya.

"What are you doing here?" he asked, furrowing his brow.

Lifting her chin, Tanya motioned to Neena and her people, "They're here to talk to Bryan. They want to get Neena's brother back."

Louie motioned with his uninjured hand. "What are *you* doing with them?"

"We had some conflict on the cliffs. I was hoping to avoid more," Tanya said over the wind. "I was hoping for peace."

Louie watched them for a while longer through the

crack, contemplating an answer, before leaving without another word. The thud of the shutting door rattled Neena's heart and her mind. She blinked hard, looking over at Kai. None of her troop had moved. They knew their plan. If Bryan wouldn't open the door, they'd camp here until they got what they wanted. Sooner or later, Bryan and his comrades would come out for water or supplies, and when they did, Neena and her crew would say their peace, regardless of Tanya.

They stood until their legs were cramped and their spears wavered, until a sound snapped them back to attention.

The door opened again, wide enough this time that Neena could immediately recognize the man coming through.

Bryan.

Taking a few steps outside, he peered through the thickening haze of blowing sand and dust.

Intimidated, Tanya took a few steps back.

Holding up her hands, she raised her voice over the persistent gale. "Bryan, we need to talk. We had some troubles on the cliff, but we have come to an agreement. I am here to facilitate a conversation."

Bryan looked past her as if she were an insect, flitting about his head, before stepping around her, holding his spear.

Neena surveyed the man who had caused so much turmoil, and had presumably killed Darius. His hair was disheveled. His eyes were ringed from lack of sleep. His clothes were tattered and worn, probably from battle, and too many days without washing.

"You shouldn't have come here," Bryan told Tanya dryly, over the wind.

Tanya stepped further away, lowering her hands.

Louie and a dozen other Watchers filtered out behind Bryan, holding spears or knives. They scrutinized Neena and her crew as if they were starved beasts wandering into a hunter's territory. One of them, a young man with blond hair, cut through and darted over to Tanya.

"What are you doing here?"

Tanya shook her head, trying to explain, but he brought her away from Bryan.

Fighting his grasp, Tanya yelled, "Bryan! We need to talk! We can resolve this!"

Her words caused a stir among some of the other Watchers, until Bryan cut them off.

"Enough!" he commanded. Focused on Neena and her people, raising his voice to be heard over the intensifying wind, he said, "You are even more foolish than I thought before."

Neena was through mincing words. "We're here for my brother," she yelled.

Bryan sneered. He studied Neena's face for a long moment, before turning to Louie.

Forcing an innocuous expression, Louie called out, "What makes you think he's with us?"

"I saw him coming down here with you," Neena returned, looking between them. "And Tanya saw him from the cliffs yesterday. Let me speak with him."

Staring between Bryan and Louie, her anger boiled. It was the same anger she'd felt when she realized her brother was gone, or when she'd felt Sherry's and her women's abuse. It was the same rage she felt at discovering what had happened to Darius. It was a rage she would let out soon, if their attempts at peace failed.

"If you have any intelligence, you'll turn back to the cliffs," Bryan warned.

"We're not going anywhere without Raj," Neena kept on. "If you get in our way, you'll feel the ends of our spears."

Bryan smiled confidently. "You aren't coming in here."

As if on cue, a dozen more armed Watchers stepped

out from the building, reinforcing Bryan's first group. Neena scanned past them, trying to spot Raj, but all she saw were more unrecognizable faces. The building was so full that they'd never get inside without being invited. And the circling sand and wind was making it hard to see them clearly. But she wasn't giving up.

Her anger driving her words, she said, "You've done enough damage to our people. This ends now."

"More than you've done?" Bryan's eyes burned with renewed anger, as he continued speaking over the gale.

"You've turned neighbors into enemies, for your own aims," Neena said, through gritted teeth. "You've kept us in our cave for too long, but now we're out, and we aren't going back."

The shuffle of feet made Bryan look behind him. In the time they'd been talking, more people had gathered at the doorway, watching with curiosity, and more than a little unease. No one had ever spoken to a Watcher the way Neena had. And certainly not to Bryan.

Feeling the pressure of the growing audience, Bryan stepped forward, jabbing his spear at Neena. "Gideon was right about you. He should've let you rot in that cell." He aimed his weapon menacingly at Kai. "And he should've let the stranger die, too."

"Or he could've killed us both, like he planned to kill Kai," Neena spat loudly.

A few of The Watchers bristled at a lie few had discussed openly.

"That's right," Neena said, motioning toward some of the people gathered in the doorway of the Comm Building. "Gideon ordered The Watchers to drag Kai from his cell and kill him in the caves, where none of you would hear. He lied on that podium. Kai never escaped."

Kai nodded, planting himself alongside Neena. "It's true," he said. "A few of the veteran Watchers dragged me to the desert to kill me. I would've died, if Neena hadn't helped me."

The Watchers looked at each other, guilt on their faces. None disputed the truth.

"Gideon had his reasons," Bryan said. "And now I understand them."

"Of course you would say that, because you are consorting with him," Neena said, venom in her voice. "Tanya told us what you were up to. She heard Sherry conspiring with him."

A few in the Comm Building conversed loudly, turning to one another. Tanya lowered her head, feeling the weight of too many stares.

"That's right," Neena pressed on. "Gideon is the reason you're down here, isn't it? You've been whispering with him in the shadows. You've been planning all of this so that he can take power back. Have you not told your people?"

Bryan's lips quivered with anger. Looking from Neena to the people behind him, he said, "Gideon has given us ideas about battling the monster, that is true."

"Ideas about how he'll return to the Comm Building, when you're done," Neena said. "Ideas about how he'll rule once again. Maybe he can tell these people more lies, or kill them, the way he tried to kill Kai, or the way you killed Darius."

Bryan took another step, thrusting his spear in front of him. Neena held her weapon up defensively. As one, the Right Cavers moved forward to protect her.

Bryan's Watchers shored up behind him.

"Will you kill us the way you killed our friend?" Neena asked, over the wind. "Will you stab us with a dozen tools, after we're dead? Or maybe you'll do it while we're alive."

More conversations started in the Comm Building. The people behind The Watchers looked confusedly from Bryan to Neena.

"He killed Darius!" Neena yelled, drilling the words in for effect. "He killed him for no reason, before marching down here with all of you. He left him dead in a cove for us to find. Perhaps that is something else you didn't know."

Realizing the trust of his people was faltering, Bryan said, "We did what we had to do to restore Red Rock."

Gasps came from the crowd.

"You killed an old man for your own selfish revenge," Neena seethed. "And now more people are dead, because your plan to attack the monster failed."

The people in the Comm Building looked from Bryan in the direction of the desert. Pain overtook their faces.

Before their pain could turn into blame, Bryan roared, "Enough!" He turned to his men, raising a signaling hand into the wind. "These pieces of trash have caused enough death. It is time to put an end to it. We will finish what we started on the cliffs!"

Samara stepped up, her face a mask of anger. "If you do that, you'll die, like Sherry."

Bryan looked from Samara to the cliffs, through the building wind and the whipping sand. Of course, he couldn't see up there clearly. He looked back at Samara. Disbelief and rage crossed his face.

"You lie!" he spat.

"I'm not lying," Samara said. "She tried to fight us and fell from the cliffs. She caused her own death."

Bryan's eyes widened. He looked from Samara, to Neena, and then back at Tanya, waiting for confirmation.

"It's true," Tanya said, lowering her head. "It happened just a while ago."

He looked from Tanya to the cliffs, struggling with a truth he couldn't believe.

"No..." His eyes widened.

He looked around at Neena and her people, as if

someone might dispute the fact, but of course, they didn't. Slowly, his denial turned to fury.

Rearing back his spear, he aimed at Samara, ready to release that fury into a throw.

Crying out, Samara raised her spear to protect herself.

A new voice interrupted them.

Everyone turned.

Cutting through the crowd of people at the doorway, holding the strange weapon and aiming at Bryan, Raj yelled, "Drop the spear, or you'll die!"

CHAPTER 68: Neena

GASPS RIPPLED THROUGH THE CROWD. People stepped back, or shielded their loved ones. No one moved to stop Raj. Fear froze their feet. Even The Watchers moved aside, not wanting to get in the way of a blast that would put a hole in their bodies.

Neena watched in disbelief as her brother moved through the crowd of frightened people, stopping within feet of Bryan, keeping the weapon trained, while the swirling sand kicked up around them. The wind had grown strong enough that they had to shout to be heard.

In a voice older than his years, Raj repeated, "Drop the spear!"

Bryan opened and closed his mouth, but he didn't let go of his weapon.

"Do it, or I'll send a spear through your body, just like we did to the stone!" Raj screamed.

Slowly, Bryan released his grasp on his spear. The weapon thudded into the sand. More wind gusted, blowing Raj's curly hair over his face. He kept his weapon aimed, and his voice even.

Focused on Bryan, while talking over his shoulder, Raj said, "Neena is right. Bryan doesn't care about any of us. He wants to use us, so that he can hold his position of power, just like Gideon. He'll kill anyone who gets in his way. I heard what he said. He killed my friend, Darius. And now I'm going to kill him."

Raj walked forward, aiming the weapon at Bryan's chest, while Bryan backpedaled, moving diagonally away from the building and to the side of Neena's group. Neena followed his movements.

For the first time ever, she saw fear in Bryan's eyes.

"The device can only hurl one spear!" Bryan reminded Raj loudly, as Raj backed him farther up the path and away from the crowd. "If you miss, you'll die before you put another one in."

In a sure tone, Raj cried, "I will not miss. Now, back up, away from the rest of us!"

Reluctantly, Bryan obeyed.

Neena's heart hammered. She looked from Raj to The Watchers. What was Raj doing? Once he used the weapon, he'd be defenseless. She searched through the faces of The Watchers at the doorway, and the confused people behind them. She couldn't tell what any of them would do when Raj used the weapon. But if they came toward him...

Stepping away from her group and toward Raj, she said, "Raj! Wait!"

Raj glanced sideways at her, but he kept the weapon poised. She lowered her voice so that she was talking only to him.

"Let me have the device."

"This is my fault, Neena," Raj said, tears welling in his eyes. "I made a mistake in coming here. And now I'm going to make it right. I'm going to put a hole in his body, so that he never hurts any of us again."

"Let me do it!" Neena said, loudly enough that only Raj could hear. "I'll take the weapon, while you get behind us."

Raj shook his head. "I can't..."

Neena let a hand off her spear and took a step toward him, but Raj sidestepped. Tears rolled down his cheeks. His hands shook. Neena felt a stab of regret in her heart. Maybe if she'd done something differently, she could've prevented this situation. But it was too late now.

"Raj! You don't have to be the one to decide what happens to him!"

"I've already decided," Raj said. "The moment I figured out what he did to Darius, I decided. I wish you hadn't come down here for me, Neena. I wish you were safe on the cliffs. And I wish Darius was safe there, too."

"The cliffs?" Bryan yelled, recoiling when he heard the words. "You mean, where your people killed Sherry?"

The Watchers shifted uncomfortably. A few looked up to the cliffs, obviously worried about their women.

"Who knows who else they have killed?" Bryan roared, picking up on their fear. "These Right Cavers come down here with their falsehoods, and yet they call me the liar!" Bryan's face reddened with rage. "Regardless of whether this boy uses his device, we will make them pay. Not only for Sherry, but for her unborn baby."

"The child was already gone," Neena called out sadly.

"Lies!" Bryan barked.

"It died before we confronted her," Kai reinforced, stepping forward. "Your other women told us."

"I don't believe it!" Bryan yelled, even though he was already looking at Tanya for confirmation.

His words carried past The Watchers, echoing off the walls of the Comm Building where his people stood, nervously clutching their clothes through the debris. The dark clouds were directly above them now. Shielding his face from a nasty gust of wind, Bryan jabbed a finger across the fifteen-foot distance between him and Raj.

"If you are going to use that weapon, make sure it kills me," he yelled. "Because if it doesn't, you'll be the next to die. And then all of you will pay for what you've done."

Raj's hands shook on the device's handle. He squinted

against the swirling sand, which had thickened enough that it was getting hard to see.

"Do it!" Bryan screamed, his rage growing. "Fire your spear! And when it's done, be prepared to face me! All of you!"

Through the sandy haze, Neena saw Louie inching toward one of the other Watchers.

And then Raj did the unthinkable.

He fired the weapon.

A loud click echoed across where everyone stood, as the weapon discharged and the spear shot out from its end. Too late, Bryan tried to move, but he wasn't faster than a powerful device. He cried out as the spear hit its mark.

Raj's aim was true, but not true enough.

The spear grazed his side and kept going, thudding into the ground a few feet behind him and splashing up sand.

A hush fell over those who watched.

Shocked, Bryan looked from the end of the weapon to his side, where only a shred of clothing was torn. Neena saw only a tiny trickle of blood—nothing that would stop an angry man.

Her heart dropped in her chest.

Oh, no!

Bryan's shock turned into a smile.

"You'll die for that!" he screamed, taking a vengeful step toward Raj. "You'll—"

An explosion of sand burst from underneath him.

An enormous, teeth-filled mouth emerged from the ground, encompassing Bryan's body, ripping him upward, just as the wind, sand, and debris grew to a shriek.

Men and women screamed and panicked.

Two things became clear to Neena.

The sandstorm had reached its peak.

And the monster was here.

CHAPTER 69: Neena

"**R**AJ!" NEENA SCREAMED, AS THE beast rose higher through the storm.

She struggled to see through the blasting sand. In mere moments, the area around her had fallen to chaos. People scattered everywhere, running away from the caving ground and the monster. The beast's enormous shadow blocked out everything but its silhouette. Neena riveted her eyes on the ascending dark shape. As soon as its tail curved over her, she skirted around the edge of the sliding sand, running blindly toward where she'd last seen Raj. The monster's guttural screech filled the air, competing with people's desperate screams. Was that Bryan screaming? Raj? Or both of them?

"Raj!"

Sand peppered her mouth and nose, making her feel as if she might suffocate, but Neena didn't stop moving. The sandstorm's shrieking gale pierced her ears.

The shadow above her made her feel as though she was in that nightmare tunnel, running through a maze without an end. But this was reality. And perhaps the last reality she would ever see.

She groped blindly through the whipping sand and dust, relying on her last glimpse of Raj for direction. Somewhere behind her, the beast crashed into the ground, taking Bryan and whomever else with it. Ignoring the cacophonous screams, Neena blinked through the storm, frantically searching for her brother.

She crashed into someone.

Arms grabbed her. Clothing brushed against hers.

Something hard hit her stomach, knocking the wind from her.

A metal object.

Raj?

"Raj!"

His hands shook beneath her as he clutched the strange device and screamed something she couldn't hear.

"Come on!" she yelled back through the pelting wind and sand. Pulling his arm toward the only place she could think to go, she shouted, "Let's get to the Comm Building!"

CHAPTER 70: Bryan

B RYAN SCREAMED, FALLING FROM ONE sticky place to another. He threw his arms out and tumbled, unable to stop his endless fall. His body shrieked with pain. He couldn't see where he'd ended up, or where he was going, but it felt like he was in a dark, winding cave.

What the hell was this?

A cloying odor filled his nose. Vomitus liquid gagged him and plugged up his ears. He spit and screamed at the same time.

He tumbled over and over, unable to find which way was up, and which was down.

And then his body struck something soft.

More of the sticky substance covered his body, binding his clothes to his body. More searing pain shot through him.

In a petrifying instant, he realized what was happening.

The beast hadn't chewed him.

It had swallowed him whole.

He was in the creature's stomach.

Bryan opened his mouth, choking on a scream he couldn't manage. Somehow, he broke away from his sticky prison, but he couldn't find his footing. Each time he got his balance, a violent jolt sent him plunging to another part of the beast's insides, where he stuck and burned. The moving beast tossed him back and forth like a piece of sand in the wind. Hot, sizzling goo burned worse than any pain he'd felt. His skin sloughed off, exposing the blood and bone beneath.

The creature's digestive juices were peeling him away a layer at a time.

More abrasive liquid filled his mouth and his nose.

No sound came from his last scream.

Searing, white-hot pain overtook him.

And then Bryan felt no more.

CHAPTER 71: Neena

NEENA PULLED RAJ THROUGH THE screaming wind, clutching his hand. The rumble of the beast and people's screams had merged into a single, frightening sound. Awful guilt filled her as she took her brother in the opposite direction from her people, who probably needed help.

It was move or die.

Billowing dust and sand barred a glimpse of whatever lay ahead. She'd lost her sense of direction. She could no longer locate the Comm Building, or anything else for that matter. Grasping her spear, she held her breath, trying not to swallow the pelting sand. The horrible noises behind them grew farther away.

Squinting, she saw something ahead.

A wall.

Neena scraped her spear along mud brick, searching for an opening while keeping hold of Raj. Uneven sand, piling along the perimeter, nearly tripped them up. They rounded two corners before they came across a door, kicking it open. She and Raj fell into a dwelling, gasping for breath, while the storm continued raging. Dragging a hand across her mouth, Neena cleared away enough sticky sand to speak.

"Are you okay?" she asked frantically.

Raj's eyes were wild and frightened. He nodded, clutching the weapon he'd managed to hang onto.

Neena's eyes flew around the ramshackle dwelling.

Cookware, bedrolls, and flasks blew back and forth. Blankets bunched up near the walls. Unslinging her bag from her back, she sifted around inside, pulled out a few pairs of goggles, and handed a pair to Raj, before donning one herself.

They looked back through the open door.

Through the whipping debris, she saw a few silhouettes, fleeing. Where were Kai, Samara, Salvador, and Roberto? Had Bryan's men made it back inside the Comm Building, or were they trapped outside, too?

Her heart fluttered with panic at the thought of her people, coming down here to confront Bryan and his marchers, only to face an unexpected battle. They'd known the risks, but no one had expected it might go like this.

She pictured Bryan flying up into the air, assumedly eaten alive. He deserved his fate, for what he'd done to Darius. But now, others might die, too.

This had to end.

Looking over at Raj, her eyes riveted to the strange, incredible device.

Pulling her brother close, she leaned over and said, "Raj! I need you to show me how to use it!"

Raj watched her with fright.

He took his bag off his back and withdrew one of the weapon's spears.

And then he showed her.

CHAPTER 72: Kai

KAI SHIELDED HIS EYES, STRUGGLING to peer through the wind and flying sand. The once-unified group of his people had descended to turmoil. Right Cavers ran in every direction, screaming into the gale. He looked frantically around, but he didn't see Neena or Raj, nor did he see any of The Watchers.

Bryan, of course, was gone.

Looking over his shoulder, he saw the tail end of the monster curve into the ground, creating an avalanche of sand, while the loud rumbling continued. Kai kept hold of his spear and ran toward where he'd last seen Neena and Raj.

An awful feeling took root in his stomach.

They'd been right near the monster when it rose.

Where were they?

Pushing through the storm and the wind, he protected his face with his free hand, while clutching his spear in the other. He didn't stop, or slow, until he reached the dark hole from which the beast had emerged. Scanning left and right along its edge, he found nothing.

Panicked yelling drew his attention right.

Kai turned in time to see a woman running towards him through the storm. The wind pinned her clothes to her body. Her face was a mask of fear.

"You have to help! They're hurt!" she screamed against the gale.

Kai's heart hammered against his rib cage. Was she talking about Neena and Raj? He opened his mouth to ask the question, but she was already hurrying away.

Sand exploded behind them.

He turned to see the monster rising up about thirty feet back — an enormous shadow cutting through the storm. With an ear-splitting boom, the beast hit the ground and tunneled to darkness.

Gasping for breath, he pressed on after the woman. Nearby screams of pain and panic told him they were close to whomever she was talking about. And then they stumbled across three figures. A Right Caver bent over Salvador and another man, both of whom lay on the ground, hollering in pain.

"What happened to him?" Kai shouted, pointing at Salvador.

"He almost fell into the monster's hole! He shattered his ankle!"

Horror overtook Kai as Salvador let his hands off the wound, revealing the awful injury. Blood leaked around a piece of jutting bone, which was twisted at an ugly angle. A few feet farther on, the other man clutched his bloodied face.

"Are you okay?" Kai asked.

"I think it's just a flesh wound!" the man cried, but given the amount of blood on him, and the way he screamed, Kai couldn't tell for sure.

To the uninjured man and woman, Kai asked, "Have you seen Neena or Raj? Samara? Roberto?"

"No!" shouted the man.

Kai stared frantically around, looking past the three people and the woman who had retrieved him. Staying out in the middle of the storm was an easy way to die.

Spinning in all directions, he looked for a place of refuge. He couldn't see anything clearly, but he could hear

222   Piperbrook

the direction of the monster. Any place was better than running that way.

"Help them up!" Kai instructed. "Come on! We need to move!"

Together, he and other uninjured man propped up Salvador, who grunted and groaned, while the woman helped the man with the bloodied face.

"Which way?" yelled the man on the other side of Salvador.

Kai pointed.

They bore in the opposite direction of the creature, hobbling for uncertain safety. Kai used his spear for balance, helping Salvador keep his weight off of his ankle. With any luck, they'd find shelter.

Two unrecognizable people tore past them.

"Wait!" Kai yelled, but they were already gone, leaving only their screams.

He had no idea if they were Bryan's people or his own.

They hurried through the storm, scanning the desert for more survivors. With each step, Salvador felt heavier. The man's intense pain was slowing him down. Kai felt as if he were in the middle of the desert, or a nightmare from which he'd never awaken, rather than in the center of a colony.

A while later, they saw the shadow of the Comm Building, looming high above them. They must've somehow circled back to it. A dozen or so silhouettes stood in front of it, holding their long, pointed spears. A few looked in the direction of Kai's group, while others huddled near the doorway. Kai slowed, wondering if they'd have to defend their lives, until he recognized some of his own people. One of them, a Right Caver with bushy eyebrows, jogged toward them.

"What's happening?" Kai asked him over the wind.

"A few of The Watchers ran inside, but they won't let us

in!" the man cried desperately, cranking a thumb over his shoulder.

Kai wasn't surprised. He watched his people pacing nervously by the door, looking out into the storm.

"We thought we might be safe near the walls," the man said, tossing up his hands in despair.

"Nowhere is safe," Kai said grimly.

He looked out into the desert, spotting another cavernous hole, and glanced at Salvador. The injured man looked as if he might collapse. They needed shelter from the monster, not an uneasy refuge at their enemies' threshold.

"What should we do?" the bushy-browed man asked Kai, through gritted teeth.

"Before the storm started, I remember seeing some intact hovels to the south of the Comm Building," Kai recalled. "Now that I know our direction, maybe we can get to them! Come on, let's go!"

CHAPTER 73: Neena

A CLOUD OF DUST FOUND ITS way inside the abandoned hovel where Neena and Raj squatted, filling the room with a murky haze. The door they'd kicked in was now broken, allowing the raging wind inside, scattering cookware and blankets from one wall to the other.

Neena looked at Raj's bag of miniature, carved spears, and then down at the weapon in her hands, which Raj had shown her how to use.

"Are we heading back outside?" Raj asked.

She glanced from her brother into the storm. The decision to go outside had been easy, when she'd first made it. Now she reconsidered. She couldn't imagine leaving Raj alone in a hovel, after going through so much trouble to find him. Nor could she imagine bringing him out into danger again.

What should she do?

"We're staying here, where we have a chance at living," she said, looking away.

Sensing her conflict, Raj grabbed her arm. "But Kai, Samara, and the others are out there. We have to find them."

Neena struggled with an answer. "It's too dangerous for us to be out there."

"What if they're hurt and need our help?" Raj insisted.

Neena bit down on a response. She couldn't ignore Raj's pleas, because she was having the same argument with herself.

Trying to convince her, Raj said, "It's my fault that they're out there in this. If not for me, they'd never be down here. Let me make it up to them. Let me make it up to *you*."

Unexpected tears welled up in Raj's eyes, causing Neena to tear up, too. He reached over and hugged her, and she hugged him back.

"I'm sorry, Neena, for all those I hurt," Raj continued. "If I could change it, I would. Maybe this is the way I can start to make it up to everyone."

"None of this is your fault," Neena told him. "It's mine. I shouldn't have ignored you. I should've paid closer attention to the problems we had on the cliffs. That's why you left, isn't it?"

Raj nodded, lowering his eyes. "I thought Bryan might treat me better than you did, but I was wrong."

"It's okay, Raj, I don't blame you."

"But you should." Raj shook his head. "I'm the reason Darius is dead. And now I'm the reason more are in danger." He smeared the corners of his eyes.

"Raj—"

"Obviously I can't change those decisions, but maybe we can change this one," Raj kept on. "Maybe we can prevent someone else from dying. Let's go out there and help them."

Neena looked from his face into the storm. The shrieking wind showed no signs of stopping. Raj was right. If something happened to her comrades—*to Kai*—she'd never forgive herself, and he wouldn't, either.

Slowly, she got to her feet.

"We'll go out a little ways. But if we don't see anyone, we'll head back inside," Neena suggested.

Raj agreed, and they reentered the storm.

"**C**OME ON!" KAI YELLED.

He didn't need to tell his people twice. Fear motivated the Right Cavers' boot steps. In the time since they'd regrouped, a handful of his comrades had donned goggles, retrieving them from their bags and slipping them over their heads. Those who had no goggles borrowed from others. A few who had nothing used their shawls. They hurried close to him, fighting the blasting sand.

A ways from the Comm Building, they veered around another giant hole, passing several mangled, dead men. The details of their grisly deaths were partially obscured by sand, but Kai saw enough to make him nauseous: blood-soaked limbs, crushed faces, flayed clothing.

One man lay on his stomach with his arms stretched out in front of him, as if he might escape his inevitable fate. Another's mouth hung agape, his tongue lolling out in a ghastly grimace.

One was a Watcher; the other, Kai recognized as a Center Caver.

Apparently, not all of Bryan's people had made it into the Comm Building.

The distant rumbling reminded them that they faced the same fate.

He swallowed, holding tight to Salvador's ropy left arm, while the other man helped him on the right. The dozen allies they'd met at the Comm Building forged ahead, holding their spears, scouting for pitfalls. Where were Neena and Raj? Each moment of separation deepened the pit in Kai's stomach.

They'd traveled a little farther when one of his men cried out, "Over there!"

Kai swiveled, spotting a person standing in the storm. The survivor shook his head wildly, covering his face with his hands. A few of the Right Cavers approached cautiously, calling out to him. Kai watched with bated breath as they reached the person, grabbed onto his arms, and shouted words he couldn't hear.

It wasn't until they brought the survivor back that he recognized who it was.

Roberto's clothing was ripped and torn; his eyes were squinted shut.

"I took a blast of sand to the eyes!" he yelled, fighting the urge to claw it out.

"It's okay!" Kai yelled. "We'll get you rinsed out! Come on!"

Herding Roberto along, they moved faster, capitalizing on their distance from the creature. Kai's heart dropped as he reached the place where he thought the hovels were located. Only rubble and bodies littered the ground. An enormous path of caved sand ran next to them.

"Keep going!" he yelled.

They passed several more demolished hovels, trekking through broken alleys and skirting more wide trenches, before reaching the back side of some intact dwellings.

Pointing at the largest one, he directed, "Inside there!"

To his surprise, a person ran alongside the wall. Kai called out, and the person turned and spotted them. His heart swelled with emotion as he recognized one his people—a Right Caver named Maria who normally kept to herself.

"Kai!" she yelled, her cry of relief filling the space between them.

Hurrying to his side, she said, "A few more of us just ran into that hovel!"

She gave him a half hug, and he embraced her back, holding her tightly enough that for a moment, he could pretend that they were all safe.

Twenty-two Right Cavers packed into the hovel, gasping for breath. Some cleaned their faces and clothes, while others tended to Salvador, Roberto, or the other injured. The wind shrieked. The rumbling continued.

"Have you seen any more of us?" Kai asked Maria.

Maria shook her head worriedly. "Unfortunately not. I followed behind these two. We were hiding in another dwelling, until the creature got too close, forcing us to flee. That's when you found us."

Kai looked at the two additional survivors from his cave, happy to see them. Both of them were men.

Getting their attention, he asked, "Did either of you see Neena, Raj, or Samara?"

The first man spoke up. "Not since before the monster came. Some others ran past us. I think they might have headed down the main path, toward the colony."

Kai nodded.

"With any luck, they're hiding in a building, like we are," the second man said.

"But something else worries me," said the first man, scratching his crooked nose. "I think a slew of Bryan's Watchers went that way, too."

"What do you mean?" Kai asked.

"The monster and the storm shook everyone's sense of

direction," he continued. "I saw some of them heading that way."

Kai and Maria traded a look. Once the monster whisked Bryan away to his death, the conflict with his people had become a secondary concern. But the thought of The Watchers out there, hiding among the Right Cavers, worried him. Who knew what those men would do, if they came across their lost comrades?

Filling the silence, another woman spoke up. "What if the others need our help?"

The question was rhetorical. No one could answer, because everyone shared the same worries.

CHAPTER 75: Samara

*S*TAY QUIET! *STAY STILL!*

Samara clung to the edge of the broken, mud brick wall, staring up the main path going north through the colony. A seam tore up the ground, coming in her direction. She blinked hard through the goggles she'd pulled from her bag. The bodies of several other Right Cavers were strewn everywhere. She could still hear their screams as the creature flung them into the air, high above the hovels, just as she could recall their bodies hitting the ground with a sickening thud.

Not one of their crooked bodies moved.

A bubble of grief filled her throat. They were dead.

And she was next.

The seam veered closer, moving south toward her.

Move!

Clutching her spear, she let go of the wall, running deeper into the branching alley, away from certain death. A sickening crash echoed behind her, as the monster's body toppled the wall where she'd just stood.

Panting, she ran faster, weaving back and forth, hoping for a miracle.

In one sense, the wind and the swirling debris confused the creature. In another, it made the beast determined to find its prey. Bryan had been its first taste of blood. It wanted more.

Samara had no idea where the rest of her people had ended up.

She was alone.

Sand pelted her clothing as she weaved around broken mud brick, scattered stones, and gigantic, gaping holes. She cried out as someone's abandoned blanket whipped through the air, stuck to her face, and blew away. She focused on putting one foot in front of the other, and the ground in front of her, so that she did not trip over any debris.

Kai's warnings came tumbling back to her.

With the creature this close to her, she couldn't hide.

Hunger consumed it.

She careened left, leaping over a rolling pot, and cut between several broken-down houses. To her relief, the hovels in the new alley were mostly undisturbed.

That meant more obstacles between her and the monster.

She tore ahead faster, scooting between them, listening to the crack of several more foundations as the creature knocked them over from underground. She glanced over her shoulder in time to see a hovel split up the middle, crack in half, and collapse. The beast's back came into view—a dark hulk of scaly flesh and protrusions. At any moment, it would emerge, soar overhead, and crush her.

Or it would erupt below her and swallow her.

Samara darted between another two hovels, avoiding another twisted bedroll.

And then she was in another alley.

The rumbling receded.

Samara slowed her boot steps, fearing she'd misjudged her safety, but the creature was moving in another direction. It had either lost track of her or gotten distracted.

Thanking her momentary good fortune, Samara gained as much distance as possible from the sickening beast. Her heart felt as though it might explode. Her legs were sore and weak. Fighting the storm made each step more difficult, and the abrasive wind wasn't helping. Pulling her wrapped shawl tighter around her goggles, she headed between more hovels, seeking out a larger building that promised more safety.

She passed several more houses before she came across a large wall.

One of the tradesmen's buildings.

Only the front wall of the building was intact.

Rounding the remaining side, she aimed to hide behind it.

And stopped.

A dozen men huddled among the rubble, obviously beating her to the idea.

Bryan's men.

CHAPTER 76: Samara

S AMARA FROZE, SURVEYING THE WATCHERS, all of whom looked back at her. Their hair was mussed and disheveled. Their clothing was caked with sand. Their goggles all but transformed them into man-sized cave bugs.

Samara swallowed and raised her spear.

If this was the end of the line, she'd face them with dignity.

To her surprise, one of the men stepped forward and pointed past her. "Where did it go?"

Samara looked back through the tempest of wind and sand. She couldn't see the creature, but she heard some distant rumbling.

"West, I think," she answered, her voice shaky. "I only know because of the main path."

The man nodded and looked at the others. They held their weapons defensively, but none of them came toward her, or threatened her. They all had larger problems.

In a hopeful gesture, Samara lowered her spear.

The man reciprocated.

The wind keened through the cracks in the wall, screeching around them.

Getting close enough to speak more easily, she held up her hands, motioning over her shoulder and elaborating. "I think it is in a frenzy."

The men nodded, grave expressions on their faces. She recognized the man speaking with her as Isaiah, one of

Bryan's close companions. Isaiah turned back to his men, who awaited direction. She looked at the spears in their hands. Surprise washed over her.

Taking an intuitive leap, she asked, "Are you going to fight it?"

Isaiah watched her for a moment through his goggles. He shook his head nervously. "What other choice do we have? It's going to continue killing us until we defeat it. We might be all dead, if we don't fight back."

Samara opened and closed her mouth. Of course, too many had already tried and failed.

Swallowing, Isaiah said, "The storm might mask us enough to get close. Maybe we can pierce its hide."

She looked at the weapons in the men's hands. Samara noticed something strange. Instead of normal blades, they'd adorned their spears with white, spiky objects.

"What are those?" she asked.

"The creature's quills," Isaiah explained. "Before Bryan died, he thought we might be able to use the creature's own body against it. A few of our men found these protrusions in the desert. We were working on creating more weapons, before...before what happened to him."

He lowered his eyes. The loss of their leader was fresh enough that it sent a ripple of emotion through the men. At the same time, they seemed conflicted.

A pinprick of hope entered Samara's voice, as she focused on the spears. "How many of those do you have?"

Isaiah pointed to his men, some of whom held two weapons. "We have enough to fill our hands, and a few extra that we salvaged from our fallen."

Whether it was the look on her face, or the way she asked her question, Isaiah sensed something. Taking a faithful leap, he took one of the extra spears from his men, offering it to her.

"If this is going to work, we could use another set of hands."

Samara took the spiky spear, holding it alongside her own and examining it. In the distance, a loud rumble reminded them that the creature was still on the move.

"Have you seen any more of our Watchers?" Isaiah asked her.

Samara shook her head. "No. How about my people?"

Isaiah thought on it. "I thought I saw some of them running toward the hovels in an alley off the main path. I can't promise they're still there, but it's possible. Maybe we can find them together on our way to fight this thing."

CHAPTER 77: Neena

"**H**ANG ON TO ME, RAJ!" Neena yelled, clasping her brother's arm and continuing through the storm.

Sand clung to their clothing and goggles. The wind blew back their hair.

Looking over her shoulder, Neena watched the outline of the hovel recede. It felt as if the wind had whisked it away, even though they'd left it behind. And then it was gone. The awful thought struck her that they might never return to it.

The knowledge of Kai, Samara, Salvador, and the others out here drove her on.

Doing her best to walk in a straight line, she forged through the storm, gripping her device.

Neena could only see a handful of feet ahead of them—not enough for an effective search. Of course, she couldn't tell their exact location. For all she knew, they might miss someone a few feet on either side of them. She studied the ground cautiously, scanning for a sliding patch of sand, or a buried body.

Neena lifted her head to the wind. Somewhere in the distance, she heard rumbling, but she wasn't sure of its direction. They walked another dozen steps, finding nothing but open space.

Raj bent, pulling her arm.

She followed his gaze to a half-buried spear. Neena picked it up, wiped it off, and handed it to her brother.

The discovery of the spear heightened her feeling that they might find the person who had owned it.

Neena's heart beat faster. For a moment, she contemplated calling out for a survivor, but fear kept her silent. Instead, they trudged warily, scanning the desert even closer.

What if they were the last people alive?

A glimpse of clothing gave her an answer. Neena instinctively jolted back, appraising a body. She and Raj bent to the sand, frantically inspecting their find. The person lay on his or her back, unmoving. She looked from the person's dirty boots upward.

And shuddered.

One of the person's arms was gone, ripped off at the shoulder. Jagged flaps of flesh hung over the exposed bone. Neena's heart sunk as she recognized the woman.

Tanya.

Tanya's face was twisted in a last, mortified grimace. Her blonde hair was stained with blood. Next to Neena, Raj cringed, his eyes wide beneath his goggles. She reached over and grabbed his arm, consoling him, while tears tracked his face.

A scream startled both of them.

Tanya sat up, grasping the air with her remaining hand.

"It's all right, Tanya!" Neena told the agonizing woman, shocked to find her alive. "We're going to get you out of here!"

Tanya continued yelling, ineffectively trying to stand. It seemed her leg was broken.

"Raj! We need to help her!"

Raj stood in a half-crouch, frantically trying to get a grip on Tanya's good arm, but shock and pain had a hold of her.

"We need you to help us!" Neena told her. "You have to work with us, so we can get you out of here!"

Instead of answering, Tanya turned her head.

Her eyes bulged, as she noticed her missing arm for

the first time. Her shrill cry carried over the wind, ringing with a terror that Neena had never heard. She groped for her missing appendage, as if it might appear, even though it was obviously gone.

A rumble started in the ground.

Oh, no....!

Neena looked frantically around, as the noise grew louder.

"Come on, Raj! Get her up!"

"I'm trying!" Raj yelled. "She keeps pulling away!"

Tanya was a screaming, writhing weight. They needed her to stop panicking. Neena tried calming her down, but the words weren't registering.

The rumble grew in volume, overpowering Tanya's scream.

Neena's head swiveled toward an incoming seam, splitting the ground.

The beast's back came into view.

In moments, it would be upon them.

She had to make a choice. She had to —

In a desperate attempt to survive, Neena grabbed hold of Raj and ran, leaving Tanya behind. A whoosh of sand pelted their backs. Neena fell, landing on her weapon, while Raj landed somewhere she couldn't see. More sand showered their bodies, covering them in its suffocating embrace.

The rumbling grew loud enough that Neena thought she'd died.

And then it faded.

Neena raised her head, spitting and choking, frantically fighting her way out of the sand. Smearing off her goggles, she looked where Raj had been. To her immense relief, he was there, sitting up and spitting fiercely.

Together, they looked behind them, finding a gaping trench where Tanya had been.

Tanya was gone.

CHAPTER 78: Kai

L OOKING AROUND THE HOVEL AT the scared and injured people, Kai said, "We have to do something."

All around him, the survivors tended the wounded, or dusted off their goggles and clothes, while sand pelted the walls. The door shuddered under the incessant wind.

"The rest of our people are out there," Kai kept on, to anyone who would listen. "And so are Bryan's men. We have to make sure the rest of our comrades are safe."

"How will we find anyone?" Maria asked in frustration. "We can barely see. We have no idea where they might be. For all we know, the rest of our Right Cavers might be hiding already."

"Or they might be lying on the ground, wounded, like Salvador," Kai argued. "More might die without our help."

He pointed through at Salvador, who gritted his teeth in pain, clutching his ankle. Guilt crossed people's faces as they looked at him. Going outside in the storm seemed like a fool's choice, but Kai couldn't help envisioning Neena and Raj lying somewhere near the Comm Building, wounded and screaming. If he did nothing, their final moments would haunt him forever.

"For all we know, our people are a few breaths from death. We need to find them," Kai insisted. "We need to head back out there."

The people in the hovel fought the terror in their hearts.

Of course, they were worried about their relatives and friends. But they were afraid of dying, too.

Fear froze their feet.

Summoning his courage, hoping to inspire them, he said, "The storm will cover our movements. We'll protect each other, and watch for the monster. If it gets too dangerous, we'll come back."

Showing his resolve, Kai stepped toward the rattling door, prepared to open it.

"Our people need us."

Whether it was guilt or duty, a handful of people moved by his side. Among them — to Kai's surprise — was Roberto.

"Let's go," Roberto said.

"What about your eyes?" Kai asked.

Wiping the last bit of crusted sand from his face, Roberto said, "They still sting, but I think I got rid of most of the sand. I'm ready to help."

He donned some goggles. His bravery inspired a few others to move for the door. With Roberto, Maria, and twelve others by his side, Kai nodded gratefully.

"We'll be back soon," Kai told those who were staying behind.

Before he could question his decision, he opened the door. A blast of wind nearly bowled them over, but he led his Right Cavers through the door, moving cautiously through the sand.

CHAPTER 79: Kai

ADISTANT RUMBLE ROSE AND FADED.

The Right Cavers looked about nervously, grasping their spears.

Falling into the pattern on which they had decided, they kept in three rows of five, spreading out, covering more distance while keeping an ear out for danger.

The gusting wind rippled their clothes. The swirling sand limited their view. Kai used the hovels for guidance, navigating to the end of the alley, heading for the main path. Maybe what the others said was true, and he'd encounter some of the people who'd fled this way. If not, they could always backtrack to the Comm Building, where some of the injured were likely to be.

At each hovel, they detoured inside, checking for survivors.

After an unproductive search, they reached the main path.

Kai looked left and right.

Dusty clouds kicked up everywhere, concealing too much of their surroundings. And then something in the distance caught his eye.

He tensed and held up a hand, signaling his party to halt.

Through the hazy clouds, on the main path, something came their way. He clutched his spear defensively. For a moment, Kai feared that the monster had detected them. But it wasn't the monster, because he could hear its sounds of destruction further away.

His heart beat faster as the moving objects solidified into figures carrying spears. More survivors than he'd ever expected to find in one place marched up the path and toward them, their shawls billowing behind them in the wind.

Kai and the Right Cavers held out their spears defensively.

A recognizable shout cut through the storm.

"Kai?"

Careful footsteps turned to hurried ones. A person broke from the approaching formation, running toward Kai and the Right Cavers. Kai couldn't believe who he saw.

"Samara!" he cried, lowering his weapon and hugging her.

Tears wet her eyes. She leaned back, inspecting him through her goggles as if he were a ghost, or a mirage.

The other dozen figures halted.

Letting go of Samara, Kai leaned back and asked, "Who's with you?"

"Some of The Watchers," Samara said, motioning to the people behind her. "They're going to help us."

Kai looked past her to the group of a dozen, rigid men. Goggles adorned their faces; spears adorned their hands. He tensed.

"They mean us no harm," Samara assured him.

Slowly, a man broke from the group and greeted him. Kai kept his spear close, searching for something in the man's posture that signaled danger. At a closer distance, he recognized one of Bryan's men, Isaiah.

Drawing up in front of Kai, Isaiah called over the wind, "We are not here for trouble."

Kai studied the man's face for deceit, but he seemed honest.

"Too much has happened since you came to the Comm Building," Isaiah said. "But we'll have plenty of time to discuss that later, if we live."

Kai nodded. Something in the man's words told him he spoke the truth. "Where are you headed?"

"To fight the monster," Isaiah said. "How about you?"

"To find our comrades," Kai answered.

"Let's go together," Isaiah said. "Maybe we can help find your people, before we plan an attack."

CHAPTER 80: Neena

NEENA STAGGERED TO HER FEET, searching the edges of the wide, gaping trench. Her effort was fruitless. Tanya was gone. A tear slid down her cheek as she studied the black hole, and the whipping, sliding sand at its edges.

A rumble ripped her attention away.

A growing seam returned in their direction.

With a cry, Neena turned and ran, clutching her weapon and her brother. They had no time to mourn Tanya further.

It was move or die.

The bedlam from the beast was like a sharp blade, scraping their nerves, pushing their feet faster. They fled in the opposite direction, fighting the chaotic storm while squeezing each other's hands. Neena waited for the beast's ugly jaws to clamp on their feet, pulling them under, or its massive bulk to crash into them.

Looking over her shoulder, she glimpsed the creature's dark, scaled back. The thing was nearly on top of them.

A spray of sand blasted their right sides.

Neena raised her hands, warding off the pummeling debris.

She looked to her right, at Raj, who was still standing.

Somehow, it had missed them.

Somehow, they were alive.

Noises under the surface of the sand told them the beast wasn't done. Neena felt like a wounded animal, waiting for a predator's last strike. She stopped and spun, seeing nothing but sand in all directions. The storm blocked too much of their visibility.

As one, Neena and Raj looked down at the weapon in her hands.

Letting go of Raj, Neena placed two hands on it, remembering what he had shown her. Finding the small piece of metal she needed to press, she aimed the weapon in the last direction where she'd seen the beast.

If they stayed still, maybe the wind would mask their location.

Of course, she'd have to contend with that wind while using the device.

Her boots shook on the sand, as the creature started another swooping pass, tunneling parallel to them. She adjusted her aim, until its bulky body rose above the sand's surface. Its dark scales and long, round curvature resembled an enormous, wriggling snake. Maybe if she landed the right shot, she'd —

Fire, Neena!

She pressed the metal, bracing for the recoil, and doing her best to account for the wind.

Through the storm, she saw the spear discharge and fly, striking its target on the top of its scales, sticking.

Black blood sprayed the air.

A guttural screech echoed from underground. The beast writhed, veering diagonally somewhere that they couldn't see.

She'd hit it!

For the first time in too long, hope washed over Neena.

"You got it, Neena!" Raj yelled over the wind, grabbing his sister's arm with excitement. "The weapon worked!"

She allowed that hope to overtake her. Somewhere out of sight, they heard the beast continue tunneling away. She listened for signs that it was slowing down. Perhaps its screech would come again, as its pain deepened. Or maybe it would disappear for a while, leaving the colony and heading back into the desert.

She prayed for a miracle.

Maybe its injury would lead to its death.

The rumbling increased in volume.

Neena clenched her eyes shut.

Dammit.

It wasn't slowing.

It was getting faster.

Despair filled Neena's stomach, as she and Raj listened to it erratically moving away, knocking down more buildings.

She let go of her foolish hope, as reality took over.

It would take more than a surface wound to stop a horrible monster.

Maybe they'd never had a chance at defeating it, after all.

CHAPTER 81: Kai

Together with Samara, fifteen Right Cavers, and a dozen Watchers, Kai walked north up the main path of the colony, walking in tight rows, scouring the desert. The irony of marching with Isaiah and his Watchers wasn't lost on Kai. Every so often, he glanced at Isaiah, still accepting their new alliance.

At the same time, he understood it.

A larger foe threatened them all.

Everyone knew it.

On the way up the path, Isaiah explained to Kai what they had done to their spears, and how they'd hoped to use them. The idea inspired Kai, but he wasn't depending on it. At the moment, finding the survivors—*finding Neena and Raj*—was more important than killing the monster.

They scanned the path quickly and quietly, looking for evidence of life, even though any boot prints were gone.

Tracking anyone felt like a lost hope.

They were operating on faith, and faith alone.

They kept precariously on, circling around holes that occupied the path, getting closer to the colony and listening to the rumbles. It sounded like they were changing course.

Not just changing course, Kai thought suddenly. *Growing louder.*

"Do you hear that?" Samara asked, grabbing his arm.

Everyone did.

The group stopped, staring intently up the main path. They uttered a collective gasp.

The monster tore up the path, coming toward them.

Of course, they'd been heading to fight it, but no one expected to see it so soon, and so unexpectedly. A tidal wave of sand lifted up the center of the path, revealing the creature's body, half in an out of the sand. It weaved wildly back and forth, tunneling toward them, apparently in some kind of craze.

"Watch out!" Kai screamed.

People shouted and scattered, clenching their spears. Kai fled west, past some buildings, continuing several dozen steps into the safety of the alley before daring to turn.

Shock hit him at what he saw.

A few brave or foolish Watchers had stopped at the edge of the main path, rearing back their modified spears. They waited for the beast to get close before flinging them. Through the storm, Kai saw the weapons stick in the beast's topside, creating splatters of black blood.

The men shouted in victory.

Their celebration didn't last long.

A blast of sand from the beast hit them, launching them high into the air and farther down the path. With screams of agony, the men fell to the ground.

"Everyone stay back!" Isaiah yelled.

The beast kept going without slowing.

And then the creature was elsewhere, and Isaiah's men were rushing toward their wounded.

CHAPTER 82: Neena

NEENA CLUNG TO RAJ, STARING at the place where they'd made their fruitless stand. Deep trenches cut the ground. The creature's black blood stained the sand. Bleeding or not, the creature was still tunneling farther away. The device hadn't stopped it. The storm blew and blew, adding to her sense of futility.

Shivering from fear and emotionally drained, she peered through her goggles at Raj.

Fear colored his face.

She'd already reloaded the weapon, but what good would it do? They were two people in the storm. Their device had done little to stop the horrid beast. For all she knew, their spear had given it the equivalent of a scratch.

In all likelihood, the rest of their people were gone.

Kai was probably dead, and so was Samara, and Roberto, and Salvador...

Emptiness followed.

Maybe they were better off retreating.

Neena closed her eyes beneath her goggles, riding a wave of despair and reliving too many regrets.

And then she heard something.

Screams.

She looked over at Raj, but he'd already noticed, too.

Other people were alive!

CHAPTER 83: Neena

NEENA AND RAJ HURRIED IN the direction of the noise, following the commotion. The knowledge that someone else had survived propelled their feet. Neena knew that heading toward the monster was risky, but they weren't stopping.

Treading carefully around the trenches, they heard the sound of distant buildings crashing.

The screaming ceased.

It sounded like the creature was now in the northwest part of the colony.

Still, the original cries had come from this direction.

After traveling a while, they came across the remains of a hovel. The sight of something other than sand gave Neena a glimmer of hope. They continued past it, shielding their faces, finding the wreckage of several other houses, and shortly after, the end of a row.

The main path!

In the center was a large, caving trench.

Alarmed, Neena and Raj stuck to the outskirts, following the small, intact strip of sand between the depression and the houses at the ends of the alleys.

A flurry of movement in the distance dispelled her fear that the screams had meant death.

Neena cleaned away her goggles.

She slowed her pace, trying to believe what she was seeing. People moved about in the storm. Not just a few.

More than a handful!

"Over there!" Raj cried in surprise.

Unable to believe what felt like an impossible discovery, Neena and Raj rushed down the path. Raj's cry had reached the ears of a few of the survivors, who dashed toward them, toting their spears. Neena studied the blurry shapes through the storm.

She recognized a familiar person's stride.

Neena couldn't believe her eyes, or her heart.

She didn't allow herself to, until she was in Kai's arms.

Neena crashed into Kai, holding him so tightly that she barely felt the pain of her scrapes and bruises. They embraced for a long moment, cherishing a time neither had expected, before leaning back.

"Neena..." he exclaimed.

"Kai!" Her eyes welled up with tears. They hugged again, overtaken by emotion. After letting go, Neena surveyed the others near him.

She couldn't believe Samara and Roberto were alive! Overwhelmed with joy, she hugged them, before doing the same with the others, including a woman named Maria that she didn't know as well, who was also from the Right Cave.

"Where's Salvador?" she asked, noticing someone missing.

"He's in a hovel not far from here with some others. He's injured, but he'll be okay," Kai explained.

"Thank the heavens!" Neena said with relief.

Her relief lasted until she saw a dozen more people appear through the haze.

Watchers!

"Kai!" she cried, voicing a confused warning.

"They're with us," Kai explained, quickly.

"With you?"

Pointing over his shoulder to the dozen emerging men, two of whom were limping, he said, "They've been helping us search for survivors."

Neena looked around in bewilderment.

Sensing her uneasiness, one of The Watchers, Isaiah, came toward her. With a curt nod, he said, "I'm glad you and your brother are alive."

She searched his face for animosity, but found none.

In her confusion, Neena fumbled for words.

Isaiah drew a long breath. Looking behind him at his men, he glanced back at her. "I know that Bryan wronged your people. I understand you're angry. I don't blame you for trying to get your brother back." Isaiah lowered his head. "I wish we could change the past, but we can't."

Neena held on to her multitude of thoughts.

"All of us heard what Bryan did to Darius, back there," Isaiah elaborated, biting his lip. "The way he killed your friend was horrific and cowardly. We had no part in it. Had we known what he was planning, we might've acted differently. Of course, it is too late for that."

Neena nodded. Emotion struck her, at the mention of their lost comrade.

"We can't change the past, but maybe we can find a way forward," Isaiah said. "Perhaps we can all work together."

Neena watched him for a long moment, judging him, but he certainly seemed genuine. She looked at Kai, who nodded. Their vindication was bittersweet. "It is what we've wanted, all along."

"Let's make it happen, then." Looking back at the rest of his men, Isaiah turned and found Neena's eyes again. "It sounds as if the creature is in another part of the colony, but it's not gone. A few of our men tried throwing spears at it, but the beast injured them."

Looking beyond Isaiah at the limping men, she asked, "Are they all right?"

"They are shaken up and bruised. I think one might have a concussion. But they are alive. It is more than I can say for many others." He glanced worriedly through the storm, in the direction of the creature's distant rumbling.

"We saw some bodies near the Comm Building," Kai told her.

Neena nodded grimly.

Isaiah's eyes wandered to the weapon in her hand. "You have the device."

Neena nodded. For a moment, she thought he might try to take it, but he surveyed it with wonder, instead.

"Have you used it?" he asked.

Neena nodded, returning to her thoughts of futility. "I shot the creature right before I came here. I made it bleed, but apparently, not enough."

"My men's spears wounded it, too. They stuck their weapons in its side, though it is hard to tell if the beast felt it."

Noticing the strange-looking spear in his hand, Neena asked, "What's that?"

"Bryan had an idea to put the creature's quills on top of our spears," Isaiah told her, holding it up. "Unfortunately, we didn't have the chance to throw ours all together." A thought overtook him. He furrowed his brow. "Where did you hurt the creature?"

"On its back," Neena said. "If I had a better shot, maybe I could have wounded it more severely."

Isaiah's thought solidified. "Maybe we can help with that." He scratched his chin. "If we can get the beast to rise, like Thorne and Bryan did, maybe we can hit it more directly. Who knows? Maybe you can even kill it. Between our spears and your weapon, we might have a chance at defeating it, where we have individually failed."

Neena nodded, but she was still hesitant. "There is still the matter of survivors. For all we know, there are more out there."

"If we don't kill the beast, more will die," Isaiah said determinately. "After we kill the monster, we'll search for them, assuming we are still alive."

"What about your injured?" Kai asked.

Isaiah looked at his wounded comrades. "Obviously, they aren't in a condition to fight. We'll need someone to escort them somewhere safer. Perhaps they can stay in the hovel with your other wounded?"

Maria stepped up to volunteer. "I remember where the house is. I can take them back. I might need help, though."

The Right Cavers and Watchers looked at one another, deciding, until a small voice interrupted.

"I'll do it."

Neena looked over, surprised to find Raj stepping forward.

Lowering his head humbly, Raj said, "I know that I'm not as well-versed with a spear, or the best equipped for a fight. But I can be useful to Maria." Gesturing to the injured men, and Maria, he added, "I can look out for the beast, and help the injured move to another hovel, if we need to evacuate. I can take care of Salvador."

"Are you sure?" Neena asked, relieved by the solution to a problem she hadn't even considered yet.

Raj nodded. Unlike before, when his eyes had blazed with rebellion, this time they shone with sincerity.

"That would be an important task," Neena said.

Nervousness immediately struck her. The idea of leaving her brother alone again didn't sit well with her.

"I'll look out for him," Maria promised. "Together, we'll stay quiet and safe. I'll make sure nothing happens to him."

"Okay." Neena opened and closed her eyes, praying to her ancestors that everything worked out.

Stepping forward, she hugged Raj.

Looking up at her, Raj told her, "Don't worry about me. Just do what you have to do, Neena. Make sure the monster is dead."

"I'll do my best," she said.

CHAPTER 84: Neena

MORE THAN TWO-DOZEN ARMED MEN and women stormed up the path, touting their quill-tipped spears and Neena's weapon, gathering their courage while heading in the direction of the noise.

Not Right, Center, or Left Cavers.

Colonists.

Neena drew a breath.

The tension of the past few weeks no longer seemed important. The threat of the larger peril made all of their former differences seem miniscule. She calmed her beating heart and walked in the direction of the commotion.

The monster's fearful rumbled accompanied the storm. In the time they'd talked, it sounded as if the creature had circled north, persisting in its rampage.

The loaded weapon felt heavy in her hands. Every now and then, she ran her hands over its smooth surface, praying she'd have better luck with it. Neena shifted the bag on her back, filled with extra spears. Too many uncertainties remained. But one thing was for sure: the monster must die.

Too many people had perished in its teeth.

She'd made the promise weeks ago to kill it.

It was time to make good on that promise.

Adjusting her goggles, she was surprised to notice that she could see farther ahead than before.

"The storm is tapering," Kai observed, looking around

through the gale, which blew at a steady pace, but not as wildly as before. "Maybe it's past its worst point."

"I hope," said Neena.

In the time they'd been walking, they'd gotten closer to the midpoint of the path, where it split in two directions, circling the Comm Building. The structure's enormous silhouette loomed in the center. In front of it were a swath of tunnels and holes. The creature had destroyed enough homes in the immediate alleys that it looked like the structure resided in the middle of a small desert, rather than a colony. Piles of rubble were the only evidence of the old houses.

Strangely, the booms had faded.

Neena glanced around, wondering whether the creature had gone away.

A new noise erupted.

All around her, people stopped and pointed.

Neena immediately saw what they did.

A seam cut the ground, creating a new path, getting dangerously close to the Comm Building's walls.

"It's tunneling near the building!" one of Isaiah's Watchers shouted in a panic. "The rest of our people are in there!"

CHAPTER 85: Louie

L OUIE STARED AT THE SHAKING walls. All around him, people hurried to the farthest corners of the building, gaining distance from the source of the noise. He looked around at the remaining few Watchers. Scant few were left. Ed and Nicholas were alive, but Isaiah and Clark were missing.

So were too many others.

Gideon's tenets rang through his head.

Preservation at all costs.

If the monster killed them all, who would be left to rebuild Red Rock?

Louie looked at the ceiling, studying the inside of the circular dome, which thankfully seemed to be holding. Luckily he'd braced the doors.

Anyone outside was on their own.

A particularly loud crash jarred the ground under his boots. The animal skeletons shook. The table in the center of the room shifted, sending the piece of the old metal satellite dish scraping and creaking from one end to the other. A few Watchers near the table scrambled to catch it before it tumbled off, pushing it back to the center.

Others looked on, frozen.

The braces in the doors rattled.

Those doors were the only thing between them, the beast, and the storm.

Motioning to Ed and Nicholas, Louie yelled, "Help me with the entrance! We need to make sure the doors stay closed!"

CHAPTER 86: Neena

EENA AND THE OTHERS SURVEYED the ugly scene. Two hundred feet away, through the now slow, but steady storm, the creature took another pass near the building from west to east, rupturing the ground. Perhaps it recalled where it had tasted Bryan's flesh.

Whatever the reason, it clearly wasn't leaving.

Maybe they could use that to their advantage.

Neena looked over to find Isaiah getting her attention.

"Let's lead it away from the building!" He gestured toward the right-hand side of the circling path. "We'll find a way to lure it out of the ground, and then you use your weapon!"

Following his lead, Neena and the rest skirted toward the edge of the wide, curved path. The sand underneath their boots shook. It felt as if the whole planet might collapse. A few blood-soaked bags lay in the middle of the path, lying next to the detached appendages of their owners. With a shudder, Neena recalled the bodies Kai had spoken about earlier. She and Raj might've been closer to them than she realized.

They stepped around several flattened bodies before reaching the western edge of the path.

The beast had disappeared underground, but its familiar noises continued.

Isaiah waved his hands, signaling everyone toward some piles of large, broken mud bricks. Without question, the group rooted around the wreckage, picking up their own stones and returning with him to a distance thirty feet from the path's edge, while Neena stayed behind.

She positioned herself in the sandy spot just before the rubble, where she could fire upon the beast when it rose.

Dozens of people glanced over at her.

Their hopes were in her weapon.

Everyone knew it.

She looked from Kai, to Roberto, to Samara, to Isaiah.

It was time to act.

Pointing toward a spot in the ground about fifty feet away that was free of trenches and holes, Isaiah reared back his diversionary stone. A flash of memory reminded Neena of Thorne and his men. They had died, but hopefully, this battle would go differently.

Together, the others reared back their arms, while Neena aimed.

Isaiah gave the signal.

And then dozens of rocks hurled through the air, knocking against one another, falling in the vicinity of the place Isaiah had picked.

With the diversions thrown, they waited.

CHAPTER 87: Neena

N EENA'S HANDS SHOOK ON THE weapon, as she trained it on the pile of thrown rocks. The others reared back their spears. The creature's thunderous noise had dissipated, so that she could no longer tell its direction, or location.

She looked down the long tube of the weapon where she'd loaded her new spear, steadying her finger over the metal piece on the handle, the way she'd done before.

One chance.

That's all she would have with the device, before it required moments of preparation.

Do not miss.

A burst of wind blew her long hair behind her. Thirty feet away, Kai, Samara, and Roberto settled into their stances with their spears. She forced herself not to blink behind her goggles, afraid she might miss the beast's return.

Her father's voice echoed in her head.

'Breathe steady. Do not move.'

A memory came back to her, of standing in the desert below the dune on her last hunt, aiming her spear up at the Rydeer. That was before that other sandstorm, and the creature.

But was this moment so different?

She was hunting then, as she was hunting now.

That idea led her to another.

Was the beast like a snake, with its organs spread

throughout its body? Or a Rydeer, with its organs clustered in one area? Neena didn't know, and she might not have long to solidify her thought.

The rocks shifted. An explosion ripped open the desert, overturning sand.

And then the beast was in the open.

Its enormous mouth opened around the rocks they'd thrown, climbing higher. Cries echoed around her as people hurled their spears.

In the split moment before her attack, Neena made a decision. She'd aim for its neck. She lifted the weapon, following the beast's ascent, and readied herself for the recoil.

Right as she fired, a heavy gust of wind struck Neena, knocking her off balance.

The small spear shot in the air—not directly at the beast, but wide of it.

Neena fell to the side as an awful truth washed over her. She'd missed.

No! No!

CHAPTER 88: Neena

NEENA LANDED IN A HEAP, the weapon beneath her. She quickly regained her footing, but not in time to effect any change. The errant shot curved away from the beast and out of sight, while the beast curved over the rubble at the path's edge. The spray of its tail was even worse for the two-dozen men and women in the line to her left, all of who tumbled like pieces of clothing in the wind.

Smearing sand from her goggles, she looked over in time to see Kai, Samara, Roberto, and Isaiah getting to their feet, their hands empty, spears gone.

And then the beast was tunneling down the alley past the edge of the path, knocking over more intact hovels.

Failure washed over Neena.

Holding her weapon tight, she hurried toward the others, who dusted themselves off.

"Did you get it?" Kai asked.

She shook her head. "I missed!"

Isaiah and Samara closed their eyes.

"How about you?"

"The spray made it hard to see what we hit," Isaiah said. "But we all threw. We need to search for our spears!"

Without further delay, they raced forward to look for them.

While they searched around the hole for their lost weapons, Neena fiddled with the device, frantically trying to ready it again. Unslinging her bag, she grabbed one of the small spears sticking out the top, removing it and stuffing it inside the tube. She pushed until she felt a familiar click, double-checking that the arrow was secure. She fished around for the winding tool.

In her peripheral vision, she saw a flurry of running, panicked feet, as the others returned to where she stood. Not all of them had their spears.

Looking up, she heard Isaiah shouting, "I think a few of us hit it! Our spears are gone!"

Toward her right, several of the hovels down the alley under which the creature had disappeared caved and crashed. Moments later, more houses shook, teetered, and fell, as the beast recklessly tore underneath them.

"We wounded it some more!" Isaiah yelled.

Some of the downcast faces of the people around her turned hopeful. Quickly, Neena pulled the crank from the bag, sticking it into the weapon and starting to wind it.

"Let's grab some rocks and reposition!" Kai yelled.

Waving a hand and his spear, he motioned for the people to follow him, grabbing more rocks and heading farther south on the path, avoiding the creature's holes and positioning diagonally, so the creature wouldn't end up near the Comm Building.

Neena followed, stopping thirty feet away again.

To their east, a seam cut up the side alley, moving erratically back and forth, coming toward them.

Neena continued winding the crank. For a moment, the grumbling grew loud enough that she thought she wouldn't finish. And then the piece of metal stopped turning, and she stuffed the crank in her bag, raising her weapon.

Isaiah readied his rock and signaled.

"Now!"

Dozens of rocks flew through the air, landing in a new area. The people with spears reared them back.

Neena hefted the device in the right direction, just as

the beast burst from the ground, soaring into the sky. Neena squeezed the metal, unleashing the small spear and sticking it in one side of the creature's flank. Black fluid — the same black fluid she'd seen before — spilled from the monster's massive body.

She'd gotten it!

Her hope compounded as she heard the thrusts of about two-dozen men and women around her. With satisfaction, she watched half of those spears land, poking holes in the side of the creature and spilling more of its blood.

The creature writhed from left to right in the air.

Its tail thrashed wildly as the last of it emerged, and it descended.

A noise emanated from the beast — not a rumble, but a guttural screech.

Cries of triumph followed.

For the first time in weeks, Neena saw joy, and not fear.

Their joy dissipated as the creature's arc took it toward the Comm Building.

It burst back into the ground, tunneling directly for the enormous structure.

More cries pierced the air — this time of fear, rather than triumph.

With a crash, the beast collided with the structure's southern wall. Stones fell in an avalanche. Screams emanated from inside. Neena's mouth opened in a yell, as if she might stop something that was already happening.

But it was too late.

The damage was big, and it threatened to kill everyone inside.

CHAPTER 89: Louie

L OUIE STARED UP AT THE ceiling as cracks rippled through the top of the dome, spraying dust and stone. He let go of the braces on the door, which he'd been holding. All around him, men faltered and fell, caught unawares by the deafening collision. Large pieces of stone shattered and flew inward, smashing into the people around him. Cries of agony filled the air. In a panic, he watched several people topple, pelted by falling rock.

The doorway had become a place of death.

Coughing, Louie moved through the haze and away from the rubble. He needed to get to the other side of the building, and fast.

In his hurry, he stumbled over a piece of rock in the floor, losing his balance and colliding with another man.

Louie and the person fell to the floor.

Louie cried out in pain as he landed on his broken arm, frantically trying to untangle himself from whomever he'd crashed into. The man cried out for help, but Louie ignored him.

Whoever he was, he was on his own.

Pain burst through Louie, as he tried rolling and getting to his feet, only to fall once again.

He landed on his side.

Panting hard, he looked over to find Ed on his back a few feet away, shouting something he couldn't hear.

Screams echoed from all over the building.

Someone he couldn't see shrieked a warning.

Louie followed Ed's eyes to the ceiling.

Panic coursed through him.

High above him, a large fracture spread across the domed roof. Pieces of stone fell from the widening crevice and cascaded to the ground.

Too late, Louie raised his uninjured arm, ineffectively warding off an incoming avalanche.

He felt a jolt of pain, and then his world went black.

CHAPTER 90: Nicholas

FROM THE AREA NEAR THE Watcher's quarters, Nicholas scanned the floor near the Comm Building doorway. Bodies littered the ground. A few of the standing Watchers groaned, massaging fresh wounds, or brushing off their dust-covered faces and hurrying for safety. Racing over to where Louie and Ed had been buried, he cleared away the rubble, frantically peeling away stones until he exposed someone. Louie's head was dented and misshapen. Pieces of grey matter stuck out from a gaping, bloodied gash near his temple.

He didn't move, not even when Nicholas tried reviving him.

He was dead.

Ed lay nearby under a pile of rock, his chest crushed by a large piece of stone. His eyes were transfixed to the ceiling.

Nicholas backed away, fighting off nausea.

A distant rumbling told him they weren't out of danger.

Collecting his wits and his courage, Nicholas looked across the room to where the dozens of other people stood crying, backpedaling away from the carnage. Others peered out from The Watchers' quarters—pale, scared people in need of direction.

Bryan's two hundred, courageous marchers had turned into a hundred confused, hiding people.

The leaders were gone.

Except him.

Nicholas looked up at the ceiling, where small pieces of the roof rained down into the building, as if the heavens were dropping them. Through a crack in the wall near the threshold, he saw a group of men and women occupying the beast.

Maybe they'd distract the thing long enough for him to protect the people around him.

One thing was certain: this side of the building was no longer safe. Raising his voice, he gathered the attention of everyone in the room.

"Stay in The Watcher's quarters! Don't come out into the main area!"

Whatever was happening, they'd wait it out.

CHAPTER 91: Neena

S TONES THAT HAD STOOD FOR generations tumbled and fell, as the wall near the threshold of the Comm Building continued collapsing. A wall of dust blocked Neena's view of any survivors within, but she could hear their screams, drifting out into the open. She didn't need to see the damage to imagine the number of bodies inside. Each ear-piercing yell jarred Neena to her bones.

She had more pressing concerns.

The people around her were weaponless.

In their satisfaction at piercing the beast, none of them realized that those might be the last shots they landed.

The spears that stuck in the beast were gone.

Even worse, Neena's device needed to be reloaded.

New cries of terror echoed from all around her, as an organized assault turned chaotic.

The Abomination churned through the ground, cutting a path of destruction in its wake, tearing up sand everywhere. Its hide came into view as it bore through old tunnels and made new ones, before disappearing again. Much of the circling path was caving inward. She no longer trusted where she stood.

"Neena! We have to go!" Kai cried, grabbing onto her arm.

She took a few, stumbling steps.

With a horrified gasp, she watched several of Isaiah's Watchers pinwheel, fall backward, and disappear into a furrow next to the creature's tunneling body, crushed by sand and the monster. A few other people fell into one of the expanding holes, shrieking for their ancestors to save them.

"Kai! We have to help them!"

"We can't!" he said, telling her something she knew.

A fresh gust of wind and sand hit her face, as they ran, listening to screams everywhere — from the Comm Building, and the people behind them.

While Neena fled next to Kai, Samara, Isaiah, and a group of others ran at a distance from them, also trying to escape the beast's havoc. The destruction felt like a nightmare that would never be over.

And then she saw something that made the nightmare even worse.

One moment Samara was running on a parallel course to them.

The next she stumbled and fell.

Neena turned to reach for her, but Samara was fifty feet away and already facedown. Samara pulled her head up, desperately trying to get to her feet while the ground behind her shook. The monster's body came into view, tunneling perpendicularly behind her.

It wasn't coming at her, but it was close.

Too close.

Neena's momentary panic faded, as she saw the beast passing by Samara.

Maybe it'd miss her.

Neena prayed for that outcome, even as its tail whipped sideways out from the trench, knocking Samara flat. In horror, Neena watched her friend mashed to the ground in front of her eyes. A living woman became a squashed, mushy pile of blood and bone.

She was here one moment, gone the next.

No scream accompanied her death.

"No!" Neena's cry sounded as if someone else had made it.

Tears streamed down her cheeks.

Despair took over.

"Come on, Neena!" Kai shouted, pulling her along. "There's nothing we can do!"

A wail escaped Neena's mouth.

In an instant, she regretted everything she had done.

She should never have come back here with Kai.

She should never have tried leading those people in the caves.

Hope was a lie that adults told children, and it would never be a reality.

CHAPTER 92: Neena

NEENA STOOD IN A HOVEL, staring around at the dozen remaining people in her group. Despair sapped their will. They hung their heads and wrung their hands, trying to comfort one another ineffectively. Every now and again, someone glanced at the door of the dwelling into which they'd fled, jerked from grief by the creature's incessant noise. Terror was an unshakeable companion it felt like they'd never outlive. Neena wasn't sure exactly where they'd ended up, but it was away from the monster.

For now.

Isaiah muttered softy to himself, pacing in a corner of the small hovel, undoubtedly reliving his men's deaths. Only three Watchers besides him had survived.

Neena swiped her thumbs over the goggles she'd taken off. Her heart felt hollow and empty.

Samara...

She could still see the desperation in the woman's eyes, as she raced inevitable death. And she'd never forget the sight of her lifeless, pulped body. Somewhere, high up on the cliffs in the Right Cave, two children awaited a mother who would never return. But that grief wasn't the end of it, because other women and children would bear equally bad news.

And so would Raj and Samel, if Neena died.

Intense worry washed over her, as she pictured Raj hiding elsewhere in a hovel with Maria, Salvador, and the other injured. She needed to get back to him. But she hadn't killed the monster, like she'd promised. That thought led to guilt. Perhaps he was better off without her. Every life she touched seemed to end in death.

Darius's. Helgid's. Samara's.

She felt dejected.

Beaten.

Neena looked over to find Roberto guarding the doorway, instinctively returning to the role he'd played in the Right Cave. He fiddled with his hands, empty without his spear.

Brushing the sand from her body, her eyes fell to the weapon on the floor, which she'd somehow managed to keep. Having it felt meaningless.

They'd obviously injured the creature. But that didn't matter, because the thing was still out there, wreaking havoc.

And no one would stop it.

Neena was so consumed by her defeated thoughts that she barely noticed someone saying her name until they repeated it.

"Neena…"

She looked over to find Kai at her side, touching her arm.

"There was nothing we could do."

Neena looked at him through a tear-stained face, and saw that he was distraught, too. She wanted to believe what her heart couldn't.

"I know it's awful," Kai said quietly. "But we would've died if we tried saving her. We both know it."

"What are we going to tell her children?"

"We'll tell him that we did everything we could."

A long moment of silence followed.

"That's not good enough," Neena said finally. "We should've done more."

Forcing away despair, Kai found strength. "We did

everything we could, at the time. We can't give up now. Did you see the way the beast tore back and forth, after we hit it with our spears? It leaked more blood than when Thorne's men struck it, and certainly Bryan's. We definitely injured it. And the way it screeched..."

"For all we know, our spears were the equivalent of a bug bite," she countered.

"That's not true," Roberto said, from his post by the door. "We injured it. I've never heard it make a sound like that. Its quills penetrated deeper than any of our spears had before. And so did your weapon."

From across the room, Isaiah muttered something no one could hear. He wasn't paying attention, but his Watchers were. They stepped forward, drawn to the discussion. Neena's attention returned to Kai and Roberto.

"It made a similar sound, when I first hit it, before we met up with each other," Neena remembered.

"All the more reason to believe it is hurt," Roberto reinforced.

"What are you trying to say? That we should go out there again?" Neena asked incredulously.

"We have no spears," Kai admitted. "But that doesn't mean we can't retrieve some."

"You have more spears for your weapon, don't you?" asked Roberto, gesturing to the device by Neena's feet.

Neena looked at the bag hanging from her shoulders, where a few of Darius's spears stuck out. "Each shot will take some time to prepare. And if I miss again..."

"So, we give you time," Roberto said. "We lead the thing in another direction, while you do what you have to. We distract it. What other option do we have? Return to the cliffs and accept a life of cowering and hiding? Or should we wait to starve, because we can't hunt or tend our crops safely?"

Neena looked over, surprised to hear him talking so

bravely. Given the amount of suffering he'd seen, she couldn't believe he'd want to continue a losing battle. But somehow, he did.

And so did others.

A few men stepped forward, then a few women, forming a small ring around Neena, Kai, and Roberto.

"When the creature attacked our colony the first time, you led us to safety," remembered a woman. "You could've run past us, but you didn't. You stopped to help us to the cliffs. We haven't forgotten that."

"You helped us stay together, even when the other caves tried tearing us apart," said a man, emotionally.

"If we go back to our relatives like this — our children — we admit defeat," one woman said, dabbing at her eyes. "But if we kill it, we give them a new life. That's what Samara would've wanted, and what her children deserve."

"Darius would've wanted it, too," Kai added.

Neena opened and closed her mouth. The strength of this small group was palpable, and it was growing stronger by the moment. Still, she couldn't fathom more death.

"What if more of us fall?" she asked, looking around at the people circling her. "What if we all die?"

"When we were out in the desert, we beat the odds and survived," Kai reminded her. "You and I know the creature better than anyone. We have the best chance out of anyone on those cliffs of beating it. And so do the people in this room. They've survived longer than anyone."

The group nodded, pulling courage through their fear.

"We have to save the people in the Comm Building, if they are still alive," Kai said.

"I doubt they survived," Neena said. "We saw how that building collapsed."

"Even in the worst scenario, if they are all dead, the people on the cliffs need us," Kai said. "Samel and Raj need you. We have to beat the creature and get back to your brother, Salvador, and the others. This could be our best chance at ridding the colony of the monster. Now is the time."

Roberto followed that thought. "Let's go out there and do what we came to do. For Samara, Darius, and all the rest that have died. Let's honor their memories and complete what we started."

Neena's conflicted thoughts tormented her.

But looking at all the people around her, she saw courage.

Despite all the things they'd survived — horrible, atrocious things — they were ready to go out and face the beast again. They were ready to risk their lives and battle the monster with bravery. They were ready to fight alongside her.

If they had faith, how could she let them down? Bending, she picked up the weapon, causing a ripple of enthusiasm among the group.

They needed someone to reinforce their courage, not tear it down.

They needed a leader.

Looking past those close to her, she found Isaiah breaking from his mournful thoughts, listening. The few surviving Watchers already stood near her. They glanced around at each of the people in the circle, and then back at Neena. She was surprised, but probably shouldn't have been, when Isaiah stepped across the room to join them.

"They're right, you know," he said. "We are the only ones who might have a chance at killing it. We owe it to our fallen."

He raised his chin defiantly.

His conviction settled her decision.

She took a step toward the door, cradling the weapon.

"Are you sure you want to be the one to carry it?" Kai asked.

Neena nodded. "I have the most experience with it. This is something I need to do." Beating back the last of her plaguing doubts, she moved toward the door with determination. "Let's go."

CHAPTER 93: Neena

HURRYING THROUGH THE RUBBLE-STREWN ALLEY, heading for the monster, Neena replayed what she hoped wasn't the group's last conversation.

"We'll need to find spears."

"Surely, some of them are still in the area near the Comm Building. We'll retrieve them carefully."

"What if the monster is there?"

"We'll lead it elsewhere."

"Where will we fight?"

"Wherever we have to."

Memories of the dead clung to her thoughts. She was doing this for them. For all of them.

She clutched her weapon, which she'd cranked and readied. A half-dozen spare arrows jostled inside her bag. Each one of those had to count. She peered through the slow, steady stream of sand that blew against her goggles.

The rumbling had stopped.

Hopefully, the monster was elsewhere.

They might not have much time to search out and retrieve any spears.

Reaching the Comm Building's destroyed path, she and the dozen around her surveyed the destruction. Holes had become gaping trenches, extending from one end of the path to the other. More than one tunnel overlapped, or crisscrossed the next. The creature's rampant churning had swallowed most of the bodies. Here and there, Neena saw a severed limb, or a fallen flask, but mostly, she saw sand.

She didn't see Samara, though she looked.

Her friend's missing body reinforced her anger.

Past the torn-up path, the southern wall of the Comm Building lay in ruins. Rock was piled in front of the area where the entrance used to be, creating a jagged, stone barricade. The smooth roof was mostly intact, though it looked like a piece was missing, and parts were cracked.

Through the steadily blowing wind, she scanned the building, but she saw or heard no one.

They had to make this fast, so they could get elsewhere.

She and her people waded through the ruined path, stepping wherever there was firm sand.

"Maybe we should split up," Isaiah said, with the same conviction he'd held in the hovel. "We'll search over there, while you search here."

Neena agreed.

Isaiah and his three Watchers walked about a hundred feet to the right of Neena's group, scouring another area.

Neena's group surveyed the edge of the nearest trenches for a handle, or a spear tip rising above the sand. Here and there, they found one, but too many were lost, or buried. After a while of looking, they'd only found three spears—and were close to giving up—when Neena checked on Isaiah.

His group had spotted something.

Below them, on a sloped part of the sand in one of the beast's vacuous holes, sat two intact, quill-tipped spears. Without a word, Isaiah and another man started down the ravine, holding their hands out for balance, while trying not to cause an avalanche of sand. The other two men stayed at the top.

A pit of dread found its way to Neena's stomach.

She searched for danger around the destroyed path, but she saw and heard nothing.

Isaiah and the man continued down the slope, somehow keeping their footing.

The wind blew steadily all around them, constantly shifting the sand.

A few steps later, their hands were on the weapons. Isaiah and The Watcher hurried up the embankment, using their new weapons for balance.

They were halfway to the top when the sand beneath their boots slid.

Mounds of sand tumbled into the blackness below, churning beneath them and pushing them back. The men cried out in terror, rushing against an increasing cascade.

Neena's people screamed in warning.

They ran a few steps toward the men, but they could do nothing from where they were.

The two others in Isaiah's group at the top of the trench rushed a few steps into it, reaching out their hands.

In a flash of instinct, Isaiah and the other man used their spears to stab the sand, using them for leverage while forcing their way up the hill. Somehow, they found the strength to climb the last few steps, while fighting the backwards momentum. And then they were at the top of the trench, and their comrades were receiving them.

Relief struck Neena and the others, who lifted their heads to the sky, praising a miracle.

Isaiah and the other man held up their new spears proudly.

They patted each other's backs, looking at the collapsed hole and the death they'd avoided.

A rumble ripped away further celebration.

Isaiah and his men backpedaled away from the hole, just moments before the sand gave way again.

A black set of jaws emerged.

The beast sprang.

It opened and closed its maw, missing The Watchers at the top of the trench and continuing its ascent. Its enormous shadow blocked out all but the shadows of Isaiah and his men. From a hundred feet away, Neena's group readied their spears, although they were in no position to throw them.

Whether it was confidence at finding the weapons, or his desire for revenge, Isaiah wasn't giving up. "Throw your spears! Strike it!"

The man-sized shadows moved, assumedly following his orders. Cries of attack split the air. A cacophonous screech followed. Black blood sprayed from the creature's underside, raining over the area outside its shadow.

Neena took a step forward, aiming her device, but her shot was uncertain.

"Wait!" Kai yelled next to her, stopping her.

They watched the creature complete its arc, burrowing into the ground at a distance from Isaiah and his men. And then it was gone, and Isaiah and his men were shouting curses after it, stumbling about blindly in the sand. Black blood spackled their clothes. Their hair and faces were tarred and slick. They smeared the blood from their goggles, frantically trying to see.

"Isaiah! This way!" Neena called out, waving her hands to guide them back.

The Watchers raced in her direction, heading for the relative safety of a group.

Not Isaiah.

Surprising her, Isaiah staggered south, covered in brackish slime, heading toward where the beast had disappeared.

Bloodlust had caught hold of him. Or maybe it was anger. Looking around the sand, he stepped carefully around a trench, scanning the ground. Neena called out his name, but he didn't respond, or stop. Instead, he continued along the edge of the trench, standing over something.

Bending, he lifted up two ends of a broken spear. Hefting one side of it in each hand, he looked to where the beast had continued tunneling. The creature's noise grew louder, as it swung back for another pass.

"Isaiah!" Neena yelled again, desperately trying to call him back to the group.

But Isaiah was a man possessed. He raced forward with the blunt end of the spear, and the one with the tip. His face was a mask of rage and determination. Rearing back the quill-tipped part of the spear, he took a stance in the desert.

His vengeful scream cut through the storm.

He stood in place, riveted, waiting for the beast, its black blood staining his face.

The beast got closer.

Neena and her people continued shouting.

A moment of clarity washed over Isaiah, just as the sand under his boots shook and caved.

His battle cry turned into a frenzied scream.

The monster rose, snatching Isaiah, catching him too soon and crunching. Only the top half of his body stuck out from between several of its giant teeth. His scream became an agonized shriek, as the creature bit down harder. But Isaiah wasn't finished. Rearing back, he buried the quill-end of the spear in the creature's gums. More black blood sprayed over him, as the creature continued rising with him in its maw. He tried striking the beast with the blunt end of the spear, but lost his grip. The second piece of spear dropped from his hands. Isaiah waved his hands in a last, desperate attempt to escape.

And then the beast rammed back into the sand, taking Isaiah with it.

The remaining Watchers in Isaiah's group watched in horror.

A few of them cried out in empathetic pain.

Neena clung to Kai.

An uneven seam rippled the ground, heading away in another direction.

Neena looked around at the last survivors around her — a handful of Right Cavers, Watchers, Kai, and Roberto.

Only three of them had spears.

Resignation washed over her.

She should never have come back out here.

She opened her mouth, ready to voice that argument, but a Watcher cut it short.

"I saw something when it rose, just now," he said, through the terror on his face. "Some sort of strange skin, by its head."

Inspired by the first Watcher, another spoke up. "I saw it, too! It might be another weak point! Maybe we can strike it there!"

Neena shook her head. How could they kill the thing, when they had no spears, and barely any people?

Echoing her frustration, Roberto told The Watchers, "It's coming up too fast. Even if we get it to rise, we'll never have a chance to strike it in time. You'd have to be almost on top of it to make a difference."

Neena closed her eyes, praying for an idea she hadn't thought of.

And then something occurred to her.

She looked from the people around her to the Comm Building, and the pile of rocks that comprised its now-demolished wall. The craggy, broken material reminded her of a formation in the desert she had climbed.

"I think I know what to do!" she said, grabbing the attention of the distraught, panicked people.

Quickly, she told them what she was thinking.

It was a hope and a prayer.

In a frantic, last-ditch attempt, she ran toward the pile of stones to get onto the Comm Building's roof.

CHAPTER 94: Neena

NEENA STRADDLED THE STONES OF the fallen Comm Building wall, balancing her weapon and her nerves. The wind tore at her clothing. In the time she'd started climbing, the storm had returned to its former ferocity. She didn't dwell on it, nor did she stop. And she definitely didn't look down. Losing her focus meant a perilous fall.

The conversation she'd just had with Kai replayed in her head.

"I'm going with you, Neena."

"No. I need you to stay here and distract the creature."

"The others can do that."

"The more people making noise, the better. You're needed there."

"How do you want me to distract it?"

"By doing whatever it takes. Use the Comm Building stones."

He'd promised her he'd try, before they parted.

Hopefully, he and the others would deliver on that promise.

She had little time to contemplate it.

Neena clambered upward, ignoring the pain of the sharp rocks, and the burn of her calves. The screeching wind pushed her in different directions, but she didn't give up, or consider defeat. A few times, she lost her grip, barely managing to hang on. One handhold and foothold at a time.

That was her goal. She climbed until she reached the crest of the rock pile.

The edge of the Comm Building's smooth roof appeared above her. A gap of about a foot and a half lay between the uppermost rocks, on which she stood, and its lip.

This was it.

The moment she worried about.

Steadying her beating heart, she leapt, catching the stone with her right arm and pulling with all her strength, while keeping hold of the weapon. For a moment she hovered, legs kicking, heart hammering. And then she was up and over the lip.

Neena climbed a little way up the sloped roof with her weapon in her hand, avoiding a section of roof that had caved, as the wind screamed around her. She turned to face the area below the building.

She could no longer see farther than fifteen feet.

She must be double that distance off the ground.

Cracks lined the lower portion of the roof's edges.

Searching for a sturdier place to stand, she climbed for a higher vantage point, holding her hands out, fighting the same dizziness she'd felt on the cliffs, or on that old rock structure in the desert, when she and Kai had climbed up and sought refuge from the beast.

She hunkered down.

She could no longer see Kai and the others. All she could see was the wind, sand, and the thirty feet of the sloping dome roof in front of her, leading to its edge.

How would this work?

CHAPTER 95: Kai

K AI LED HIS SMALL GROUP away from the Comm
Building, carrying the rocks they'd picked up from
the bottom of the collapsed wall — or, in the case of
three of them, their quill-tipped spears. It felt as if the entire
colony sat on the edge of a treacherous abyss. He no longer
trusted his steps.

Looking over his shoulder at the Comm Building, he
scanned for Neena. A short while ago, he'd watched her
clamber up the rock pile, but the intensifying storm had
stripped away his visibility.

The screeching wind drowned out the monster's
incessant rumbling. Of course, he no longer saw any sign
of it.

It felt as if their plan was doomed to fail.

Still, he pressed on.

Gripping his rock and his spear, he led the small group
to a position alongside the Comm Building, but not too
close. Motioning to half his people, he instructed them to
pile their rocks in a spot parallel to the wall.

They needed to coax the thing back out of the ground,
getting it in a position where Neena could strike it.

He cocked his head, hoping for a clue as to where the
beast was located, but he still couldn't hear anything. The
intense wind was probably confusing the beast, but he knew
one thing that would draw it.

Loud vibrations.

They were his only hope.

Instructing his group to do the same, Kai knelt down with his rock, banging it violently against the ones they'd set down.

CHAPTER 96: Neena

A PERSISTENT GALE PICKED UP, FLAPPING Neena's clothing behind her and pressing her shawl to her face. From somewhere far below her, she heard the rocks clanking together. They were doing it! They were following the plan!

Her relief was short-lived.

The wind was strong enough that it blew her in several directions. She fought to keep her footing. Every so often, a pebble rolled over the round dome, whipping past her and falling out of sight. It felt as if she was on the top of that secluded rock formation in the desert, far away from everything else, even though she could still hear the bangs of Kai and his people far below.

Abruptly, the clanking noise stopped.

Quiet reigned, other than the storm's din.

She fought the awful feeling that Kai and the others had suffered some unseen fate. How would she know? She might be the only one left in Red Rock, other than the people on the cliffs. Neena waited a long while, straining to hear the sounds of the monster's rumbling, or more rocks, but the wind shrieked too loudly.

Each passing moment stoked her unease.

She waited until she could wait no more.

She needed to do something.

This might be her only chance to lure it. She needed to take advantage of it.

Kneeling, Neena held the device steady.

She might never use it, if she couldn't get the monster close.

Looking around the rooftop, she searched for something to throw — anything with which to draw it. Her fingers met sliding sand and debris. Of course, she had no spear. She looked at the bag over her shoulder. Other than the small spears, it contained only clothing, a few blankets, and a flask. Nothing helpful.

She needed something heavier.

Looking down the sloping roof, she found the spot where she'd climbed up. Most of the rocks on the pile on which she'd stepped were large, but there had to be a few that were the right size to throw. Neena edged down the roof, heading down the slope and avoiding the caved section again, hoping she could reach down and get her hands on something. It was a hope and a prayer. She steadied herself with her hands and boots, using her bottom to scoot. After carefully working her way down, she reached the edge and peered over the drop.

The stones were a few feet away.

Tucking the weapon under her arm, Neena positioned herself so she was on her belly, reaching, while pressing the rest of her body against the dome. The roof's hard stone ground into her ribs, aggravating old wounds. She bit down on a cry of pain. Still, she didn't stop reaching, until she'd grabbed hold of a fist-sized rock, pulling it close to her body and retreating.

She spider-crawled up the roof, heading for her sturdy perch, up high.

Regaining her old position, she turned on her haunches, looking down at the rock she'd managed to grab.

A crash vibrated the dome.

Kai! Her mind instinctively screamed.

Something slammed on the roof's edge, in the general direction where Kai and his group had been making noise.

The rock flew from her hand, bouncing off the stone, rolling down the roof's slant. Neena followed the path of its descent.

And saw something horrific.

Thirty feet away, on top of the Comm Building roof, the beast's mouth opened and closed, as it writhed back and forth. Gigantic teeth—nearly the size of a human body—mashed together, searching for prey.

Neena cried out, fumbling with the weapon in her hands, trying to aim.

Giant fissures spider-webbed up and down the roof's surface, as the beast's movements broke away more stone on where it had landed.

How had it gotten here?

She had no time to question it.

Neena put out a hand to stop herself from falling, but a hole caved in where she placed her hand. Rock crumbled and fell inside the building. She yelped and pulled her hand away, rolling to the side in time to avoid another caving section of roof. It felt like the building was coming apart around her.

With a cry, Neena felt herself sliding toward the creature's mouth.

CHAPTER 97: Kai

"**N**o!" KAI SCREAMED OVER THE wind.

His heart pounded as the creature slammed against the Comm Building roof, thrashing back and forth. Somehow, his judgment had been misguided. Somehow, the beast's enormous bulk had landed on the top of the structure.

Or maybe they'd been foolish in thinking they could guide it at all.

All around him, his small group screamed and shouted, trying to correct their awful mistake. They found rocks and hurled them.

The beast screeched, but its position didn't change.

It was stuck on the stone.

The creature was large and dark enough that he saw it, even through the storm. The roof groaned under its weight. From somewhere out of sight, Neena screamed. Those screams stabbed his chest like a thousand spears.

"Neena!"

Sand filled Kai's mouth as he uselessly shouted. He needed to do something. Running toward the beast's arcing body, he reared back one of their last spears, hurling it. Through the storm, he saw the weapon pierce the beast's hide, saw its body writhe, and heard a hideous wail. Two Watchers near him also threw their spears, finding their target, to no avail.

With empty hands, Kai and his group got close enough

to see the thing's hard scales and the puncture wounds on its side, from some of the spears they'd thrown earlier. A few were still stuck inside the thing. Blotches of black blood marred the creature's exterior.

Nothing stopped it.

Perhaps his worst fears were right, and the thing couldn't be killed at all.

Kai rushed a few more feet, frantically searching for something—*anything*—else to distract it. His people clustered around him, shouting things he couldn't hear, over the creature's screeching and the grinding sound of the Comm Building's crumbling roof.

Kai never saw the trench in front of him until it was too late.

Judging by the screams around him, neither did the others.

Kai's boots flew out from under him.

His wind left his body.

He plunged into one of the beast's deep, dark holes.

CHAPTER 98: Neena

NEENA FOUGHT FOR BALANCE ON the shaking roof. All around her, pieces of the Comm Building caved and fell inward. With each thrash of the beast, she felt herself pitching forward into its mouth. She envisioned her death in between its grinding, vicious teeth.

Too many of her nightmares came flooding back to her: its skeletal body rising above her, dripping bile, searing her flesh, and reducing her to bone.

Her corpse, decomposing in its stomach.

Perhaps this was the culmination of too many bad choices.

The rancid smell of blood and flesh from its mouth filled the air. Neena raked at the Comm Building roof with her nails, keeping hold of the weapon with one hand, while trying to stop her inevitable slide down the slope to the edge, and the beast's mouth. Her grip was giving way. She pictured Raj hiding in that hovel, or Samel huddled in the caves, waiting for her.

No!

These couldn't be her last moments.

Letting go of the roof, Neena spun and slapped her free hand above her, catching the edge of a crack. Pulling with all her strength, she managed to get further up the slope and away from the creature, tucking her boots into the crevice and pressing her back against the dome's slant. Extending to full height while lying on her stomach, Neena rolled onto her back, aiming the weapon onto which she'd managed to hold.

The thrashing creature opened and closed its mouth. Six folds of brown flesh contracted into one point, before gaping open again.

Terror and disgust swirled inside her.

So did fear.

This might be the last spear she'd have a chance to use.

Once it was gone, she might never be able to reload.

And then she saw something.

On the side of the beast's head, just below its closed mouth and underneath its scales, something contracted and expanded. For a moment, Neena thought she was imagining it. And then she realized what it was: a heart, beating inside it and rippling its flesh.

Just like a snake, she had a moment to think.

Perhaps The Watchers had been right, after all.

Neena gritted her teeth, aiming at the moving piece of skin. Her hand shook as she put her finger on the piece of metal. This was it. Her last shot before she'd need to reload the device.

If she failed... She couldn't think about that.

She took a breath, waiting until the beast's mouth was fully closed before pressing the metal on the device's handle.

The spear flew from the device; the weapon recoiled.

Metal pierced flesh.

Black fluid sprayed out of the creature, splattering the Comm Building roof with gore and darkening the swirling sand. The foul substance pelted Neena's body, covering her clothes and her goggles. A screech louder than any she'd heard emanated from deep within the beast, rising above the wind, echoing off the rounded dome.

Reaching up a shaky hand, Neena smeared her goggles clean, certain that she'd find the monster wriggling higher and about to swallow her. Not this time.

The creature's mouth opened and closed once more, as if the beast might score a last, grisly meal. And then its mouth stayed shut.

Dark blood spewed from the gaping wound on the side of its neck.

Neena's heart pounded.

For a moment, the world went silent, save the storm.

And then she heard a groan—not the beast, but the edge of the building, creaking under the weight of an enormous, dead thing. The beast rolled sideways, sliding down the stones, pitching off the roof, and disappearing from sight.

An enormous thud rippled through the landscape.

More broken stones toppled.

And then Neena was alone on the roof once more.

CHAPTER 99: Neena

F OR A LONG WHILE, NEENA sat in place, covered in brackish sludge, staring into the wind. At any moment, she expected the creature to leap up again, crash against the building, and resume its savage attack. It took a while for her to believe it was over.

After a while, she slid across the dome, taking care for the new holes and cracks that surrounded her. The creature's fetid odor wafted from her clothes, filled her lungs and nose, and gagged her. Fighting back her feelings of sickness, she moved toward the edge of the building from where she'd climbed, but she didn't descend.

Not yet.

Hands shaking, she rose to full height instead, scanning the ground, as the wind petered out. The storm seemed done at last.

So was the beast.

The Abomination lay in a massive, unmoving heap.

A sigh that felt as if it had been stuck inside her for weeks escaped.

Neena turned, slowly lowering herself down the side of the broken building. With each precarious step, she anticipated a noise from the creature that would change her course and prompt her retreat. Nothing.

And then she was on the ground.

Neena's boots crunched over broken stone and sand, as she approached the creature through the calming wind.

The long, scaled beast lay half in and half out of one of its many trenches, occupying most of the path, extending all the way to the edge. A thin layer of sand — the last debris from the storm — dammed up its bloodied wounds.

In a strange, sickening way, it had prepared its own burial ground.

For a time, she held her unloaded weapon, staring at the Abomination's enormous jaws, which were motionless, and would never move again.

Neena opened and closed her eyes. A relief she couldn't process washed over her.

Covered in the beast's gore, she spun in a slow circle, taking in the ruined path, the newly destroyed hovels, and the shattered hulk of the Comm Building. Farther out, she saw only more ruined structures.

Relief turned to panic.

Where were Kai, Roberto, and the others?

Keeping a buffer from the beast — out of instinct, rather than fear — Neena hurried over the path, avoiding piles of fallen rubble and searching the holes and trenches. She scanned the ground underfoot, and the alleys she could see. She yelled Kai's and her people's names. Nothing. With each fruitless step, her pace quickened. After a while of ineffective searching, she walked to the head of the main path, staring down the trenched middle. She saw no evidence of Kai, Roberto, or any of her people. Nor did she see Isaiah's Watchers.

Neena blinked hard.

They couldn't all be gone.

She searched for a while longer, unable to believe their deaths.

A bubble of despair stuck inside her throat.

Her thoughts turned in wild circles.

Eventually, they landed on something.

Raj.

Finding him was the only thing she could think to do.

Maybe the others were somehow with him.

Changing direction, she hurried for the hovel where she'd left him, praying her brother had survived the chaos with the others. With each step, she convinced herself that Kai and her other comrades had somehow made their way back to him. Panic strangled her breath. She no longer felt the sticky blood of the creature on her body, or smelled its foul innards.

Traversing the colony felt foreign and strange, with so many holes, and so few hovels. Twice, she backtracked, changing her path. Eventually, she spotted what she thought was the right hovel.

Neena's heart pounded when she saw the partially collapsed roof. Stones littered the outside of the structure; cracks fissured the walls. The door was gone. Shadows surrounded the doorway, which was cracked and partially covered by a pile of sand.

Falling to a crouch, Neena dug at the buried entrance, screaming for her brother. She'd scooped only a few handfuls away when she saw someone crawling toward her.

"Neena?"

Raj came from the shadows.

He immediately leapt for her arms.

Sand matted his hair. A few scrapes marred his face. But he was alive. *Alive!*

Neena hugged him so tightly she never thought she'd let go.

Stepping back from the doorway, she saw Salvador, Maria, and the others crawling out, revealing themselves, taking her in with shock.

It took her a moment to realize what they must see: a woman, covered in the creature's black blood, and dirt and sand. It wasn't until she spoke again that they believed it was her.

"Neena!" a woman cried. "You made it!"

Neena hadn't known the extent of joy until now. Heaving a sob of relief, she embraced them all.

CHAPTER 100: Neena

EENA AND RAJ WALKED ALONGSIDE Salvador, who hobbled between Maria and another man, while the others walked alongside them. Slowly, the storm clouds receded and the light of the sun returned, illuminating the ruined paths as Neena and the others threaded back through them.

Eventually, they made their way back to the Comm Building path, taking in the horrid scene. The women gasped. Raj and Salvador stood with their mouths agape.

Silence fell over the group, as they studied the creature from its giant maw to the end of its tail. Neena wouldn't have believed it was ever alive, if she didn't know better.

The smell of blood filled the air. The carcass was fresh, but in a short time, the sun would bake its body.

"Were you the one to kill it?" Raj asked.

"Yes." She nodded with emotion. "I used the device from the roof of the Comm Building. It landed there, before I shot it and it fell."

Neena didn't need to tell any more. The story was written in the creature's massive carcass, and its gaping wounds. It was written in its blood, which covered her, and in the rubble-strewn wall of the Comm Building. It was spelled out in the sections of the roof that had collapsed, or been damaged.

"Where is everyone else?" Raj asked, staring at the distant structure. "Are they inside, searching for survivors?"

His words trailed off. Everyone could see the damage the building had suffered, and the piles of rubble. Neena shuddered as she imagined the crushed bodies inside.

No sound came from within.

"I don't think anyone's in there. I haven't heard anyone," Neena said, hoping to protect Raj from what was surely an ugly scene.

"Then where are Kai, Roberto, and Samara?" he asked, spinning around.

His words reignited her panic. Neena hurried back to the nearest trench. She couldn't accept that Kai, Roberto, and the others were dead. Not like Samara. She'd search everywhere twice, or three times, if she had to: every hole, every hovel, every pile of sand. She needed her hands busy, so her heart wouldn't process something she didn't know if she could take. She scanned from one end of the trench to the next.

"We'll search the Comm Building," said Maria, leaving Salvador in the care of a few others, while she and another man hurried toward the fallen structure.

"Be careful!" Neena yelled.

She had only searched for a few moments when Maria called her name.

"Neena!"

She looked over to find that her and the other man had halted near one of the cracks in the building. They took a few steps back, startled. Through a gap in one of the Comm Building walls, Neena saw shadows.

Moving shadows.

Surprise struck her, as a nervous line of people worked their way out from the building, staring between her and the monster. Men and women filtered outside, holding one another up. The people kept coming, until nearly eighty survivors were standing outside in a large group, huddled together in disbelief.

A Watcher named Nicholas stood at the head of the group, watching Neena and the others as if they were ghosts.

"It's okay!" she called over. "The beast is dead."

The line of people stayed in place, riveted by the massive carcass from which no one could look away. What had once been a threat had become a spectacle. Men and women held onto one another, talking and pointing. A few of the bravest people talked about getting closer. Others gaped at the arrows embedded in the creature's side. Neena could already smell the reek of its insides, wafting over the area, prompting some people to cover their mouths.

After inspecting the creature for a long moment, Nicholas walked away from the others and drew up to Neena. Gone was his look of disdain. In its place was a look of wonder.

"You did it," he said incredulously.

Neena nodded.

At the same time, sorrow dulled her celebration. Before Nicholas could ask another question, Neena asked, "Did you see anyone else out here?"

"This is all of us," Nicholas said, reinforcing what she feared. "We hid in some of the side rooms on the other side of the building, where we were protected from the cave-in."

Tears swelled up in Neena's eyes. She spun again, searching the landscape, but nothing else moved. The sorrow in her gut turned to emptiness.

So this is our price for killing the beast, she thought.

Still, she wasn't through. She'd search the colony for days, months—however long it took until she verified the awful truth.

She'd gone only a few steps when a voice shouted from the gathered crowd.

"Over here! I see something moving!" Raj said, pointing into a trench.

CHAPTER 101: Neena

HOPE STIRRED IN NEENA'S HEART as she raced toward Raj and the ditch, fighting to move faster in her sticky, blood-drenched clothes.

"Over there!" Raj yelled, as she approached. "Do you see it?"

Neena followed his pointing finger to a collapsed hole at the bottom of the trench, where a hand poked from the sand, clenching and grabbing. A stream of people gathered behind them, peering down at a new spectacle, talking loudly.

Another hand appeared, and then a head. Groaning, a sand-covered person tried pulling himself from out of a collapsed hole, blinking through his sand-covered face. Neena's heart leapt as she recognized him.

"Roberto!" Neena cried.

She, Raj, and a few dozen others skirted down into the trench, heading for the battered man and helping him the rest of the way out. Roberto tried standing, but his legs wobbled. A circle of people helped him stay upright. The next words he spoke made Neena's heart leap.

"There are more people down here!" Roberto rasped, coughing and spitting sand.

While some people assisted Roberto, Neena, Raj, and a bunch of others knelt and dug, throwing back sand, exposing more of the hole from which Roberto had crawled.

Voices emanated from within. Neena and the other, digging people shouted back to them.

"Can you hear us?" Neena cried. "Keep crawling! Follow our voices!"

A groan echoed from somewhere deeper in the tunnel, but no one could make out the words.

"They're stuck!" Raj worried.

Neena, Raj, and the others pawed frantically at the ground, tossing away sand and debris and widening the hole. While they dug, they continued calling out to whomever was inside. Soon, they'd made a larger opening. Neena peered into it. Far below the top layer of the sand, the ground became a harder mixture of dirt. With dismay, she noticed that tunnel narrowed for a long while before it widened again. She'd never fit past a few feet.

"I'll go in!" Raj said, looking at her and the others with wide eyes. "I can get to them quicker, while you all continue digging."

"Raj..." Neena protested.

"I'll be careful," he assured her and the crowd. "I'll just need a torch!"

Hearing his words, a few of the people behind them scrambled up the hill, heading quickly for the Comm Building, while Neena, Raj, and some others kept tunneling. After a little while, a man scampered down the hill, handing Raj a lit torch. Before Neena could argue, Raj hurried into the hole.

Neena's pulse beat fiercely as she watched his light recede.

"Keep talking to me!" she called, while continuing to clear away sand.

Neena's heart hammered as she and the others worked frantically to catch up. Raj might be crawling into a dark space from which he'd never return. If the tunnel collapsed...

"Raj? Can you hear me?" she called after him.

"I'm okay!" he called back. "I think I hear where they are!"

After a handful of nerve-wracking moments, she'd widened the tunnel enough to follow.

"We shouldn't have too many people in the hole," someone warned. "The tunnel might collapse."

"I'll go in!" she said.

"Take a torch!" someone said, handing one to her.

With the blazing light in one hand, Neena scurried into the hole, taking care not to brush the sides. Her pants scraped against a firmer, darker layer of soil. The restrictive hole smelled like waste and wet rock. With a shudder, she imagined the monster tunneling through it, leaving a trail of excrement.

She kept going, shining the light and looking for her brother.

"Raj?"

"Over here!"

After a while of crawling, she caught sight of him, hunkered next to a woman from the Right Cave. The woman coughed and spat, her hair covered in sand. Behind her was another man whom Neena recognized from the last, tense battle with the creature.

"We fell down here when we tried helping you," the man explained, smiling through his obvious pain. "We've been trying to get out, but it's dark and hard to breathe."

"The tunnel collapsed a few times," the woman added. "We kept digging, hoping we'd find a way out."

"We heard all the noise above," the man said with fright. "And then it stopped. Is it over?"

Neena nodded. "It's over. You're going to be all right. Are you injured?"

"We're scraped and bruised, but we can move."

Neena shined her light past them, trying to see more of the tunnel. "Is there anyone else here?"

"I think," the woman said, after a cough.

Neena looked over at Raj, who took a flask from his side

and offered the people a drink, while ushering them in the direction of the surface. He traded a look with Neena.

"I'll lead them out," he offered.

He handed her the flask, in case she needed it.

And then he was herding the people back the way they came, crawling through the tunnel on hands and knees, clenching his light. Neena watched them go for as long as she could, before turning and using her torch to battle more blackness. The tunnel narrowed again. At one point, she had to dig through more dirty rocks and sand, uncovering a better place to crawl. Perhaps the man and woman had been mistaken, and they were the last survivors.

Claustrophobia made her stomach clench. Still, she forced herself onward, taking a turn in the dark tunnel.

A figure lay at the fringes of her torchlight, sitting upright against the wall.

"Hello?" she called, to no response.

A shimmer of fear wormed through her gut, as she realized her luck had ended. She crawled until she reached the person, holding the torch out and assessing their condition.

The person's hands lay idle on their lap. Their head sagged in the other direction.

Reaching out, she gently moved the person's sand-covered face toward her.

Kai's cheeks were splattered with mud. His eyes were closed. He looked strangely serene, as if he'd made peace with his death before succumbing to his sandy grave. Tears slid down Neena's face. Her heart felt like it might hurt forever. Reaching up, she brushed a strand of hair from his forehead, revealing his markings, before reaching down and holding his hand. Sorrow and guilt ached in her stomach.

So, this is the cost of victory, she thought.

"Neena?" he croaked, opening his eyes.

Her heart leapt. "Kai? Can you hear me?"

Kai nodded, groaning and turning his head. "I can hear you."

"Can you move?"

"I think," he said, wiggling his fingers and then his legs. "I crawled for so long that I got tired. I could use a drink." He coughed hard, and then looked at her, his eyes as blue and wide as the first time she'd met him.

Neena smiled through more tears, reaching for the flask Raj had given her. "Take it."

"It looks like I owe you again," he said, with a small smile.

CHAPTER 102: Neena

NEENA WALKED SOUTH DOWN THE main path of Red Rock toward the Comm Building, pushing an empty wagon. A few people wheeled past her, headed toward the desert behind the eastern formation, where she'd just been, maneuvering around the massive trenches and holes. Still others worked along the path, clearing the wreckage and filling in smaller holes that might catch a boot and trip someone.

She smiled at a former Center Caver passing by her, before heading down the path. The woman gave her a hesitant wave. A day after the battle with the monster, old alliances no longer seemed important to Neena, but she knew that mending their old emotional scars would take time.

Right now, they had an important task.

Reaching the area of the Comm Building, she followed the trail her people had been using, heading toward the grisly carcass at the colony's center. Men and women knelt on either side of the massive beast, carving up its flesh, depositing it into people's waiting wagons so they could dispose of it. Farther down, others carefully cut away the scales on the beast's side and piled up its quills.

Rolling up her wagon in a line behind a few others, all of whom waited for pieces of the monster, she found Kai approaching her.

"How is everyone doing in the desert?" he asked.

"We're burying the beast far enough away that we shouldn't have to look at it anymore, or smell it," Neena said.

"It will take a lot of work to cut up the bones, but we'll get it done," Kai said confidently. Reiterating the colonists' decision, he added, "I think it makes sense to use its parts, rather than burning it."

"I agree. The quills will be useful for our spears, and the scales will reinforce our hovels," Neena said. "The pieces we bury in the desert will bring scavenging animals, so we can hunt them."

Kai nodded. As disgusting as the beast had been, it had its uses.

"Are the guards still watching for predators?" Neena asked him.

"Yep. We have a group of men taking shifts on the outskirts of the colony," Kai said. "They'll alert us if they see any wolves that they can't handle. The blood from the enormous carcass is sure to draw them."

Neena's gaze wandered to the people working on the monster. Every so often, they changed shifts, while others rested their arms, or recuperated.

"At least our people are working together," she said, with relief. "I thought we might have some trouble."

"The colonists are glad to be out of the caves," Kai told her. "And they're happy the monster is dead. Everyone knows you're responsible for killing it. You saved their lives."

Neena enjoyed a rare moment of warmth.

Her eyes returned to the people working on the beast. They'd already removed a pile of organs from the creature's neck. She shuddered as she saw some people working near its stomach. She was certain they'd find more bodies inside, as well as more of the dead in the rubble. But hopefully, they'd be past it all soon.

Kai sighed, looking toward the cliffs. "Do you think you'll ever go back up there?"

"No," Neena admitted. "I'm glad to be down here."

"Raj and Samel seem happy, too. The heavens know they've been through enough."

"We've all been through enough," Neena said. "Hopefully, we can move forward."

CHAPTER 103: Raj

AJ AND ADRIANA WALKED THROUGH the colony alleys, treading a path they hadn't walked in a while. In between watching for the rubble, Raj stole glances at her. Adriana's long, dark hair swayed over her shoulders, blowing with a gentle breeze. Her eyes were radiant and blue. She looked even more beautiful than he remembered. Or maybe it was the light of the natural sky, under which they hadn't strode together in too long.

"Where are you taking me?" Adriana asked, a curious expression on her face.

"You'll see." Raj smiled.

He led her through a path between broken hovels, weaving around the fallen stones, or the leftover piles of sand that swooped up along their edges, which no one had had a chance to clean. For the first time in a long while, he was free of his plaguing fear, and his doubts.

"It's so strange to walk through the colony without worrying about the monster," he said.

"You're sure that no one minds us coming here?" Adriana asked.

"They won't miss us for long," Raj said. "We'll be back soon. Besides, Samel is safe with the other children in the tradesmen's buildings."

Adriana nodded. They'd both been working hard to assist with the cleanup of the monster, and the transport of its body to the desert. Raj figured they needed a break.

They wound through the alley, watching their footing, until they reached a batch of familiar structures. Some of the buildings in the alley had fallen, but one stood out. Adriana opened and closed her mouth.

"My house!"

Raj nodded, smiling.

"I had heard it survived, but I hadn't seen it until now," she said, incredulously.

"I hoped it might be a good surprise," Raj told her.

For the past few nights, they'd mostly slept in the intact buildings at the front of the colony, keeping together, where they were protected from predators. Only Adriana's parents had been here. Walking up to the door, Raj carefully pushed it open and inspected the dwelling.

"No wolves," he said, adding, "or dust beetles."

Adriana walked inside, a smile plastered to her face. She looked around at the dwelling, finding a few bedrolls and pieces of cookware inside.

"My parents told me some of our belongings survived," Adriana said. "I can't believe how everything looks the same. It's so strange."

"You were definitely fortunate," Raj said.

"I'm sorry that your house didn't fare as well," she said.

"It's fine," Raj answered. "We'll rebuild. Our next house will be even stronger, Neena says."

Together, they took a seat on the floor, glancing between each other and the open doorway.

"This is the first place we officially met," Adriana said, reaching over and taking his hand.

"I remember," Raj said.

They met each other's eyes, sharing a nostalgic moment, and then a kiss.

Raj closed his eyes, enjoying a moment he'd wished for too often, in his many days in the colony without her. Her lips tasted the same way he remembered — soft, but familiar. Leaning back, he felt the same, dizzy feeling in his stomach.

He wanted that feeling to last forever.

If he was lucky, it might.

Far in the distance, other colonists chatted, or clanked tools. The smell of the cooking fires brought Raj a security he hadn't felt in too long.

Raj squeezed her hand. "Neena told me how you tried sneaking out of the caves to find me."

Adriana nodded. "I was worried about you."

"You didn't have to do that."

"I wanted to." Adriana looked at the ground. "I felt bad about some of the things that happened in the caves. I'm just glad that everything worked out the way it did."

"So am I," Raj agreed.

"I heard how you dug out Kai and the others, in one of the monster's tunnels," she said, giving his cheek a soft punch. "You are a hero."

Raj blushed and let go of her other hand. "I don't know about that."

"I mean it," Adriana said, leaning over and eyeing him playfully. "You crawled in there without fear, the same way you did in that passage in the caves. If not for you, those people wouldn't have been alive. And no one would've had the device to kill the monster. Who else would've found it?"

Raj couldn't help a humble smile.

"Maybe when things settle, we'll do some more exploring," Raj said, with an adventurous grin.

"Back in the caves?" Adriana frowned.

"Or in the desert, after I learn how to hunt," Raj said.

"I think I've had enough of the caves." Adriana made a face.

"Yeah." Raj laughed. "Me, too."

CHAPTER 104: Neena

U NDER THE LIGHT OF A new day, Neena looked out over the two hundred people facing her at the edge of the graveyard. High above, the morning sun shone down on them, providing a comfortable warmth. The survivors consoled one another quietly, wiping their eyes and holding on to their children. Far up on the cliffs, several men stood on the ledge, watching for sandstorms, keeping Red Rock safe in the same way The Watchers had.

She smiled softly as she recognized Roberto among those men, performing his new duty.

Beside her, Kai, Amos, Nicholas, and Salvador stood with their heads lowered, their hands folded. Unlike the hunters in the desert, who'd once watched her with disdain, the crowd regarded her with deference, even affection. The past few days of working together had healed some bonds, and forged new ones. Their lives weren't perfect — and they had much work to do — but for the first time in a long while, the colonists could see a path forward.

They consoled one another, leaned on one another's shoulders, and dried each other's tears.

Their undeniable loss bound them together.

Sucking in a long breath, Neena glanced over her shoulder at the long rows of freshly dug graves. For most of the night before, she'd lain in bed, contemplating the old speeches of The Heads of Colony. She'd even recited a few of them quietly in her bedroll. Now, she could think of none of them.

Looking out over the crowd, she let her own words guide her.

Putting a fist to her chest, she said, "For the past few weeks, we've faced challenges that no one expected. But we faced them with courage and valor. We fought with pride, and we defeated a horrific monster, the likes of which none of us have faced before, so that those who are left might walk this colony without fear. And the people behind me— the relatives we lost—did a service that we will never forget. They fought bravely, so that our children may grow old, and so that our colony may continue. It is a future that many of us never thought that we'd see."

The colonists squeezed their relatives tightly.

"I'm not sure what comes after our lives; I don't think any of us do. But wherever our loved ones are, I'm sure they're looking down at us with pride. They know that we honor them. And they know that we love them."

Neena swallowed past a lump in her throat, thinking of Darius, Helgid, and Samara, while the crowd openly wept. "We should be proud. Not just of what we have accomplished, but that we persevered. Our hearts will always feel a little emptier because of the people we lost. But their courage will live in us, as we protect our children, and our children's children. Our people—the people of Red Rock—will never be forgotten."

Neena lowered her head, turning to face the rows of graves. For the past few days, they'd worked tirelessly to bury their loved ones.

Now, they would live their lives in honor of them.

Neena walked slowly next to Kai as they made their way to

one of the plots they'd dug together, in the back of the new rows of graves. All around them, people filtered through the graveyard, speaking with one another in quiet tones, saying their goodbyes. Stopping next to a large, beautiful rock they'd pulled from inside one of the caves, they knelt down together over it, clasping hands.

"I think Darius would've liked this rock," Neena said, tears stinging her eyes. Her gaze roamed to the top, on which they'd carved a familiar, circular marking.

Darius's marking.

"He loved the caves, despite their dangers, or maybe because of them," Kai said, pulling Neena close. "I think it's only fitting that we buried him next to his lost friend, Akron."

Neena glanced over at the rock next to him, which they'd marked with Akron's triangle. After most of the other bodies had been found and buried, they'd headed to the caves, transporting both the boy's remains and Darius's to a more suitable resting place.

"May they forever be exploring, wherever they go."

They nodded, overlooking the plot in silence for a few moments, before moving on to Samara's plot. After a few tearful words, they joined Raj and Samel, who kept vigil near Helgid's empty grave.

"Are you holding up all right?" Neena asked Raj.

Raj nodded, tears in his eyes. "I'm going to miss her."

"We all will," Neena agreed, doing her best to console him.

"Helgid was like family. And I will miss Darius, too," Raj said, opening and closing his eyes. Some of his guilt had abated, but he'd always carry the grief. Everyone would.

"You remind me of him," Neena said, smiling as Raj tucked his hair behind his ears.

"I do?"

"He was proud of your sense of discovery," she said. "I think you have his spirit of exploration."

Raj smiled back through his grief. "I could only hope to be as wise as he was."

"One day," Neena promised.

She leaned over and hugged him. She was surprised when he not only returned the embrace, but hugged her more tightly than she expected, burying his face in her shoulder. Samel joined in on the hug, and then Kai. Together, they stood by the stones, the wind blowing gently around them, a band of survivors in a colony of the fallen.

CHAPTER 105: Neena

"**W**E HAVE ONE LAST THING to discuss," Kai said.

Neena looked over at him, following his gaze to the cliffs.

For the past few days, while the colonists had tended the dead and started repairing Red Rock, Jameson had kept his post in the dark cove in the Center Cave, tending to one patient. Most of the colonists had avoided the disturbing topic of the old Head of Colony, discussing it only in whispers, while burying their lost loved ones. But everyone knew they had to deal with him eventually.

"He's still up there," Kai said.

A dark shadow clouded Neena's mind. The thought of Gideon dredged up dark memories of the past: his lies, his treatment of Neena and Kai, and the things they'd learned from Nicholas, in the days since the monster's death.

Too many were gone, because of him.

His lies were evident in every person they buried, in the hidden monster carcass in the caves' bowels, and in the way he'd feigned incompetence with Neena, Kai, and Darius. If not for him, many more people would've been alive.

Now, his lies were exposed.

Everyone knew about his plans to return to power, and the way he had rallied up Bryan and the others, because everyone bore the consequences.

"He would've killed us, if he had the chance," Kai

reminded Neena. "And I still believe he would've let you rot in that jail cell, if you didn't persuade him to let you out."

"And he ordered The Watchers to slit your throat," Neena remembered. "He would've dumped your body in the caves."

"No one has forgotten the lies he told that day on the podium," Kai said. "In a way, he was responsible for the deaths of half your people."

"And he sent away yours, all those years ago," Neena recalled.

"Too many times, I've wondered how that might've gone differently." Kai blew a long breath. "But none of that makes our decision for us. So what should we do?"

Neena's gaze wandered to the cliffs. Despite the atrocities their former leader had committed, she couldn't imagine harming or killing him, especially in his crippled condition.

"His body bears the result of his choices," she said, after some thought.

"And yet he continued to plot against us," Kai said. "Maybe we should put him in a jail cell in the Comm Building, once we fix it. Or we could construct another one."

Silence fell between the two of them, until another option surfaced in Neena's mind.

"Perhaps we could do nothing at all."

Kai looked at her, confused, until she explained.

"Perhaps we have Jameson come down here with us, and we leave Gideon to his cove. We won't punish him. We won't hurt him. But we won't help him, either."

"You mean we'll stop tending him?"

"That's all," Neena said, with a firm nod. "It is more mercy than he showed you, when he ordered you killed."

"And it is certainly more courtesy than he showed his people, by lying to them for all these years." Kai nodded, thinking that through. "Do you think the rest of the people will have an issue with that?"

"I don't think anyone will," Neena said. "In fact, I think we will all sleep easier, knowing that his lies will never hurt us again."

CHAPTER 106: Gideon

GIDEON STARED AROUND THE DARK cove, watching his bedside torch flicker. His empty stomach growled. Waves of pain washed over him, as the last of his herbs wore out. It'd been almost a day since he'd seen Jameson, and even longer since he'd heard any commotion from the women and children in the Center Cave. He still recalled Jameson's strange expression before he'd left.

He'd barely looked at him.

What was going on?

Perhaps he'd forgotten to have someone take his place.

Gideon struggled to move his arms and legs, but too many days of inactivity had made him weak. He couldn't stand, and of course, he couldn't walk. Maybe if he tried his hardest, he could crawl and find someone to assist him.

He was contemplating trying to move when he noticed his last torch dying out.

In the time Jameson had been away, he'd burned his last light down to the end. Gideon's uneasiness grew, as the flame shrank, wavered, and died.

Blackness enveloped him.

Gideon waved his hands, clawing at the inky darkness, as if he might beat it back. But it was useless. It was all around him. He'd need another torch. And in order to find one, he'd have to venture out of the cove. What if there were none around?

Something skittered down the main tunnel.

"Jameson?" he cried.

Gideon's voice echoed and died. The smoke from his dead flame and the odor of his last meal hung in the air. Where was everyone?

"Jameson!" he yelled, more insistently. "I need you to get me something! Now!"

The skittering grew closer. Something sniffed the air.

Not a person. An animal.

Gideon cried out and grabbed at his sheets, but he couldn't move quickly: his muscles were atrophied; his leg was lame. He tried rolling and catching his balance, but fell to the ground instead.

Gideon landed with a painful thud on the side of his bed. He cried out, trying to get to his feet, momentarily forgetting that he had only one leg remaining. He tried dragging himself, but his movement was limited.

Even if he could get out of the cove, where would he go?

He was directionless and in the dark.

His eye roamed the pitch-black room, scanning for whatever occupied the cove with him.

A growl pierced the room.

For the first time in a long while, fear shook Gideon.

"Jameson?"

With effort, he managed to turn, grabbing his bed and trying to pull himself back up.

He never made it.

The wolf's first bite tore into his empty pant-leg, causing no pain, but the next one punctured his arm, and the one after that, his shoulder. Agony washed over Gideon. He screamed as more wolves joined the first—a pack of feral animals chewing his flesh, ignoring his frantic flailing, and ripping off pieces of his body.

No one came, even when he screamed for them.

Nor did they come, when the wolves tore into his neck, turning a scream into a gurgle.

And then Gideon felt no more.

Epilogue

SHOULDERING THEIR BAGS, NEENA, KAI, Raj, and a dozen others stood in the middle of the hunter's path, facing the hundred and eighty colonists who had gathered to see them off. Studying the faces of the people in front of them, Neena couldn't help the nostalgic lump in her throat. Three months of working together, sharing plentiful meals, and rebuilding their homes had forged bonds she never would've imagined. She'd always felt close to her brothers, but now it felt as if she had a newer, larger family, two hundred strong.

Walking forward from her group, she met Roberto and Salvador, who watched her with affectionate concern.

"Are you sure you want to leave?" Salvador.

It was a formality, rather than a question.

They'd discussed their plans ad nauseam. She knew they'd take care of things here, just as they knew that Neena and her group would be careful. A few of the children in the crowd shifted anxiously, looking at the fifteen leaving people with inquisitive eyes. Neena's attention turned to Samel and Adriana, who broke away from the crowd to see them off.

Samel reached Neena first.

"You behave for Amos, okay?" Neena said, hugging him.

She looked over at his shoulder at Amos, who smiled in his grandfatherly way.

"I will," Samel promised.

"One day when you're older, I'll take you on a trip, too." She glanced over at Raj. "Or maybe your brother will."

Raj nodded proudly at Samel, before saying goodbye.

And then it was Adriana's turn to step forward. After a brief farewell to Neena and the others, she moved over to Raj.

"I want to hear all your stories when you get back," Adriana told Raj, clutching him tightly.

"Don't worry, I'll save them for you," Raj promised.

They leaned in, kissing briefly.

And then it was time to leave.

Neena looked at the people around her. Their nervous posture reminded her of the meetings they'd held in the caves, but this time, they had hope. She glanced at Red Rock a last time, scanning the buildings and the hovels.

Her colony would always live in her heart, no matter where she went.

But now, it was time to trek between the soaring, auburn spires and into the desert.

"Do you think we'll find them?" Raj asked Neena and Kai, after they'd put several klicks between them and Red Rock.

"If the heavens are with us," Neena said.

She adjusted her bag, glancing up at the twin moons. In their collective sacks were enough supplies for several weeks in the desert—enough to provide a good chance at finding New Canaan, if their luck held.

"If we don't find them on this trip, we'll find them on the next one," Neena added.

Turning to Kai, Raj asked, "How do you think they'll react when they meet us?"

"I'm not sure," Kai admitted nervously.

The risk of being thrown back in jail was a very plausible fear for Kai. And he had no idea how his parents would react, if he found them. Still, he was committed to reuniting with his family, and potentially improving the lives of both Red Rock and New Canaan.

Sensing his nervousness, Raj said, "You know what I think? They'll consider you a hero when you prove that the creature is dead, and show them the piece of its heart, and the quills on our spears. I'm sure of it. You helped to save both our people and your own. You are no criminal here."

Kai smiled, wiping some of the beading sweat away from his markings. "I appreciate that, Raj."

"If the worst happens, you can come back with us to Red Rock."

"We'll be there with you, vouching for your honesty, and what you have done for us," Neena vowed. "Whatever happens, I think it's time for both our people to work together. Years ago, the people of New Canaan reached out a hand. Now, it time to extend the hand back."

Kai nodded. "Maybe we can find a new way of life that will be better for all of us."

They traveled for a long while, drinking from their flasks, keeping cool from the morning sun, while making headway.

When they'd hiked about half a day from the colony, Neena abruptly changed course.

"Where are you going?" Kai asked.

"I was hoping I could show Raj something," she answered. "It's not too out of the way."

She looked around at the other dozen who accompanied them, none of whom objected.

"What is that?" Raj asked, furrowing his brow.

In the distance, a tall, circular formation of rocks appeared.

"Is that another place you stay while hunting?" Raj asked.

In the time they'd been out, he'd marveled at every landmark, and every story Neena told.

"It is a special place," answered Neena vaguely. When they'd gotten within fifty yards of it, she turned to the others and asked, "Would you mind if Raj and I went alone?"

The group agreed.

Sunlight glinted off she and Raj's faces as they trekked across the desert, reaching the reddish rocks and heading into the middle of them.

Nostalgia washed over Neena as she reentered a place she'd been many times, but not in a while. She and Raj stood in the center, enjoying a reprieve from the day's heat, while Raj turned in wonder and studied the rising rocks.

"This is where Dad taught me to hold my spear, when he first took me out to hunt," Neena said.

"When you were thirteen?"

Neena nodded. "I'll never forget the long talk we had here. It is the place where he told me to be strong, if anything ever happened to him." Emotion welled in her throat, as she looked toward the sand in the center. "It is also the place where I buried him."

Raj opened and closed his mouth, as understanding set in. "Is that why you brought me here?" His voice wavered with emotion.

"Dad knew we couldn't come after him when he was sick, due to our tradition. But I think he came here as a final message to me...to us. He wanted us to know that he was thinking of his children, even in his final moments."

"Dad..." Raj whispered.

Tears sprang to his eyes, as he collapsed in the sand.

"I'm sorry I didn't tell you sooner, Raj. I meant to."

Emotion filled Neena's heart as she walked over to him, huddling down and embracing him. For a while, they held each other, sharing in their grief and loss, until all their tears were spent.

After drying their faces, Neena and Raj sat among the circular rocks.

"I'm sorry I didn't tell you sooner," Neena said.

"It's okay," Raj said, still hanging his head. "I thought you might be waiting for the right time."

"I knew this day would come," Neena said. "I just wasn't sure when." Looking down at her new, quill-tipped spear, she said, "If I hadn't lost Dad's spear, perhaps we could've practiced with it."

An eager expression crossed Raj's face, as he looked down at the spear in his hand. "Why don't you show me using this one?"

"Do you think you're ready?" A competitive smile sprang to Neena's face.

Raj nodded excitedly.

For the first time since they'd arrived here, Neena felt a true sense of warmth.

Walking over to her brother, Neena had him open his hands, while she showed him what her father had taught her. "First, you'll want to find the spear's balance point."

"Like this?"

"You've got it. Now, relax your hands, and I'll show you how to grip it."

"This way?"

"Perfect! You're doing great."

Raj beamed. Neena could almost hear her father speaking to her in the desert, all those years ago. With those memories to guide her, she finished showing her brother how to hold the spear.

"Perhaps I'll be even better than you, when I'm done learning." Raj looked up at her mischievously.

"We'll see," Neena said, with a sisterly smile.

"Are you all set?" Kai called out to Neena and Kai as they returned to the group.

"I was just showing Raj one of my favorite places to rest," Neena said.

"And she taught me how to hold my spear," Raj added, rearing it back and taking some practice heaves.

"It sounds like he's picking it up quickly," Kai said.

Neena smiled at him. "I think he'll impress all of us."

She and Raj shared a happy glance, while walking alongside the others.

Together, they traveled through the desert with the group, traversing over long stretches of sand, until they reached the dunes where she and Kai had met, passing them to whatever lay beyond.

THE END

Afterword

It has certainly been a blast writing the SANDSTORM series.

There is always a possibility I'll return to the world and characters (I have a few ideas), but for now, I'm happy to leave you with the last image of Neena, Kai, and Raj heading off under the desert sun.

That image somehow feels right.

If you're looking for something else to read, THE LAST SURVIVORS and THE RUINS are similar, though a bit more post-apocalyptic.

If you'd like to receive an email when I have new releases out and get a free story, sign up for my newsletter at: http://eepurl.com/qy_SH.

Thanks again for checking out my stuff. With so many choices for entertainment, you chose to spend some time with me, and that means a lot.

Talk soon!

Tyler Piperbrook
January 2020

Ps. If you've enjoyed WAR TORN, please leave a review! Reviews go a long way in helping other readers find what they like.

Email & Facebook

If you're interested in getting an email when my new books come out, sign up at: http://eepurl.com/qy_SH.

You'll periodically get updates on other books but no spam. Unsubscribe at any time.

If you'd like to get a bit more involved, you can find me on **Facebook** at:

http://www.facebook.com/twpiperbrook

Other Things To Read

Looking for another series to read after SANDSTORM?

THE LAST SURVIVORS might tide you over. It's a sci-fi series that explores what happens 300 years in the future after the apocalypse, where man has rebuilt and gone back to a medieval society. The full series is available now in paperback.

Printed in Great Britain
by Amazon